SCAVENGERS FROM THE SEA

SCAVENGERS FROM THE SEA

A Historical Thriller Novel

LEGEND OF THE ENGLISH BOOK 1

ROB MACKINTOSH

ISBN: 978-1-63161-047-9

Published by TCK Publishing

www.TCKPublishing.com

One must wait until evening
to see how splendid the day has been.
~ SOPHOCLES

1

ROME ARRIVAL
May 589 AD

MY HEAD SAGGED in the drowsy afternoon sun, a trickle of sweat running down my back. A voice called from the riverbank. I looked up and saw my younger brother Godric holding out a small wooden carving as a gift for me. The voice called again, and my dream dissolved.

"Not far now!"

I opened my bleary eyes. Godric had disappeared. In his place, a young boy about my age stood on the towpath, his team of oxen attached by a thick rope to the prow of our vessel.

Felix, the skipper, called out from the stern in his bullhorn voice, "How far?"

"Maybe two miles, maybe less."

"Make it less!"

The ship rocked slowly beneath our feet. I straightened up, the chains on my wrists rattling across the oar resting on my knees. I gazed at the landscape but saw no signs of life. No ducks paddled on the river, and not a single starling chattered in the trees. No cows, sheep, or goats grazed on the riverbanks. Not even a dog barked. The only sounds coming from the shore were the lowing of oxen and the sharp *crack* of a herdsman's whip.

A sigh escaped my lips as a vision of my sister Tola drifted before my eyes. More than four months had passed, but I still missed her bitterly and ached all the more for home. Cadmon, sitting near me, guessed what I was feeling and gave a sympathetic pout of his lips.

I glanced down at the river as something, drifting just below the surface, bumped against the vessel. I guessed it was a log, but it rolled over, and I stared in horror at a fully clothed body. Its face was down in the water and its arms trailed with palms upturned. In a few moments, the corpse had floated past and disappeared downstream.

Attracting attention on Felix's ship brought trouble, so I sat in silence as a stab of anxiety twisted in my stomach. I glanced nervously upriver. What kind of place was this? Cadmon saw my expression and raised his eyebrows. I drew a finger across my throat and nodded towards the river.

On the riverbank, the oxen hauled our ship past an imposing basilica, its white-columned porticoes facing the river. Along the whole winding length of our journey from the port of Ostia, we had seen farm buildings razed to the ground, blackened roof beams poking into a pale blue sky. Only the basilica we were passing remained undamaged. Felix seemed to have seen all this before; he made none of his usual comments as the landscape slowly unfolded.

During the previous five or so months, I'd had plenty of time to observe the skipper at close quarters. I guessed Felix to be a little older than my father Galen, perhaps forty years. He stood over six feet tall, bow-legged from his years at sea, his muscular arms and broad chest showing beneath his jacket. Felix's clean-shaven head and exposed skin were burnt from a life under the sun. Dark eyes glared out from beneath thick eyebrows, penetrating, ever watchful. An old scar ran down his left cheekbone. A trimmed moustache and short beard framed his full lips. I looked away when he caught me watching him, and returned my gaze to the winding river.

Further upstream, on yet another bend, an unforgettable sight came into view, one still vivid in my mind years later. Towering walls surrounded a city we had only heard spoken of in awe: Rome! A hill rose high within the city walls, covered in trees; their leaves burnished a fiery copper as the spring sun dipped towards the horizon. The River Tiber sparkled in a magical evening glow, casting a soft hue over the landscape. On the opposite bank of the river, an aqueduct stepped carefully down a hill that was thick with vegetation, and tall umbrella pines gave the appearance of marching along its ridge.

As we drew near to a stone bridge, Felix cast the ship adrift from the team of oxen. Heaving on the oars, we turned the ship about, facing downstream on the dirty green waters, and moored alongside a broad, tree-lined avenue. The river seemed deserted, with none of the hustle and bustle of the North African coast where we had anchored a few weeks earlier. The only ship at the moorings belonged to Felix, the only sign of life a few men sitting idly at the door of a dilapidated warehouse. With our ropes now tied to the moorings, the ship sprang into action. Felix, as usual, did all the shouting while our slave-crew, in a well-worn routine, rushed to make ready for market the next day.

We all slept on board that night. In the early hours, a dream spoke to me: *This is the day*. I remained awake for a while then whispered this to Cadmon. He lay still for a long moment, then nodded, rolled over, and went calmly back to sleep.

In the cool of dawn, we washed on the quay. I now felt sure our journey had come to an end. But *how* would it end?

I splashed some water at Cadmon. "You smell like crap!"

"You look like crap!" Cadmon's finely woven woollen tunic, with threads of blue, grey, and white, was unrecognisable beneath months of accumulated filth. My woollen leggings lay in tatters at my feet, my shoes long since rotted away.

"You won't be needing those anymore!" Felix boomed, kicking our clothing into the river. "Put these on!" With our clothes disappearing downstream, Felix thrust white loincloths into our hands. As I tied mine around my waist, I looked back at the ship gently scraping against the quay, but Cadmon's eyes were fixed on the bridge upriver.

I shivered as I stood barefoot on the stone quayside, but not from the cold. Miserable as life was on the ship, I knew what to expect from Felix, his first mate Souk, and Anaxos, the ship's navigator. Until my dream the night before, I had not reckoned that Cadmon and I would be part of the day's merchandise. A thrill of anticipation and also a shudder of fear ran through me. As in all the weary days before, we lived one moment at a time.

Back on deck, Felix rummaged around in his sea chest at the stern of the ship. Particular about his appearance, he rubbed a potion all over his bald olive-skinned head and swarthy face, adding a few dashes of ointment to his neck and under his arms. By noon our small group had started to make its way up the tree-lined avenue, pushing through a crowded marketplace. As usual, Felix led the procession, an outrageous hat perched on his shaven head partly covering his long scar. A sleeveless blue tunic showed off his dark torso, and his legs were clad in theatrical striped trousers, acquired from some Eastern magician.

Three of us followed behind: Cadmon, Edoma—a slave Felix had bought on the African coast—and me. We formed a single-file procession, our feet fettered in chains and our necks linked by a rope, shuffling along behind Felix, stumbling to keep pace, carrying two tightly rolled carpets resting on our shoulders. The remainder of the slave crew followed, hauling carts crammed with exotic wares—a carved ivory chest, hand mirrors, bone hairpins, silver jewellery boxes. More merchandise lay stashed beneath heavily embroidered fabrics at the bottom of the carts.

Stalls jammed the crowded marketplace, traders selling cloth, fruit, jewellery, and housewares. A stench hung in the air from sweaty bodies and rotting garbage, only partially masked by the smell of strong spices and perfumes wafting from market stalls. Clothes worn by the locals seemed drab and shabby compared to market days back at our home in Sandwic Haven. Far worse were the baggy trousers laced with strips of leather worn by many of the Roman menfolk, clearly marking them out as barbarians, whereas we Saxons typically wore tight-fitting woollen hose. Was Rome not boasted to be the apex of sophistication? And the cadaver drifting downstream the day before—what evil did the city nurture in its soul that led to such a grave?

A basilica bounded the bustling market to our right, and to our left, a stone bridge spanned the Tiber. The market was one of Rome's major hubs, bordered by districts and landmarks whose names I would come to know well. On the edge of the forum a small, dilapidated rotunda lay close to the river with a derelict, rectangular temple just beyond it. Felix pressed on past both of these, strutting across the forum towards an abandoned theatre. We stumbled on, shuffling onto a street that followed the theatre's curved wall.

All around us brown-brick *insulae*—apartment blocks five or six storeys high—hunched over narrow alleyways shutting out any hope of sunlight reaching the streets below. Several upper rooms were abandoned, their roofs collapsing, broken tiles scattered about in the narrow streets. Dogs sniffed for scraps and cats crept in and out of buildings and courtyards searching for vermin. It all overwhelmed me, so different from the cleanliness of any of our Saxon hovels at home. We had heard reports of Rome's glory and splendour at every port around the Great Sea, but instead of glory, we saw dirt and dereliction at every turn.

Our procession shuffled on. Felix forced his way through the crowded streets using his ivory staff topped with its monkey-skull handle. He shouted in his booming voice, "Spices and ivory from Africa! Jewels from the East! Finest fabrics you will ever see from Gaul! Slaves for your villa!"

His words brought a mocking laugh from the bystanders who lived in the overcrowded apartments surrounding the markets. Still, we began drawing a growing throng into our wake, and I guessed from their interest in our wares that merchants like Felix did not often come calling on Rome.

These were the ordinary citizens of the city, mostly tradesmen with their wives, children, and slaves. Some bystanders scowled and spat at Cadmon and me as we shuffled by. Our fair skin and straw-coloured hair gave us no advantage in Rome. The only people who looked like us were ruthless and murderous Langobard warriors who had seized their farmlands and torched their homes.

Felix turned our procession on to the Field of Mars, the *Campus Martius*, heading towards an imposing rotunda we later knew as the Pantheon. We stopped just short of this forlorn temple and entered the imposing colonnaded courtyard of the Septa Julia. This was Felix's destination—the slave market.

While our king's royal hall at Raculf in the Kingdom of Cantia had seemed enormous to my young eyes, it was no match for the sheer scale of the buildings I saw that day. I stared open-mouthed at the colonnade surrounding a temple at the centre of this vast square. Surely giants—no, gods—must have built all this? But neither giants nor gods were anywhere to be seen.

Felix pushed through the bucket-carrying residents of Rome vying for clean drinking water around the Aqua Virgo fountain. Two magistrates in dark robes, supervisors of public auctions collecting taxes on imported slaves, came over from the Prefect's Office. They pointed Felix to a place between two portico columns to set up his stall, and we began to lay out his wares.

On our long and brutal journey by sea, I sometimes wondered why Felix had waited so many months to sell-off Cadmon and me. His usual practice boiled down to buying in one port and selling in the next. Months had now passed, and we were still with him. Had he needed us for his crew? But there had been a plentiful supply of healthy young men at every port we visited, and none of the slaves who were in the vessel when we were captured at Sandwic Haven were still with us now. So why? Perhaps because our appearance was different as we came from a northern climate? I had noticed nearly everyone in the crowd had dark hair and much darker skin than either Cadmon or me. Our faces, necks, and arms were brown from the sun, but standing in our loincloths, everyone could see our skin was as pale as a goat's udder. I had no answer unless perhaps Felix had miscalculated the market value of two Saxon boys who, unfortunately, looked like those hated Langobards?

I glanced at Edoma, bought as a slave only a few weeks earlier. He was much more promising; a little older than Cadmon and me, perhaps fifteen or sixteen years old, well-built, handsome, his skin dark as polished ebony. Felix's first mate, Souk, stepped forward and whitened our feet with chalk dust from a bag. I thought, *How ridiculous, Cadmon's stepped into bird-shit, and Edoma's wearing a pair of white shoes!* Felix hung a scroll around each of our necks, advertising our name and country, and stating we were free from disease and defects of body and character. Whatever Felix might have declared, he certainly wouldn't roost in Rome long enough to be exposed if what he claimed wasn't honest.

I understood little that anyone said at the slave auction that day; comprehension came much later, thanks to others who were present, but what I *did* understand was the nauseous taste of fear. I began to tremble as Souk pushed Edoma on to a pedestal.

Turning to the crowd, Felix bawled, "Now! Gather round! Look at this fine specimen of youth, worked in the household of a wealthy merchant, housetrained, in superlative condition! Just look at his teeth! Notice his eyes! Not a mark on him! What's my first bid, then, you lucky people?"

A woman expensively dressed, wearing a silk headscarf over her grey hair, pushed forward. She had two slaves with her. Her eyes were cold, her nose giving her a hawkish, predatory appearance. She gave a ringing smack of her hand on Edoma's thigh. Felix smoothly intervened, expressing all the concern of a gardener protecting his prize melon.

"No, no, madam," he said in a manner both warning her off and ingratiating at the same time. "You may test the merchandise more closely *after* you have paid the price! Now, what do you offer me for this fine young man?"

The woman made her first bid for Edoma, then another woman followed, and then a man. Despite the grisly nature of the business at hand, I found myself admiring the skill with which Felix managed to keep the bids rising. The crowd pressed in, eagerly following the two bidders remaining in the auction; one a man, and the other, the woman with the headscarf. Then it was over. Her household slaves threw Edoma into the back of a cart and swiftly trundled away.

I had not seen a slave market in action before. A feeling of panic now began to rise as I looked at the jostling crowd, my eyes darting left and right for some chance to escape, but to no avail. So who might buy me, and for what purpose? My fevered imagination began to take hold—I would become a slave to a harsh taskmaster, given impossible tasks and subjected to cruel punishment, beaten and finally put to death at a whim, because of some minor infraction.

I looked at the crowd in front of us. Would our buyer be the woman with a dark cloak, her face lined and severe, scowling at us with hostile, piercing eyes? Or the man with brick dust in his hair, tool bag slung over one shoulder, his stocky legs bare from the knees down? I could foresee my new life, carrying bricks up and down building sites, my back permanently bent and aching, my strength oozing away like water through beach sand. It took all I had to hold myself together.

Souk grabbed Cadmon and me by our elbows and pushed us forward. Quaking, I put one unsteady foot on the pedestal, then the other, and stood near naked in full gaze of the crowd. My dream had spoken truthfully; our day had come.

2

THE SLAVE MARKET
May 589 AD

FELIX THRUST A finger in our direction as we stood before the throng, while my eyes searched the faces of the crowd jostling in front of us. I glanced at Cadmon to my left, as calm and composed as if he was doing the buying, and the crowd was on offer.

"Who'll start the bidding for these two fine young lads then? Sons of a king from the Misty Isles at the far ends of the earth! Fine specimens both! Just look at their teeth! Look at the colour of their hair! Young, strong, plenty of life in them! What will you bid me? Come on, now! You won't see fine young lads like these again!" Potential buyers began jostling forward to give us a closer scrutiny.

Then a man, poorly dressed in a rough woollen robe belted at the waist, came to the front. With some people, you can see their authority before they speak. I noticed the two magistrates came to greet him warmly with respect, but the crowd also deferred to him. He called out to Felix above the hubbub.

"Slaver! Where exactly are these young boys from?"

Felix looked up, noticing the bidder's rough clothing, and appeared to recognise him. Another, younger man similarly robed stood beside him. Even though this second figure was the taller, he seemed somehow to stand in his companion's shadow.

"And what would you be wanting with a pair of young slave boys, eh?" Felix sneered.

The bidder treated him to the full, contemptuous stare of a Roman aristocrat. He pointed to the sign around my neck and repeated his question slowly, as one might for a child, or for someone with a feeble mind: "Where are these boys *really* from?"

"These fine specimens are Saxons, from the Kingdom of Cantia. Now, are you going to make a bid, or are you just wasting my time?"

The onlookers had swelled in the last few moments. At the same time, the open space around these two men seemed to have widened. It felt as though a fight was brewing and the crowd wanted to see what happened, but no one else came forward to bid once they saw our robed bidder showing an interest. The shorter figure looked at the two of us again.

"So," he said to Felix, taking charge and speaking slowly and unhurriedly, "are these Saxons you speak of so barbaric they sell their children?"

I stole a quick glance at Felix. He scowled, not making eye contact with the bidder. "You know these savages. They sell their grandmothers if there's money in it."

"No, I don't know anyone who would sell their grandmothers or their grandchildren into slavery. But, like a good godfather, I will redeem them. Now, what is your asking price?"

The taller of the two men paid our redemption price from his belt-purse without haggling. Souk released our legs from the irons using a hammer and awl, knocking out the pins holding the metal clamps around our ankles.

"So, you are Alric?" our new owner asked, pointing to me, "and you are Cadmon?"

We nodded, hearing a stranger speak our names for the first time in months, but not understanding what he said. Our new owner beckoned, "Come with us."

We quickly left the Septa Julia, pausing only to acquire two square-necked tunics to cover our nakedness and some leather footwear. We hurried on, looking like any other young boys on the streets. My sense of relief began to grow as we put more and more distance between Felix and us. We still did not know our fate, or our destination, or who had purchased us, or why. We had changed masters, but would we be free to return home?

Our new owner kept a hand on Cadmon's shoulder as we hurried on through the crowded streets, a bow-wave of space mysteriously opening ahead of us. The taller man and I followed swiftly in their wake, my hand firmly grasped. His hands felt soft, not a labourer or fisherman's, though his grip was firm when I stumbled on the uneven cobbles. Easily taller than his companion by a head, his dark hair lay tonsured around his crown. His lips gave the appearance of a permanent half-smile beneath a pronounced Roman nose.

The ground floor rooms of the apartment blocks we passed were mostly tradesmen's workshops. On our left, a key-maker; across the street, a family of ironworkers were beating out barrel hoops; from ahead of us the delicious aroma of freshly baked bread wafted into our nostrils. Crowds of people, carts, and donkeys blocked our path in the narrow passageways. Several times we stopped as passers-by greeted our two rescuers, who seemed well known and well respected judging from the profuse greetings and smiles. I noticed that they called him 'abba' and later discovered this meant 'father.'

We crossed a square that brought us to the foot of a low hill and climbed a long flight of steps to a paved piazza. Three stone buildings confronted us. To our right, a crumbling and forlorn building that I later learned was the Temple of Jupiter; to our left, an imposing citadel; and directly ahead, the City Records Office. Our rescuer took a path to the left of this four-storey building, leading down into the Forum Romanum. From here onwards a vast swathe of Rome extending from northeast to the southwest was all but devoid of human habitation. Entire suburban districts disappeared beneath a haze of uncultivated trees shimmering in the afternoon heat. Far beyond this verdant landscape snow-capped mountains sloped away to the distant horizon.

The ancient Forum Romanum, once said to be the bustling heart of Rome, lay deserted compared to the streets we left behind. Ancient temples crumbled away beneath the forces of neglect and the ravages of time. Dogs scavenged among ruins lying half-buried beneath the dry sand. We hurried past a small market near the disused Republican Senate House. Over to our right, another slave market was underway, tucked behind a derelict basilica once housing the law courts of the Roman Empire.

Above us, in the pale blue sky a lone eagle hovered, the living and ancient symbol of Rome. A good omen, perhaps? As we stumbled along the uneven path, three vultures flew from the direction of the Palatine Hill. The weary eagle slowly flapped its wings and wheeled away towards the east, the vultures trailing behind with long, mournful cries. My tall companion followed their flight for a few moments, a grim line replacing his usual half-smile. Our new owner also looked up and, taking in the sight, snorted. No, the omen wasn't good.

Adding to the atmosphere, the imposing Palatine Hill to our right cast a long afternoon shadow into the Forum. We hurried past a guard of soldiers, lounging on a flight of stairs that led up to derelict palaces that once were the homes of emperors.

A triumphal arch, dedicated to Emperor Titus, stood at the far end of the Via Sacra on which we were walking. Beyond it stood a colossal amphitheatre that dominated this part of Rome's landscape. We turned onto a path to our right, passing through the Arch of Constantine. Olives and fig trees grew wild in this narrow, overgrown valley between the Palatine and Caelian hills. Some goats slowly chewed their way towards us on the grassy track.

Our journey neared its end as we passed beneath the brick arches of an aqueduct. In better days, this Aqua Claudia had carried water to imperial palaces and scented gardens on the Palatine, but now the broken water channel ran completely dry.

A further fifty paces across a small piazza brought us to our destination—a large Roman town house.

Cast iron gates separated this cloistered sanctuary from the outside world. Set back at an angle to the road and enclosed behind a high stucco wall, the urban villa possessed an uninterrupted view of umbrella pines and other trees adorning the Palatine Hill. Broad marble stairs led up to the villa's shady courtyard where potted flowers filled open spaces between the pillars. A few men, robed similarly to Abba and my tall companion, paced slowly back and forth in the open courtyard, deep in contemplation. They greeted our new master with smiles as we arrived. Cadmon and I exchanged puzzled glances. It seemed strange to us that poor people could inhabit such a magnificent house!

My attention turned to a carefully tended pair of olive trees that stood on either side of a large door, leading into the house. We found ourselves shepherded through this imposing entrance into the atrium, a cool and spacious interior room where a well stood at its centre. Sunlight filtered through an opening in the roof, a bright patch creeping across the mosaic floor. Abba dipped an urn into the well, filling several tumblers with cool, clean water that tasted quite unlike the bilge we had drunk on Felix's ship. After our long, hot day, I felt my bone-weariness slowly drain away. We had entered a very different, evidently gentler world.

So far, I had mostly only seen Abba's heels as we made our way swiftly through the city. Now while we drank, I could observe him more closely. He was perhaps in his late forties; his manner authoritative, his movements as he spoke were quick, and he usually spoke with a sense of urgency. Above his interrogating eyes rose a high, intelligent forehead. His slightly thinning hair was tonsured after the Roman manner—the same as everyone else we saw in this large house—falling long and carefully curled on both sides of his head. His face was a pleasant Sicilian olive colour, further darkened by the sun. His nose, thin and straight, appeared slightly hooked. His lips were thick, cherub-like above his handsome, prominent chin. His hands were not rough and chapped as ours were, but smooth and soft, the hands of a Roman patrician unaccustomed to manual labour. I clasped my grimy hands together, hiding my own rough skin.

Several small rooms led off this atrium. Their occupants came and went through this concourse, glancing only briefly at us, but to my relief, with none of the hostility we had experienced earlier as we passed through the marketplace. Our companion—I did not know his name until this moment—spoke with someone who addressed him as "Augustinus", and the two slipped away to attend to some business. Now I knew his name, but nothing else.

Abba gestured us to follow, and we hastened past large murals decorated in bright reds, yellows and blues. One striking picture showed a wealthy Roman aristocrat and his family. This, we later learned, portrayed our rescuer's deceased father and mother, and also our rescuer depicted as a young boy. The smartly robed, imperious youth who stared out from the mural looked very much at odds with the man he had now evidently become—the spiritual father of his household, wearing the coarse woollen habit of a mendicant monk.

We arrived at a room where another plain-robed man rose from behind a desk. He was youthful with curly, tonsured hair, and large dark brown eyes. Abba spoke with him for a few moments, and then, introducing us to Prior Pretiosus, handed us over to this man whose ready, welcoming smile told us we had nothing to fear.

Rising from his desk, Pretiosus beckoned us to follow, and we trotted to keep up, our sandals slapping on the smooth flagstone floor before we entered the monastery's steamy laundry. The prior disappeared into the mist, returning shortly with undergarments, two brown habits, and belts. By now, most of the white chalk on our feet had worn off, and he noticed our swollen and cracked feet. Pretiosus signalled again: "Come with me."

We went to another room. In the days to come, I knew it as the infirmary. A physician sat at his bench, as plainly dressed as our guide. His name, as we later discovered, was Justus. He and his brother Copiosus had both entered this community as monks and physicians, after studying at the renowned medical school of Alexandria. Like several young men drawn to Rome from around the Mediterranean world, Prior Pretiosus—who came from Hippo Regis in North Africa—was inspired by thc abbot's passion for a holy life in these troubled times.

Justus looked up from his workbench, covered with manuscripts and glass bottles, liquids of different colours, and a pestle. Prior Pretiosus explained our problem, and Justus sat us down, kneeling on the floor while he examined our hands and feet. Fetching a bowl of water and a towel, he carefully washed away the dirt, opened a jar, and gently rubbed some thick creamy ointment into our palms and the soles of our feet. Justus wiped our grimy sandals with a towel and, handing the pot to Cadmon, made it clear by gestures that both of us should apply the ointment until our cracks and sores healed. We did our best to thank him and left, our experience so different from our long journey with Felix, whose business was inflicting, rather than alleviating, pain.

Pretiosus next hurried us to the refectory with its beamed ceiling, wooden tables and benches for the community's meals. The refectory reminded me of King Ethelbert's royal hall, only very much smaller, and I felt more at home. Windows opened onto a small inner courtyard, letting in the noise of building work. Pretiosus disappeared into the pantry, returning with some flat pieces of bread and goats' cheese, served on a plate. Cadmon and I were the only people eating in the refectory. We ate like starving pups.

Unlike Cadmon, the son of an earl, eating off fired pottery was a new experience for me. We wolfed slices of bread with cheese, followed by fruit, and gulped down tumblers of fresh spring water. It was our first real meal in months, a far cry from the rotting scraps Felix tossed at us like starving animals. We finished up, gulped down another tumbler of water, our stomachs beginning to ache. The prior led us quickly back to his office with a short detour to the dorter, an indoor latrine near the refectory.

Back in the prior's office, a few chairs stood in a semi-circle in front of his desk. A striking image of a face, painted on wood, hung on the wall. It showed the head and torso of a bearded man, circled in a golden halo, his right hand raised, a book in his left, his gaze both unwavering and unnerving. Books were new to me, but here bound manuscripts lay casually on top of the desk; several more lined the shelves on one wall. Broad planks formed the ceiling, unlike the thatch we used at home. Terracotta tiles covered the floor, different from our dried mud covered with straw and bracken matting. Pretiosus left us briefly to call the abbot, and we found ourselves alone for the first time in months.

"What's going on?" I whispered to Cadmon. "I don't know what's happening here!"

"Nor me, but it may just be better than slaving for Felix!"

We could hear the sound of footsteps coming down the passage.

He whispered, "We'll know soon enough!"

Pretiosus returned with the abbot and Augustinus, accompanied by the monastery schoolmaster who had the appearance of a thoughtful and intelligent man, and this proved to be the case. Neither Cadmon nor I, of course, understood Latin, which the monks spoke amongst themselves, but I followed every movement and gesture intently, every tone and pitch, to discern what we could not otherwise understand from their words.

When everyone had taken seats around the desk, the abbot began with a warm smile, gesturing to the schoolmaster to translate for him. The schoolmaster spoke in a Frankish-Germanic dialect that we could more-or-less understand.

Introductions came first. "Boys, I am Brother Petrus, and this is Abbot—or Abba—Gregorius, as you may already know. He is the 'father' of this house, who redeemed you in the slave market today."

Abba Gregorius, it turned out, was formerly Prefect of Rome, the highest office in the highest civil authority, which perhaps explained why so many stopped to greet him on our way. He was also the founder of this monastery, as well as its first postulant member, and now served as the abbot.

Petrus continued, "And this is one of our monks, Brother Augustinus, who also accompanied you back from the Septa Julia. And this is Prior Pretiosus, whom you have already met, and he is in charge of the day to day running of San Andreas monastery. So, on the abbot's behalf, we welcome you here as part of this community! Although Abba paid redemption money for you in the slave market today, in this house, there are no slaves; you are free. But in Rome, because you are so young, you are still regarded as children; and as children, someone takes responsibility for you until you are sixteen, and old enough to make decisions for yourselves. For this reason, our prior," he looked towards Pretiosus, brow furrowed as he made notes, "will be your guardian while you are with us. And I, Brother Petrus"—he pointed to himself—"will be your teacher. You will also join fully into the life of the monastery, and you will have much to keep idle hands occupied!"

Augustinus, seated between the abbot and me, nodded encouragingly.

"Also, Alric and Cadmon, you are safe with us here—while you are within the walls of this monastery; but you must take care when you go outside the gate, because Rome is not a safe place, particularly at night."

After months at sea with Felix and his first mate Souk, Cadmon and I knew what 'unsafe' meant; and the body floating down the Tiber carried a message about the state of Rome. In the calm order of this monastery, we felt secure.

Brother Petrus said, "Is there anything you want to ask of us before you tell us your story?"

I half raised my hand and looked from the abbot to Augustinus.

"Yes! My sister Tola! She was also captured by Felix, along with Cadmon and me. Felix sold her to someone on our journey. I promised to find her. Can you help me?" I pleaded.

The abbot nodded as he sat up. "There is someone who can!" He turned to Augustinus. "Go to Felix's ship at once! He must know. His ship may still be tied up at the Imperial Wharfs." Abba glanced at the two of us. "And take the boys with you. We'll gather tomorrow afternoon again to hear how you came to Rome!"

Our sandals clattered loudly on the steps as we hurried to the street and turned towards the vast, silent Circus Maximus, a hundred paces away. Weeds grew unchecked on the abandoned circus floor and through cracks between the marble seats. A cool breeze had sprung up with sunset. Shafts of evening light dazzled from the direction of Trans Tiberim on the far bank as we hurried towards the river. We turned left at the Forum Boarium, alongside the riverbank towards the crumbling Imperial Wharfs, where we had set off earlier in the day.

Augustinus breathed a heartfelt *Deo Gratia*, thanks be to God, as we saw Felix's ship still moored, slowly rising on the incoming tide. The carts that carried Felix's wares earlier in the day stood empty on the quayside. Felix has had a good day, I thought, still feeling apprehensive at the prospect of coming face to face with him. Flies swarmed around the carts, and a rat ran down the mooring rope. Anaxos and Souk were on watch, gambling and drinking. Souk cursed as the dice switched winnings back and forth between the two men, hardly noticing our arrival at the gangplank.

Augustinus called out, "Deo Gratia! Where can I find your skipper, Felix?"

Souk looked up, annoyed at the interruption.

"And who is asking?" Then he recognised Augustinus.

Anaxos said, "Felix is in a tavern in town, you won't find him back here before morning. Late morning."

Augustinus gestured towards me. "One of these young boys has a sister, about seven or eight years old. Where did you sell her? And who did you sell her to?"

Souk focused his bleary eyes on Cadmon and me, hardly recognisable in clean woollen habits and sandals. He sneered when he finally realised who we were and I felt hatred rising like bile in my mouth. Souk took a swig from his flagon. "Well, we've been to a lot of places these last few months. Maybe the slave market at Bordele. But I don't know who bought her. Some rich bloke; paid a good price, mind you." He leered. "A very good price!"

Augustinus pressed Souk further. "Do you mean, a man *from* Bordele?"

"Don't know; maybe he came from somewhere else, or bought her for somebody else."

We walked swiftly back towards the Forum Boarium, crossing the marketplace for the second time that day. The last few stallholders were packing up for the night. Through a break in the clouds, I noticed the moon rising over the Palatine. Empty and sightless windows stared down at the ruined city below. Lights flickered from one of the palaces where the Emperor's representative in Rome had his quarters.

Just ahead of us we came upon an evening shift of the Vigiles, Rome's police-cum-fire brigade, their sturdy horse-drawn cart loaded with buckets of water, sand and centones—fire-blankets made of woollen patchwork and soaked in vinegar. The cart also carried several amphorae of water and a syphon-pump for drawing water from the Tiber. They came from their barracks in the Trans Tiberim district, their motto "Where there is suffering, there are the Vigiles!" It seemed that night-time in Rome overflowed with dangers, not only from dark, narrow alleys that waited for the unwary but the risk of a careless fire that could spread from street to street in a matter of moments.

Augustinus called out to the night watch as we came up behind. "Glad to see you, Remus! We need your help!" The captain cheerily returned the greeting; the two men apparently knew each other well. "We are looking for Felix, the skipper of the ship that's moored down at the Imperial Wharfs. His henchmen say he's in a tavern somewhere in town."

"Well, Rome's not short of taverns! But he probably hasn't gone too far from his ship, so let's try a few and see if we can find him for you."

The first two taverns had no news of him, but we were lucky with the third, its painted sign creaking back and forth in the breeze. The tavern was a seedy place on the ground floor of an insula block, noisy with patrons who worked on the river. We scanned the customers for a few moments.

"That's him over there." I grabbed Augustinus's sleeve, pointing at a table. I felt my legs turning to jelly. What if they seized us again and we ended up back on the ship? Augustinus made his way over to Felix. The slaver's hat sat perched on top of his monkey stick, resting after a hard day's work. Felix looked up at Augustinus before shifting his bleary gaze to me and then to Cadmon. He burst out laughing.

"Well, well! Look who's come back! The brats too much trouble for you already, eh? Well, I might just take 'em back if you make me a good offer!"

Felix reached for a flagon on the table and poured another tumbler of cheap sour wine. Two of the Vigiles pressed past us, standing on either side of Felix. Remus drew out his sword a couple of inches and commanded, "Keep both hands on the table!"

The noise in the tavern fell silent. The landlord, wiping his hands on a cloth, came over, looking anxiously back and forth from Remus to Felix.

Augustinus put a hand on my shoulder and said to the slaver, "You sold this boy's sister into slavery somewhere on your journey. Where was it? Who bought her?"

Felix shrugged. "We stopped at many places."

Remus drew his sword out a little further from its sheath.

"Well, now that you've cleared my head, let me think. Perhaps Bordele. Yes. It's a big centre for slaves."

Augustinus glanced at Remus for comment.

"I know of it—in the land of the Franks, near the sea. But it's a long, long way from here."

Augustinus said, "Who bought her, then?"

Felix theatrically opened up his hands and puffed out his cheeks before answering. "Someone buying for a client. He didn't say who, or where he came from. That's not my concern. You're wasting your time. There's no way to find out, even if you go back there."

Augustinus's eyes bored into his, probing for truth or lies.

"All right", he said at last. He turned to Cadmon and me, indicating with an apologetic shrug that he could do no more. The Captain of the Vigiles slid his sword back into its sheath. I glared at Felix as he let out a sigh, relaxed, leaning back. His colourful coat opened, exposing his broad chest, and I saw the gold coin that he had taken from me at the start of the voyage. It now hung on a thin gold chain, dangling around his neck, just visible in the opening of his coat. With my heart thumping and my anger soaring, I lunged forward, the chain snapping as I jerked my gold talisman from his neck.

"You little bastard! That's mine!"

"No, it's mine! My Queen gave it to me on the day I was born, at the old fort near my home!"

Cadmon joined in. "Yes, it's true! That is his coin! It definitely belong to Alric!" I looked pleadingly at Augustinus, standing next to me. I said, "He took it from me the day they took us! It belongs to me!"

Augustinus couldn't understand a word I said, but he caught the gist of it, as I pointed to myself and back at Felix while I babbled out my story. He stretched out his hand for the coin. After a few agonising moments of intense struggle, I dropped my gold amulet into his palm. He examined it briefly, turning it over in his fingers, squinting in the dim light of the tavern. Augustinus read out the inscription on the face of the coin, "*Charibertus Rex* – King Charibert." For the first time, I heard what those markings meant – the name of Queen Bertha's father, the long-dead King of Lutitia, inscribed on this coin that she had pressed into my hand on the day I came from my mother's womb.

Augustinus sighed and, to my horror, returned my coin to a grinning Felix. It was only much later that I understood his reasoning, even though I struggled to accept it. As Brother Petrus later explained to me on Augustinus' behalf, "You did not have the coin when Abba redeemed you, and he could not spend the monastery's money buying gold when we have already redeemed what is worth far, far more. He means *you*."

In the tavern Cadmon put a consoling arm around me, and with a heavy heart, we retraced our steps to the monastery, no further forward in knowing what happened to Tola, and with my hopes of retrieving my precious coin now completely dashed. Augustinus removed a small, wooden cross from around his neck and placed it in my hand. His simple words needed no translation: "Have this, Alric. It means more than a gold coin."

By the time we returned to the monastery, darkness had fallen. The prior took us to a small upstairs cell and we fell upon our beds. Here, for the first time in five months since Felix snatched us away from the Haven, I slept like the dead until long after daybreak.

When I finally opened my eyes, Cadmon was still asleep and snoring. Everyone was up and presumably about, but silence ruled. I lay back, and my thoughts drifted to a time nearly eleven years earlier when all this began.

3

RATTEBURG FORT

May 579 AD

REMARKABLE EVENTS SOMETIMES happen in unremarkable lives. Such, I confess, is mine. These events had begun with my parents, Galen and Erlina, at Sandwic Haven in the Kingdom of Cantia, home of the Cantwara people.

My parents remained without issue for three anxious years after their betrothal. Then Helga, my mother's sister and a midwife, made an offering to our ancestral matriarchs, took her newborn child and placed her in my parents' bed for the night. Nine months later, I came from the womb at the annual spring market held in the shadow of an ancient Roman fort we called Ratteburg. For the next nine summers, Erlina told and retold this story around the time of the anniversary of my birth. By my fourth year, I knew all the essential points. By my seventh, I could recite the story by heart, and I have no difficulty recalling it once more.

From early morning on that day, wagons and handcarts clogged the ancient paths leading to Ratteburg fort guarding the coast. Occasional wispy clouds drifted across the heavens, a good omen for a thriving market. Fires roared into life on the open ground, between the Earl's mead-hall and the crumbling flintstone walls of the old fort. By early afternoon most farmers and craft workers in the district had arrived, eager to barter crops for handiwork and tools for cloth. Many country folk also stayed over until the following day. They came with their families, on foot, and on donkeys, but most came over water, as my parents did. A fleet of small boats, roped to the quay below the walls of the fort, bobbed on the rising tide. Landowners in the district, together with churls—such as my family who fished the rivers and farmed their lands—also swelled the numbers. Womenfolk bartered for embroidery and earthenware while men inspected sheep and spilled their wisdom as they examined newly crafted ploughs.

Earl Sighart, the king's nobleman and overseer of both the fort and district, rose well before dawn, preparing for the market. The earl and his wife, Odelinda, were greatly respected for fairness to their churls and generosity in hard times. Storehouses, guest-huts, workshops, stables, servants' hovels, a bake-room and several small family shrines surrounded Sighart's manor and spacious mead-hall. Enclosures for animals stood to the rear, near the grain stores and a training area for Sighart's warriors, who comprised his household guard. Not far beyond these buildings was a wide, circular hollow dug into a small hillock of rising ground, lined with ancient crumbling stone seats. It had served as a small theatre in Roman times, but for now, several shaggy sheep occupied this hollow waiting for their wool-clip. The theatre's magnificent view overlooked the countryside and, just visible in the distance, a hilltop shrine dedicated to our chief god, Wodin.

Odelinda mingled easily with the crowd, offering a kind word and listening ear as she inspected each stall. Her two-year-old son, Cadmon, trotted confidently beside her, while Derian, three years older, clung whining and pulling at her skirts. From early morning a wild boar donated by the Earl turned slowly on a spit, expertly sliced by Alfric the charcoal burner. Few noblemen in our part of the kingdom were as generous as the earl. Alongside the hog roast Wulfwyn, a widow, set up her stall and gave out thick chunks of course bread—also thanks to Sighart. Another shelter erected alongside Wulfwyn's did a roaring trade in light honey-beer and dark cider; this too from Sighart's estate.

My father did not hail from Sandwic; he came from Eccles, a small hamlet on the Medd-Wey, which means "the river of golden mead." Part-Briton and part Saxon, he too owed fealty to Sighart. My parents' hovel was in a fishing hamlet, open to the ocean tides and waters of the broad Wantsum Channel. My mother was a local girl, now heavily pregnant with me, and nearing her term. She debated the wisdom of undertaking this journey to market, but then she would have regretted staying behind. Besides, Helga would be on hand as the midwife if anything happened.

Cadmon pulled his mother's hand, dragging her towards old Jorg. Grey-bearded Jorg, a venerable warrior from days of yore, whose great-great-great-grandfather had fought bravely at the battle of Badon Hill, sat on a log surrounded by young boys eager to hear of his spellbinding exploits. The youngsters sat motionless, eyes fastened on the huge jewelled sword that Jorg held aloft, its patterned blade as undimmed as the day it was forged more than a century before. Already, Cadmon dreamed of becoming a warrior. He was too young to follow the story that old Jorg was weaving, but his passion for possessing the sword grew ever stronger as Jorg, in his gruff voice, spun his tales of valour in battle. Occasionally withdrawing a glimpse of steel blade from its ancient scabbard, Jorg finally removed it from its sheath as his tale of valour reached its end.

New arrivals swelled the market as the afternoon wore on, children running and shrieking as one game turned into another. Hens clucked around the stalls, scratching the earth for worms, while dogs scavenged for bits of hog meat and gristle dropped by the children. Seagulls swooped down from the walls of the fort, snatching scraps of bread and pork missed by the dogs. So far, events continued as they always did.

In the midst of all this, two long, drawn-out blasts on a bull's horn sounded from the walls of the fort, alerting the earl and his warriors to a small flotilla approaching from the sea. The horn-blasts stopped all revelry, and the hubbub from the market died away. All eyes turned to the sea as a wave of anxiety swept through the fair.

The three ships turned directly towards the fort. As they sailed nearer, curiosity overcame anxiety, and the crowd pushed towards the edge of the cliff. Others, more agile, climbed the fort walls and yet more scrambled down to the jetty below. The ships entered the estuary, beginning a long, sweeping movement towards the fort. The faces of half a dozen of Earl Sighart's helmeted warriors appeared along the eastern wall, staring across the water, as the small flotilla sailed past our home at the Haven. These were not ships that anyone recognised, except that the leading vessel was a man-of-war, round-painted shields hanging from its sides, warriors drawing steadily on the oars as their sail began to furl.

The third ship, a merchant's vessel, struggled under the weight of its merchandise. The middle ship, however, was very different. As it drew closer a Frankish insignia on the white sail became visible. A lookout on the walls of the fort shouted out he could see the richly decorated deck of the ship, partially obscured by a tent-canopy stretched over the rear. The vessel drew nearer, and onlookers could see half a dozen young women dressed in white, standing on either side of the canopy, their cloaks billowing in the breeze. A tall man in a purple robe and carrying a shepherd's crook, stood boldly upright in the prow, his steady gaze sweeping the crowd as the three vessels made their final approach to the jetty.

"They are traders, come to barter," said one man.

"No, the middle ship is boldly decorated," argued another. "Can't you see the gold glittering on the front of the prow; the gilded masthead? And the symbol, emblazoned on the sail?"

A third man spoke up. "You're both wrong! They are raiders from afar, come to grab what they can before returning with their spoils."

The only thing everyone agreed on was that they had never seen the likes of this before.

Earl Sighart called his household slave. "Saba! Bring my best cloak! We have guests to welcome!"

On the cliff, a few hundred feet away from the fort, Sighart's impressive manor house and mead hall stood overlooking the sea, befitting an Earl of the Realm and Alderman of the District. The house rested on the brow of a gentle slope, offering magnificent views over the channel and the sparkling sea. Although Sighart was somewhat stout and no longer in his prime, he ran from the manor to the fort with surprising speed. Reaching the dilapidated south gate, he entered the derelict fortress and hurried down a flight of rotted wooden stairs to the jetty. The swirling river and scouring sea had slowly eaten away the base of the soft chalk cliff on which the fort's eastern wall rested.

As the earl reached the jetty, the ships made their final approach to the landing place. Some seafarers noted, with murmurs of admiration, how carefully and skilfully these craft edged towards the jetty at the base of the fort. The crowd could now clearly see that beneath the canopy sat a young woman gazing out at the assembly, a golden diadem on her brow. A tall man standing in the prow wore an unusual pointed hat, and a silver cross glinted on his chest, something that none of the onlookers had seen before.

Sighart stepped on to the jetty, commanding everyone standing there to leave. With groans of disappointment, onlookers grudgingly yielded their vantage point to their chieftain and his warriors. The earl called out, "Greetings, most excellent travellers! What brings you to us in such splendid craft? How may we know your intention? Be it good, or be it ill?"

The imposing figure standing in the prow motioned with his hand and boomed, "We have come in peace from the Kingdom of Francia, bringing Princess Bertha to wed her betrothed, Prince Ethelbert of this great and blessed Kingdom of the Cantwara!"

A gasp of surprise swept through the onlookers, but before Earl Sighart could respond, Princess Bertha's protector, who was undoubtedly a man of high rank, turned to his charge, sitting beneath the shady awning, and stretched out his hand to her. The princess rose and came forward. From her long raven hair tied with a ribbon, to the pearls that studded her shoes, she shone radiantly in her regal finery. The air resounded with gasps of admiration as the princess stepped ashore, accompanied by her maidens. As she turned to those on the quay, her smile was so glowing she could have melted the heart of a blindfolded statue—or so my mother said, although I'm sure she had never actually seen such a thing. Utterly enchanting, and in full command of proceedings, Princess Bertha turned to Sighart with a most charming and regal smile.

"Now, good sir, would you kindly inform the Prince that his bride awaits his arrival?"

In her surprise, my mother took half a step back, tripped over a thick tuft of grass and landed firmly on her buttocks. Erlina laughed at herself; others turned around to see what had happened and laughed with her. A moment later Erlina cried out, clutching her womb. "Galen! Galen! My waters are breaking! My child's coming!" My father swept her up in his arms and carried her to a nearby tent. Helga arrived swiftly and opened her bag of potions, beginning her examination. In only a few minutes, I came out yelling into the world.

A little while later, as my mother lay cradling her firstborn, the earl's wife entered the tent with Cadmon in tow, bringing soft pillows for Erlina. Cadmon stretched out his hand, pushing a fat finger into my face as Princess Bertha herself appeared at the tent door. She knelt beside my mother, looked at me, and said, "What a beautiful child! A boy?"

Erlina stammered out, "Yes, your highness."

"May I?" The princess reached out, and my mother placed me in her soft, warm hands.

"What will you call him?"

"His name is Alric, your highness, after his grandfather," my mother said proudly.

The princess rocked me gently for a few moments before returning me to my mother. Then she fished out a gold coin from the folds of her robes. The coin bore the image of Princess Bertha's father, his face in profile and clean-shaven, long hair tied in a band on his head. Around the coin, letters were inscribed, meaningless to my mother and understood by me only many years later. To my mother's great surprise, the princess squeezed this token into my tiny hand.

"This is for you, young Alric," she said, "in honour of this auspicious day!"

Later, Erlina made a small leather bag with a cord to hold the coin, and when I was old enough, she hung the coin around my neck as an amulet, my lucky charm. But at that moment, as the princess squeezed my tiny hand around her gold gift, she asked my mother, "What do you think your child will become?"

"Oh, he'll be a fisherman, your highness, just like his father!"

Princess Bertha's reply, so mysteriously worded as to make little sense to my mother, was nevertheless delivered with such quiet solemnity that she never forgot it: "One day, may the Almighty bring him to the place of the great Fisher of Men!"

The princess put her hand on my tiny head and said, "May God bless you, Alric!"

My mother believed that my Orlag, the course of my life, was laid down at the moment of my birth. Even as I came from the womb, the Three Fates, the Wyrdae, had already set up their loom in the heavens, weaving my future from a thread of life supplied by the goddess Frigg. Only the intervention of the gods could change it.

Little did we know just how much I was going to need Princess Bertha's blessing.

4

KING EORMENRIC

Raculf, Mid-Winter 588 AD

THE OLD KING lay dying.

Eormenric's guard, we learned later, carried him from his royal quarters across to the royal mead-hall, near the crumbling walls of an ancient Roman fortress we Saxons called Raculf. News of Eormenric's illness spread swiftly throughout his kingdom, causing deep uncertainty as much as great sadness. Longships bearing the king's earls and warriors had been arriving for the past three days. The king's men gathered in the timbered hall, murmuring in low tones as they ate and drank and speculated about what might come next. Once the king breathed his last, others would contend for his place; and who could be sure the winner would be Prince Ethelbert, his son?

With mid-winter came nights of icy cold. On the rain-spattered balcony overlooking the sea, the queen made a comfortable bed of soft animal skins for her king. Here Eormenric could smell the sea air and gaze over the waters of the Temes Estuary, as he waited for his end to come.

The Midwinter Feast at the king's palace called for vast supplies of food and drink. Earl Sighart summoned my father to bring a boatload of fish from Sandwic to Raculf, in part-payment for the food-rent the earl owed to the king. My father, in turn, owed Earl Sighart for his fishing concessions at Sandwic Haven. The earl had already left for Raculf a few days earlier to attend at his ailing king's bedside.

And so my father and I found ourselves carefully rowing our heavily laden boat through the Wantsum Channel on my first journey to the king's royal hall. My father had only made this crossing a handful of times; but now, with the king failing, we answered the urgent summons to Raculf.

Before daybreak, my father and I arose and filled the boat to the brim with baskets of eels, perch, pike, carp and sea bass, taken from our holding pools at the Haven. Only a few natural havens, like ours at Sandwic, were able to provide adequate shelter from the storms, so we managed a good passing trade. For this journey, we could not raise our mast and sail for fear of overtipping in a squall, so we stowed them with the catch and used only our oars. We had no concerns about the boat, built for this coastline with its long stretches of beach and countless inlets. The boat's weathered planking was light enough for two of us to carry through the surf and up the beach, and also strong enough to launch into heavy breakers on a stormy sea. The shallow draft also made it possible to beach the boat without tipping and losing our catch.

I had laboured with my father for nearly four years, since my sixth birth-feast, setting his traps, clearing the fish baskets, cleaning the nets and angling on our lines from both the shore and the boat. We also believed that success or failure in making a livelihood depended as much on the whim of the gods of sea and sky as on our skill.

At dawn, the Haven finally slipped away behind us. Erlina waved goodbye from the gate of our little hamlet, near the shore. My sister Tola clung to Erlina's arm with Godric and Greta, my younger siblings, holding on to mother's skirt. She knew well the dangers that might lie ahead on the open channel and stayed watching and waving until we disappeared from view.

Our course took us past Ratteburg's sombre fort, lying to the west. Looking east, a long low ridge of sand and flint stone shingle lay between the fort and the open sea. This spur of land belonged to Hrothgar, Earl of the Isle of Tanet, and also the village of Stonar that clung to its stony shore. Fishermen worked furiously at the water's edge, scraping shellfish from the rocks, loading their catch into boats for their long journey to Raculf.

My father steered a course between the marshes off Ratteburg and the treacherous shores of the Isle of Tanet. After a time we drew near to a small island in the estuary that stood clear of the water, even at high tide. Here, the remains of an old Roman burial shrine lay partially hidden beneath the roots of a gnarled old hawthorn, growing through broken burial stones. Tales of spirits from this island, luring sailors to their doom, abounded in these parts and no one ever dared set foot there. A shiver ran down my spine as I remembered stories of the souls of the dead, mysteriously transported by night from the Frankish coast to this tiny island, all in the space of a single hour. My father called out, interrupting my dark thoughts. "We turn here, son!"

This haunted island marked our westward turn further into the Wantsum, towards the night-rest of the pale winter sun, and following the deepest part of the Channel. Here the Great Stour, hidden beneath the waves at high tide, became exposed when the tide went out, leaving mud flats exposed to scavenging herons and gulls. It took us a long while to reach the confluence of the Great Stour that flowed from the ruined Roman town of Cantwaraburg towards the Wantsum River, where the salt waters of two seas met at high tide. Low ridges of land rose in the distance, as drab and grey-brown as the sea and sky, and I caught sight of fishing boats from Stonar in our wake.

We had set off from the Haven on a rising tide, and for the last part of our crossing, the ebb tide would draw us towards the Temes Estuary. We shipped oars for a while to ease our aching shoulders, drifting slowly northwards. The wind had dropped, and even the gulls in the darkening sky had ceased screeching. Nothing seemed to stir on the low hills in the distance, the world coming together in an utterly silent moment as the boat gently rocked on the grey Channel water. I clambered around so that my father and I sat facing each other, sharing a few pieces of smoked fish and bread cakes from our belt pouches, washing the meal down with water from a leather gourd. Soon, Galen nodded and reached again for his oars.

"Is it much longer, Pa?" I asked, climbing back over the bench.

"Before dark, my son," he said; and while I worked out what that meant, we pulled steadily towards the royal palace beneath a streaky sky.

An icy on-shore breeze sprang up blowing Galen's long hair, partially covered by his woollen Phrygian cap that drooped over his dank forehead. A jacket of sheepskin hid his tunic, his legs covered with thick, woollen hose down to his shoes. I shared my father's slim build and medium height, my growing hands large and rough from fishing, repairing and rowing. But unlike him, and very much like my mother Erlina, I had corn-yellow hair, while his was dark, interspersed with flecks of grey. Celtic blood flowed in his ancestry, he said, from even *before* old Roman Britannia, and that was common in our parts. A man of few words, like most fishermen, my father confined his conversation to work at hand. Despite his lack of conversation, a close bond existed between father and first-born son, and he treated me kindly and taught me carefully.

The waters could be rough and choppy at the meeting point of the two seas and the river of the Great Stour, where it branches northwards into the smaller River Wantsum and flows towards Raculf. However, with the high tide on the turn, rowing became a bit easier as we rounded the shoulder of the Isle of Tanet towards the Temes Estuary, and rowed past the fishing village of Sarr where the waters swirled the strongest. Our boat rocked unsteadily for a few moments, but we righted and rowed on past a broken Roman lighthouse, set high on a hill at some distance from the shore. A foul, overpowering stench arose from the nearby marshes, so strong we could scarcely breathe.

My father called out, "Look Alric. See that old hall on your right? Up on the bank?"

On the western shore of the River Wantsum I could just make out the ruins of an old hall, its roof collapsed, a pitiful remnant of better days. My father paced himself between each hard pull on his oars as he continued his tale. "Used to belong to Gilling, the frost giant a long time ago. Met his end through treachery, right here on the Wantsum."

"What happened, Pa?"

He pulled on the oars for a few moments, choosing his words carefully. "Gilling died by drowning at the hands of two dwarfs. You know they are not to be trusted?"

"Yes, Pa, so I've heard." The dwarfs usually dwelt deep beneath the earth, with a renowned reputation as smiths, but in these parts, there were no mountains and only a few low hills, so dwarfs were few – so few, I'd never seen one myself.

Galen continued, "Well, they sank Gilling's boat in the middle of this river. Legend says that for this deed his son Suttung punished them. He tied the two dwarfs to a rock in the path of the rising tide and left them to drown."

When he paused, I said eagerly, "What happened then, Pa?"

"Well, they begged for mercy vowing to give up their magic mead that never runs out in exchange for their lives." Many, it seemed, regarded Suttung's mead as the finest in the world. "Some say our king also received some of this magic mead as a gift and now he gives this to his favourites at his royal hall."

My father rowed in silence for a while as we laboured on dark waters towards our destination. I wondered if we would be given some of the magic mead when we arrived at the hall.

Pa added, "Some say the ghost of Gilling still walks these waters on a dark evening such as this. So keep your eyes peeled!"

I shuddered, looking nervously about for any sign of Gilling, a sense of foreboding settling on my narrow shoulders. Spirits dominated our world at every turn; keeping on their good side or out of their way was a big part of life. I touched Princess Bertha's gold amulet coin around my neck, and we picked up the pace as we rowed past the rock where two dwarfs once lay bound on a rising tide.

My father was anxious to reach our destination without delay, as we had rowed for much of the day towards the king's great hall, perched on the cliffs facing the Temes Estuary. The sun began to set, leaving a yellow streak of sky beneath the grey cloud, looking like a giant's half-closed eyelid. In winter, it always seemed to me, the Sun God both rises and sets in a low arc to the south. But that, I supposed, was the prerogative of a deity, just like Suttung and his mead.

From my childhood legends and myths, I feared that Loki, the Norse god of cunning and deceitful tricks, might cast his bleary eye upon us, weighing up whether to allow us to make landfall, or to toss us with our catch into the inky-black waters. I touched my amulet again, glad that I had slipped into our family shrine before we set off, to make an offering to Neorth, god of the seas and fishermen. I had left three small fish and a piece of barley bread on the altar. I would have left some ale, but drinking was forbidden for one my age.

The dark outline of an old Roman fort, a ruin a quarter of a mile or so from the king's palace, came into view. Several longships were beached below its southern wall, bringing noblemen and warriors from all parts of the kingdom. They had come for the Winter Solstice, and also for the great meeting of the Witan of ruling elders, earls, and aldermen of the Kingdom of Cantia.

I recognised Sighart's warship, built only the year before, with its yellow carved dragonheads fore and aft. Fires were lit on the sand near the ship, warming the night watch; and I saw Weal, Sighart's slave in charge of the vessel, fussing about on board. We waved a greeting as we passed, but he did not recognise us in the gloom.

At last, we arrived at the great hall. I jumped on to the shingle as we beached the boat, my tired and cramped legs buckling beneath me as I landed. Together we unloaded and carried our heavy baskets to the kitchens and returned to lift the boat clear above high tide, turning it over and securing with a rope and an iron spike driven deep into the beach. Far too late to make a return journey and too weary anyway, we made our way to the entrance of the king's hall. The king's guard stood by and a steward greeted us as we entered the antechamber, directing us to a long bench at one of the dozens of wooden tables inside the hall.

I found myself completely overawed by this, the largest building that my eyes so far had seen. Huge carved ash and oak trunks supported the intricate woodwork holding up the thatched roof, giving the appearance of some giant ship turned upside down. Burning torches flickered on the columns, casting long shadows that disappeared into the cavernous ceiling. A carefully tended fire blazed in the centre of the hall, warding off the cold night air.

On one side of the hall, behind a long table, stood the king's magnificent carved and gilded throne. A smaller seat stood beside for his queen and other lesser chairs for his sons and the chief men of the kingdom, all of them unoccupied. Magnificent woven hangings framed the throne, the jewelled chair sparkling in the flame of torches on either side. Everything spoke of the wealth and prestige that attended the king, and somehow everyone who saw it also basked in its glory.

I picked out some of the noblemen and their warriors, sitting at the far end of the hall, come to pay their respects to the ailing king and attend the Witan. The great hall also hosted a few visitors to the kingdom and several humbler folk, churls like us. We greeted our table companions while the young women servers laid down jugs of beer and haunches of pork and fish in wooden bowls. Hungry and still thawing out after our long journey in an exposed boat on a windswept day, we voraciously attacked the hot food; but we were not offered the magic mead, only beer for Pa, and I felt disappointed.

Earl Sighart sat near to the king's empty throne, his sons Derian and Cadmon beside him. Cadmon had already reached his twelfth year. He had left his childhood behind with his eighth, beginning the journey to a warrior's life in the service of his father as one of the warrior lords of the kingdom. I provided the friendship Cadmon needed—through his visits to Sandwic Haven, part of his father's substantial estate.

As the son of a churl, I found that life demanded more of me than that of a son of a nobleman. While I spent long hours on my own with fishing lines and nets, rising early at first light and returning at dusk after a full day, Cadmon pitted his strength in wrestling contests where he fought as fiercely as a bear protecting her cubs. He could ride any horse. I had been on the back of a beast only once, and that was a donkey.

My particular gift was patience, catching any creature that lived in the water. Cadmon's skills were evident with horse, sword, and spear. He now joined boar hunts in woodlands surrounding Ratteburg fort and the hamlet of Eastringe, a few miles from Sandwic Haven. His outgoing manner and natural charm made him popular with everyone—except his older brother Derian.

The rivalry between the two brothers had grown intense, yet it was because of Derian that I came to develop a friendship with Cadmon. Whenever Earl Sighart went away on the king's affairs, Cadmon escaped to the Haven, by boat or on horseback. Here he spent several days with our family until word came that the earl had returned so that Cadmon could return safely home. Erlina made a fuss of him and my siblings—Tola, Godric, and Greta—followed him around like ducklings. But mostly we worked together in the Haven, fishing in silence from a boat among the reeds.

I looked up from my meat and saw Sighart talking to an enormous hulk of a man with long straggly reddish hair and a full beard, his exposed arms ringed with gold bands.

"That's Hrothgar," my father said, "Earl of the Isle of Tanet." The earl quaffed deeply of the king's mead, dominating the conversation with a few words, punctuated by long silences. Sighart listened, occasionally making some comment or shaking his head in disagreement. Unnoticed by Sighart, I saw Derian threatening his younger brother, jabbing a finger at Cadmon's chest.

My father finished his meal and rose to talk to some fishermen nearby. I helped myself to the dregs of his beer and, resting my head on my arms, drifted into an exhausted sleep.

A hand, roughly shaking my shoulder, interrupted my slumbers. Cadmon put his mouth to my ear. "Everyone's busy talking and drinking. Come on, Alric, this is a good time to explore!"

5

Mothers' Night

Raculf, December 588 AD

I FOUND MYSELF at Cadmon's side, passing the guards at the door and stumbling into the cold winter's night. "Where are we going?" I demanded, as we rounded a corner of the hall, our backs turned to an icy wind coming off the sea.

"Always wanted to explore this old fort! I wonder if it's different to Ratteburg? Come! They won't notice we're gone!" I didn't believe that for a moment.

"Let's be quick then!" I acquiesced.

We stumbled through the dark for what seemed an age, a full moon slipping in and out from behind the clouds until the broken wall of the old fort became faintly visible ahead of us. We picked our way around heaps of rubble, finally entering the fort through a dilapidated gateway on the west side. The barracks were in ruins, abandoned for nearly two centuries. The only building still standing lay within a large, enclosed courtyard. No one ever came to this dismal place, haunted by tales of ghosts and evil spirits discouraging anyone from entering, either by day or by night.

I shivered, and not only on account of the cutting wind. A sense of evil swirled around us in the blackness; I could feel it and smell it, but not see it. Cadmon pushed at a gate leading into the courtyard. The tiled roofs that once surrounded a portico had collapsed, and rubble lay scattered all around. As the moon slipped away again behind the cloud, we carefully picked our way towards the building and a large doorway in the centre. We crept closer then froze against the peeling wall, unable to breathe as a door creaked open on the far side of the building. A few moments later the door slammed shut. A dim light flickered through high, broken windows to our left and right. Inside, two men were talking in low voices as they walked into the hall.

The first voice said, "All is ready. They're stacked in here, waiting for your signal."

We could hear his companion grunt in approval, then say in a deep, rumbling voice, "Good. While that pup's burying his father, these spears will surround the Witan. You will propose me as his successor, and the rest will vote in favour. If they don't, they will know what will follow, and I will have the throne either way."

The first voice said, "Yes, my lord, we have the hand of surprise on our side. At a stroke, the whole kingdom will be yours!"

Cadmon, listening with his ear pressed against the door, suddenly swung around to me. Pieces of masonry scattered noisily under his feet, and the voices inside fell silent. We froze. I pointed to the columns around the courtyard that had once supported the roof, and we tiptoed as fast and silently as we could. We had scarcely reached the cover of two columns, pressing ourselves against the rough stone, when the two men inside reached the doorway where we had stood only moments before. The flame from their torch spilled its light into the courtyard, swinging from left to right as they stared into the gloom.

"Who's there?" demanded the deep, rumbling voice. Panic seized me. What if they discovered us? We would be lucky to get out of here alive! Just as my fears reached fever pitch, a startled pigeon hooted and flapped as it fled the roost in the alcove above the hall door. Bats followed next, swooping down from the rafters. After what seemed an eternity the deep voice grunted again, and the two men turned back into the hall. We heard their footsteps crunch across scattered pieces of masonry on the floor, followed by the creak of a door on the far side. Their footsteps sounded in the direction of the east wall of the fort, towards the river.

We waited for what seemed an eternity without moving a muscle, scarcely breathing. At last Cadmon signalled and carefully led the way back to the hall doorway. We listened hard for several more minutes, making sure no one lay in wait for us and pushed open the door. We inched our way slowly into the large room, the last place I wanted to be. The musty smell of decaying brick and plaster, mingled with the strong odour of a man, hung in the air. The full moon again obliged, and in its cold light we could make out scores of spears, stacked around the walls of this former headquarters of the old fort.

A low whistle of surprise escaped Cadmon's lips.

"This is treason!" he whispered. "And I know who it's coming from!"

We hurried back to the royal hall, retracing our steps to avoid any chance of running into the two plotters in the dark. A strange sight greeted us as we arrived. Outlined against the leaping flames of a log fire were huge, black, horse-like shapes, their teeth snapping at the watching crowd as the figures circled the fire. Some of the king's warriors also gathered around this spectacle, celebrating a hunter-gatherer god, a wanderer, and shaman called Wodin.

As we drew closer, I saw the horse-heads were wooden carvings, mounted on poles. The horses' thick necks, made of soot-blackened sacks, cloaked the person holding the pole. We had stumbled into an annual hoodening festival, where groups of farmers, facing a grim winter as the Solstice approached, travelled from village to village performing at mead-halls, and begging alms that would see them through the hungriest part of the winter. Modranicht, Mother's Night, the night of bloodletting, marked the turn of the year. Any livestock that farmers could not feed through winter were slaughtered.

Usually, young boys darted in and out of the crowd, bags held open to collect food or jewellery; but this group didn't seem concerned that no one was collecting. Wooden teeth snapped loudly only an inch above my head; I ducked to escape and noticed the feet beneath the cloth and the bottom of the stick holding up the horse's head. I turned and pointed Cadmon towards the shuffling feet. These were not farmers' feet, and the pole was not the staff of a threshing stick. Instead, the shoes were the shoes of a warrior, and the stick the shaft of a spear.

A hand flashed out from beneath the horse's cloak, dragging me into the circle of gyrating, snapping horses, swirling around and around the great log fire. I saw a huge hooden horse, towering above the rest, appearing in the midst of the figures, disappearing and reappearing in another place in the circling ring, over and over again. The circle of horses seemed to spread out wider, coming closer and closer to the entrance of the royal hall. I struggled to get free, and pulling my fishing knife from my belt with my free hand, I thrust it into the leg of the hooded figure holding me in his grasp. He released my arm with a cry of pain as someone else grabbed my free hand, pulling me out of this frightening, prancing ring. It was Cadmon, and together we ran for the entrance to the great hall. As we stumbled in, my father and Sighart came striding towards us, their faces like thunder, a sure forewarning of serious trouble.

"Where've you been?" Sighart shouted. "Didn't I tell you not to leave the hall without my permission?" Sighart directed his words to his son, but his eye also fixed on me. Cadmon blurted out where we'd been and what we had witnessed. The earl stood stunned for a moment, taking in all Cadmon had said. He dragged us back into the entrance hall and commanded one of the king's guard, "Send for the Captain! These two have a tale that he must hear at once. And don't give entrance into the hall to any of that hoodening crowd outside; the king's life depends upon it!"

The entrance doors to the royal hall slammed shut.

"Let Hama keep guard!" the night watch on the great door cried out, calling upon the god who kept watch over the rainbow bridge leading to Asagard, the home of the gods. In moments, we found ourselves bundled upstairs into the vestibule of the king's chambers, surrounded by the Captain of the Guard, together with Sighart, my father and, to my surprise, Prince Ethelbert.

Cadmon told again our story about two men in the old fort, less than an hour ago.

"Who were these men?" the prince demanded.

"We didn't see their faces, my Lord, but by his voice and his smell, I'd swear one of them is Hrothgar of Tanet! I sat only a few feet away from him at supper – his stench is unmistakable!" Cadmon had seen him on several occasions at various gatherings of the earls and had supped that very night only a yard away from him.

"And the other voice?" Ethelbert snapped abruptly.

"Belongs to Falk - his son!"

"That I can believe of them both!" the prince exploded, his face turning red. "Hrothgar claims descent from Horsa. They have schemed to seize the kingship from the line of Hengist from the beginning!"

The Prince was speaking of his royal lineage in the legend of two brothers, Hengist and Horsa, founding fathers of the Kingdom of Cantia. My father had told me the story that they came from Saxon people across the sea and journeyed to ancient Britannia as mercenaries. The request came from Lord Vortigern, a Roman-British overlord, desiring to protect Britannia's coastline from pirates and opportunistic raiders. However, the two brothers soon fell out, and the descendants of Horsa believe to this day that Hengist murdered his brother. My father said the stronger story is that Horsa died in battle, but in every generation since, one of Horsa's descendants has used this as an excuse to seize the crown from the family of Hengist. Hrothgar, the Earl of Tanet, had now come forward as the most recent pretender to the throne.

The Captain of the Guard said, "My lord, the men of Tanet have been arriving here in great numbers throughout the day."

"It is no coincidence that they arrive while the king is at death's door, and I fear he will not survive the night," said Ethelbert. "In the morning, our warriors are standing by, ready to drag the king's ship up the beach and prepare the burial barrow for him." He thought for a moment. "All this could take place by nightfall tomorrow. Hrothgar won't make his move until then. Nor will he delay for long after the burial!" Ehelbert returned to the matter at hand, instructing the Captain of the Guard, "Place a watch on the old fort so that Hrothgar cannot arm his men."

"We already have under guard the weapons from Hrothgar's men who are here in the hall, so they will find it difficult to take you by force," said Sighart.

Ethelbert said, "His only recourse, then, will be to put himself forward at the gathering of the Witan. And that he will lose."

Sighart hesitated before responding. "I believe you are right, my Prince. But not everyone welcomes a king whose queen is not one of their own, nor follows the traditional ways."

Ethelbert knew this well enough. He nodded. "Send up the King's Guard, one by one, so we do not arouse suspicion. I will take an oath of loyalty from each man in turn, so there is no treachery on the morrow. Do it now!"

The Captain of the Guard hurried downstairs and returned with the first of forty warriors who had formerly sworn fealty to their king.

As I watched each one take the oath, I felt in my bones that we were witnessing the dawn of a very, very long day.

From daybreak, cattle, sheep, pigs, eggs, cheeses, fowl, pulses, barley beer, flour, and other produce, arrived in large quantities from neighbouring estates to feed ever-growing numbers. Local fishermen were already taking to the water, rowing out to fish their weirs strung out along the banks of the river. I found the sight of so many boats on the water, bobbing on the swell of the incoming tide, both unusual and reassuring. Fishermen did not usually work together in such numbers, and fishing, for me at least, was a solitary business.

Later in the afternoon a ship under sail, with a dozen oarsmen, nudged its way into the Wantsum River to a landing place below the ancient walls, on the south side of the old fort. "Traders," my father said, inspecting the vessel as it passed. "And slavers too. But strangely, they have come very late in the year." Few ships crossed the seas to our shores once winter began, the sea rising high and the winds unpredictable. It took an exceptional skipper to take risks like this.

The ship moored, and we could see the skipper's distant figure swaggering up the beach, followed by a line of men, headed in the direction of the royal hall. They were laden with trunks of goods to trade; weapons, jewellery, glassware, Frankish wheel-turned beakers, gold from the Mediterranean and garnets sourced in the Far East.

I thought no more of this as I threw our nets over the side of our boat again and again for hours without respite, trailing baited hooks behind us, tipping fish into baskets, rowing back to shore with our catch and out again to fresh fishing grounds. Strong backs and hands helped land mounds of oysters, mussels, eels, sea bass, plaice, and herring, from a dozen boats on the stony shore.

The last rays of a red western sky had begun to fade. From beyond the king's hall, the blaze of cooking fires shot sparks into the night sky. At last, we turned our aching backs towards the shore and our oars drew us slowly to land. I noticed the merchant ship again, carved swan-neck rising high above the aft, and the skipper only just visible in his black sleeveless jacket, shouting at his crew.

We returned to the royal hall as a group of warriors in solemn procession bore the body of their king, wrapped in a bearskin, to his great warship that already lay half-buried on the beach. The rigging, sail, and mast had been removed, clearing a space for the frame of the wooden bier on which his body rested. Eormenric lay surrounded in death by the weapons and goods that served him in life; a fortune in gold plate, cups and jewellery, stowed in chests alongside his body. Eormenric's shield lay close to his head, helmet at his left side, sword in his hand at the right.

The grieving Dowager Queen, together with Princess Bertha and her children, stood watching from the balcony overlooking the sea. In sympathy, I touched the coin she had given me as I noticed her face—pale, drawn and anxious.

A little distance from the king's ship, a rope-fence marked off a sacred site for an altar and an offering—a prized bullock from the king's herd. The beast lay stunned and trussed on the altar, awaiting ritual slaughter at the hands of Coifin, the king's High Priest. He carried himself with authority, a tall, slim, bearded figure, his white, flowing woollen garment covering his feet.

Although of a distinguished lineage, this Chief Priest of Wodin neither carried a weapon nor rode a horse, making a distinction between his own sacral role and that of the warlords of Cantia. His son, who would be expected to follow in his father's footsteps, stood a little to one side as the sacrificial blade in Coifin's hand rose and fell. Blood spurted into a golden bowl beneath the bullock. Coifin removed the bowl and placed the bull's blood at the feet of the departed king, as an offering to Wodin.

Next, Wilfrid, Captain of the King's Guard, came forward and gave the prince a burning torch that he thrust into the altar's kindling. Flames spluttered and leaped into life, burning fiercely until both the bull and the altar were consumed. All the while, the women who had served Eormenric's household sang a dirge and wailed their grief.

Ethelbert, his head bowed, laid a hand on the king's warship for the last time. Eormenric and his great chariot of the sea were then buried deep in the sand by his warriors and covered by a mound of rocks. After this, twelve horsemen of Eormenric's Guard circled slowly around the burial mound. They sang songs of praise to their departed king and hero in battle, as he passed from Middangard—the realm of the living—into the realm of his ancestors, the Great Mead Hall in the heavens.

We all left the beach and made our way to the royal hall where a night of ritual drinking and songs lay ahead, in honour of our departed Warrior-King. Earl Sighart hosted as feast-giver, the Master of Ceremonies, approving or disapproving boasts and oaths made during that long night. Odelinda, the earl's wife, took the role of Ale-bearer for the gathering. She poured the first drink of the evening and, moving gracefully around the hall, dispensed mead and beer, accompanied by her ox-horn bearers, giving a kind word to each person with smiles and compliments. Young boys and girls of the king's household stood by, making sure the horns remained filled to the brim.

The Dowager Queen sat in her place beside her late king's empty throne, Ethelbert, and Bertha at her side. As the night wore on, toasts were made to Eormenric. He was their departed war-band leader and hoard-sharer; he was his warriors' ever-generous gold-friend. Despite this, hostile glares came from further along the king's table, marring the celebration of this sacred gathering of remembrance. Hrothgar made no toast and promised no loyalty to the king's heirs; instead, he drank liberally of the king's mead all through the night.

Meanwhile, with the patience of eternity, tireless sea-fingers had already begun the work of probing into Eormenric's sand and rock-covered burial chamber. Grain by grain, stone by stone, boulder by boulder, entrance would be gained. In the fullness of time, powerful waves would pound the exposed ship into splinters; the king's mortal remains and his treasure-hoard ferreted out by succeeding tides and dragged remorselessly into that great maw of the hungry sea.

6

THE VACANT THRONE

Raculf, New Year's Day 589 AD

MORNING BROKE TO a watery sunrise. Prince Ethelbert pulled chainmail over his tunic, strapped on his sword belt and took up his helmet. Lifting his heavy, painted shield, he walked to the cliffs and down to the beach where his father lay buried. Wilfrid and the King's Guard followed close behind.

The beach formed a natural amphitheatre of smooth, damp sand, and here Earl Sighart had drawn a large circle where the tide had drained away. The kingdom's earls and chief councillors gathered beyond it, and a semicircle of warriors gathered behind their respective chieftains. The warriors made way for the prince to enter the ring, then closed behind him. I wondered for whom the circle would open again in an hour's time.

I had passed the night as best I could, sleeping fitfully in the king's hall. Unable to sleep, I spoke in a low whisper with Pa, asking what would happen if Prince Ethelbert should lose the fight. "If Hrothgar emerges the victor, it won't take long before someone tells him who betrayed his secret stash of spears in that old fort and broke the news to the Prince. Things might go badly for Earl Sighart – as well they might work for us."

"Perhaps we shouldn't have said anything," I said.

"No, you did right, my son; you boys were brave, and spoke the truth. Had you not, we might all be dead by now. As it is, I'm by no means certain that Hrothgar will have the victory." Eventually, I fell into a fitful sleep, with all the events of the night swimming around in my tired head.

We arose early, backs stiff from lying on the hard table, and made our way with everyone else to the cliff top overlooking the Estuary. I felt excitement and fear churning in my stomach, wondering how this matter would end; and not least, what the outcome would mean for our family.

Cadmon and I sat together in the cold morning amongst the crowd of onlookers above the beach. My father stood watching events from a few paces behind us, his arms folded, his gaze sweeping the hilltop, the beach, and the horizon. Screeching gulls swooped towards us, turning at the last moment to glide away along the cliffs. In an atmosphere thick with tension, warriors from all parts of the kingdom thronged around us. Hrothgar's men from Tanet stood a little apart, nervous, speaking in low whispers. If Hrothgar lost this contest, their future would also be very bleak.

Falk waited anxiously down on the beach, holding his father's gear. The Watchman for the Coast, a seasoned warrior, sat on his restless horse. He switched his gaze from the horizon to the assembly on the beach below and back again to the water, alert to any danger from the sea.

I looked down at the backs of warriors and their helmets, their palms resting on jewelled pommels of their war-blades, thick woollen cloaks billowing in the icy wind. Those in the forefront were the noblemen who comprised the Witan, the king's council of some twenty aldermen of the kingdom—Earl Sighart among them—and behind each one, a servant holding his lord's battle-gear of helmet, spear, and shield. Behind the aldermen stood their thegns, seasoned warriors of ability and character, who rode with their lords in battle and managed their estates in peace. But at this moment, none of us knew which it would be, war or peace, as the two men prepared to face each other on the beach below.

During the night Hrothgar's weapons hoard in the old fort had been recovered, and Ethelbert's bodyguard seized the men from Tanet sent to collect them. Rumour was now rife that Hrothgar was the author of a plot against the Kingdom. Cadmon shared his father's opinion with me; Hrothgar's opportunity to take the Witan by force had passed; it was near impossible that he would win a vote of confidence from the aldermen and ascend the Throne of Cantia. Hrothgar's only recourse was to challenge Eormenric's son and heir in a contest to the death, and this he had finally declared in the mead-hall only a few hours before dawn.

Hrothgar was late, his hangover prodigious, his temper furious as he stumbled out from his all-night drinking. He stopped, his face confused and agitated at the sight of a woman dressed in black, sitting outside the door of the king's hall, spinning wool. Many of our kin believed that a man who comes across a woman as she spins must turn back from his path, or misfortune would befall him. I reckoned the woman could only have been there at the command of the widowed queen, or perhaps even Princess Bertha. Both women had everything to lose if Hrothgar emerged the victor.

Hrothgar recovered himself, gave a dismissive grunt and pressed on to the beach below the royal hall, leaving his nauseously strong odour in his wake. Even his warriors blew out their cheeks and leaned aside as he passed by. Hrothgar had rejected his body-armour, leaving his pale-skinned chest and belly exposed. A sheathed sword hung on his belt, and in his colossal grasp, Hrothgar dragged a long-handled battle-axe behind him like a club. He had slung his shield over his back, held by a thick leather strap across shoulder and torso. Beneath his helmet, his red face bore nothing but contempt as he brushed aside his fellow aldermen and entered the ring.

With a clear view from the cliff top, I noticed Hrothgar stood much taller than Ethelbert. He was an experienced warrior, decades older than the prince. None of the onlookers would have placed a wager on the outcome between the younger but less experienced man and a battle-seasoned warrior with a colossal, throbbing hangover.

Hrothgar stopped just inside the ring, standing across from Ethelbert who stood patiently waiting with a sword, shield, helmet, and mail. Everyone awaited the insults that preceded every combat, wounding words that allowed no compromise and no peace between the two men.

Hrothgar broke the silence in a deep, slow and bored voice.

"Well, boy, you are pretty enough, I grant you, for someone born of a foreign bitch and wedded to another!"

Ethelbert said nothing, weighing every word, not rising to the bait, watching for the slightest movement.

Hrothgar's voice now boomed, "But you are no warrior! You turned your back at the battle of Wibbandun when Ceawlin drove you shitting yourself back to Cantia, leaving my brother Oslaf behind on the battlefield as a feast for the frigging crows!" He paused and spat on the sand. "Cowards have no place ruling a kingdom of real fighting men!" A few grunts of support arose from Hrothgar's supporters, but everyone else remained silent, tense and watchful; few warriors had witnessed a contest such as this in their lifetime. Hrothgar raised his heavy axe and pointed beyond Ethelbert's shoulder to King Eormenric's burial mound several paces behind. "Soon, boy, you'll be dead like that bastard behind you!"

Ethelbert waited until Hrothgar had finished. Now all eyes now turned to the prince. He stood at ease, his shield resting on the sand, lightly held between thumb and forefinger, its weight leaning against his leg, his hand resting on the pommel of his sword. Cadmon thumped my arm, pointed to the weapon and whispered, “That’s the ancient Blade of Hengist – you know, who first came to these shores? My father says the old king gave it to him moments before he died!”

Down on the beach, Ethelbert finally spoke. His voice was clear and echoed back from the cliff. “It is indeed a sad day for us to hear a windbag like you tell such lies before an assembly of honest men such as these!” He swept his hand towards the warriors lining the beach. “You well know, Hrothgar, that I held the middle of the shield-wall, where you would expect your prince to be, while Oslaf was given the task to hold our left flank. His men were overwhelmed, the centre could not hold alone and we drew back to protect him. Yes, Oslaf died, but not with a spear in his stomach or a blade through his heart, but from an arrow – in his back – as he ran from the field!”

More shouts rose as Hrothgar spat again in contempt, shook his huge shaggy head with a roar, lifted his axe and advanced a couple of steps into the ring.

Ethelbert said, “Turn your words into steel, Hrothgar, you who have attempted to steal the kingdom by stealth like a scavenger from the sea! Now we shall see, and let this lay to rest at last all the enmity between my hall and yours!”

The two men began circling each other warily, each sizing up his opponent, positioning for best advantage. There was no sun to dazzle their eyes. The morning was dry and clouded, dismal and cold. From across the Temes Estuary, rain was coming.

The whole assembly fell silent, as tension sucked air from our lungs. With one explosive movement, Hrothgar swirled his axe above his head and advanced towards Ethelbert. The prince took a few paces to the right, turning sideways-on to his opponent, shield guarding his left side, sword held close to his body, pointing upwards towards his assailant. Hrothgar lunged forward, rapidly closing the distance between them, his axe swooping down in a vicious arc. Ethelbert took the blow on his shield and the two men disengaged. The circling continued, each probing the other, looking for an inner weakness that could prove crucial to victory. Hrothgar lunged again, disengaged, lunged one more time, reversing his grip to bring the axe-handle sharply against Ethelbert's shield. Ethelbert did not flinch or retreat and Hrothgar drew swiftly back again.

The two men had edged around the circle, exchanging initial positions. As Hrothgar moved to engage him again, Ethelbert struck for the first time, his sword coming down on Hrothgar's padded upper thigh. The older man lunged forward, striking his opponent's shield on its central boss, then swung around and away, his shield guarding his back, taking another blow from Ethelbert's sword.

With a surprisingly nimble movement for a man so heavy, Hrothgar swung around again, his long axe catching the inside edge of Ethelbert's shield. The prince closed in on his opponent, but once more Hrothgar swung away, his shield taking the full force of a blow to his shielded back. He twisted around to face his opponent again. This time Ethelbert led with his shield, driving the heavier man back on the defensive, their movements becoming a blur to the ring of warriors who stood watching the battle in tense, unnerving silence.

A curtain of steady winter drizzle now reached the shore, churning the sand into mud. Hrothgar swirled around again, Ethelbert closing in as his opponent lifted his axe above his head for another blow. The prince struck again and again with his sword, heavy blows that drove Hrothgar back on the defensive. As Hrothgar swirled around one more time, Ethelbert's blade struck hard against Hrothgar's leather-twined axe-handle and the weapon slipped from the older man's grasp. Hrothgar stumbled and slipped backwards, reaching for his sword. The prince's blade plunged towards the exposed stomach and Hrothgar staggered back one step, another step, then slipped and fell heavily on his back in the mud. Ethelbert kicked aside the axe and stood with one foot pinning down Hrothgar's sword scabbard. The tip of Ethelbert's sword pressed into his opponent's throat. The circle of warriors fell silent, waiting for the final thrust.

Ethelbert was breathing hard, his chest heaving. His opponent said nothing as he lay on the sand.

After what seemed an age, the prince finally drew himself upright. "My kingship will not begin with the spilling of blood; not even yours." He stepped back a pace, withdrawing his sword. "Instead, I banish you from these shores! You will leave this day and never return!"

A collective gasp of surprise rose from the hundreds of men holding their breath on the beach and cliff top, and I felt that a shadow of fear had lifted from every person watching. Ethelbert looked up at the earls and aldermen of Cantia standing in a circle around him and his gaze fell on Falk, Hrothgar's elder son.

"And you, Falk, you will keep your father company on his journey into exile!"

Then his gaze found Hrothgar's second son. "And to you, Rollo, I give all your father's lands as his successor, when you swear your oath of loyalty this day to me, as your king!"

It was an astute ploy on Ethelbert's part. At one stroke, the prince removed the two most troublesome men in the kingdom and yet he also honoured the warriors of Tanet by giving authority to the one son on whom Ethelbert could most rely to remain loyal.

Alongside me, Cadmon let out his breath. "That's far more than *we'd* have got if this had gone the other way!"

He was right. Our two families had been marked for a very bad end, and I realised with a great sense of relief that we had come out well from this affair. My father was a freeman, a churl like other local farmers and landed householders, but he was also considered a companion of Sighart's household and always welcomed at table in his mead-hall. We were accepted as a respected family in our district, like many who worked the land and formed the mainstay of the Realm of Cantia. But now, the part that Cadmon and I had played could only strengthen the bond between our two families. Cadmon thumped me on the back and I clasped his hand in relief. Our fortunes had changed dramatically in the short space of little more than a day. I had also lost my childhood ignorance of the darker affairs of men—the lust for power, and the pursuit of kingdoms.

But our two families were not the only ones who had stood to lose everything that day. Had Ethelbert lost this contest, the prince's lifeless body would have been thrown to the wolves, and Eormenric's widow put to the sword. Hrothgar would have slain Bertha's children and seized her as his bed-slave. Death would be a friend compared to a fate such as this.

Below on the beach, Ethelbert gave a great bellow of triumph, beating his raised shield with his victory sword. His royal bodyguard joined in, and in moments the air rang to the drumming sound of swords on shields echoing from the cliff. The Dowager Queen, Princess Bertha, and her children came out on to the balcony, their faces wreathed in smiles of relief and tears of joy at the outcome of the contest for the crown. Sighart seized Ethelbert's arm and raised it high above the young king's head.

"My Lords and Councillors!" he cried several times before the din died down. "My Lords and Councillors! Ethelbert, Prince of the Realm, rightful heir of King Eormenric, has this day proved himself in open contest as the Chief of our people! He is the one to guide us through these turbulent days into calmer waters. Freemen of the Realm, *here is your King*!"

The assembly roared approval. Ethelbert raised his sword and shield in the air again, turning to acknowledge the support of the nobles who stood chanting and stamping their feet in the circle around him. The king's guard seized Hrothgar, bound him, and dragged him away together with his son.

Ethelbert shouted above the noise, "I convene a Council of the Witan! To the mead-hall!" The new king thrust his sword into its scabbard and, followed by his Guard, walked swiftly to the royal hall.

My father and I left for the Haven as the Assembly of the Witan began. Carrying our empty baskets from the kitchens, we hurried back to our boat and lifted it across the shingle to the water's edge. As we pushed out from the shore, the sound of hurried footsteps crunched on the shingle behind us, and in the distance Derian's angry voice shouting, "I'll kill you, you little bastard!"

I leapt into the prow, turning to see Cadmon splashing into the water after us. A moment later he hurled himself into the boat, scrambled on to my seat and grabbed one of the oars, pulling hard to put as much distance as he could between himself and the spear in his brother's hand.

"He means it!" Cadmon panted to Pa, out of breath. "He says I made him look a fool last night when we discovered what was going on and didn't tell him! He's a shithead! One day I'm going to take his place! But he doesn't want to see me live long enough to do it!"

Derian's figure diminished on the shore as my father steered us further into the Wantsum River. Lowering his spear, Derian turned away walking up the beach, and soon we lost sight of him in the rain. We rigged the mast and sail, but there was little wind, so we lowered the sail again and rowed on, hoping to make landfall at the Haven before dark. Cadmon proved to be a strong rower, and between the three of us, we made good progress into the Wantsum Channel and down towards our landmark, the funeral island.

It was now so gloomy that all contrast seemed washed away. The old Roman burial shrine loomed a hundred yards ahead when my father first noticed the mainsail of the trading ship at Raculf coming up, barely visible behind us.

"Strange," said my father, "they can't make the sea crossing at night, and the tide is all wrong. Perhaps they are trying to make the anchorage at Ebbsfleet for the night, and catch the morning tide? We'll find cover, and see what they're up to."

We rowed hard towards the small funeral island and in a short while slid beneath a canopy of bare, overhanging hawthorn branches. We tied both ends of the boat to some thick, knotted roots. Lying low in the boat, we waited for the ship to pass, hiding low beneath some of the sacks stowed in the keel. Our boat rocked slowly on the tide; my teeth began to chatter in the cold and a warm trickle from my bladder told me I was no longer holding it in.

My father reached over and clamped my mouth shut. "They can hear your teeth rattle," he hissed, "and your piss can be heard five hundred paces away!"

Time seemed to drag by agonisingly slowly. We lay flat in the boat. I was still clutching my gold amulet as the ship came clearly into view. The rain had blown away and the moon slipped out from behind high, feathered clouds, creating a circle of light that lit up the water—and our hiding place—but the shadows of the knotted branches helped disguise our small craft. We could just make out dark shapes of three figures standing fore and aft, while rowers pulled hard on the oars and sails flapped feebly in the light breeze. The crew made no effort to mask their presence; the skipper bellowed at the oarsmen, his whip cracking over their backs. The splash, splash of oars digging into the black waters carried clearly as the ship left behind a silver trail of moonlight. The ship was heading in the direction of Ratteburg fort, but why? And why at this time of night?

Once the ship was out of sight we gingerly sat up, stretching our cramped limbs.

"What now, Pa?"

"Now we wait. They'll be back."

He was right. After what seemed an age the ship returned, passing by our small hideaway to make anchorage at the small haven at Ebbsfleet. The shouting and whipping on the ship had ceased and the pace of their oars was slower. Winter light had faded and it would be impossible for them to make out our boat, pressed against the shore beneath bare, overhanging branches. We lay hidden as before. More time passed; the ship disappeared behind our small island, heading for their overnight anchorage.

"Let's make sure they've gone," Cadmon whispered. My father grunted assent and remained in the boat as the two of us climbed out in the eerie moonlight and up through the island's thick, knotted roots from overgrown vegetation. I held my fears in check as the legend of this small island of the dead came into mind. We ascended through loose clumps of stone and brick until finally we came upon a small bell at the pinnacle, suspended on a rusted chain. A rotting length of rope was still attached, knotted at the end and swaying in the breeze, occasionally tolling the bell as it had done for hundreds of years.

A tree hunched low at the summit, its roots buried deep in the masonry below. Clinging to its thick branches, we looked towards the low, sloping spur of land called Ebbsfleet and its small anchorage in this corner of the Wantsum Channel. Our pursuers had entered this sanctuary a thousand or so paces away to our north. Lamps shone fore and aft and I could hear an anchor splash in the water. It looked as though they were settling down for the night. "Let's go," said Cadmon and we scrambled down to Galen, waiting anxiously for us in the boat.

"They've settled for the night, Pa," I said in a low whisper; "let's go!" But Cadmon was still anxious. "Why's this ship following us? I don't like the smell of this!"

"Lets move on and put some distance between us," my father said and we pushed carefully away from the shelter of the island, dipping the oars slowly and quietly into the waters. We had covered several hundred yards when suddenly the bell on the island began to ring out—not the usual slow, mournful tolling in the wind, but the urgent ringing of someone who had taken hold of the rope and was sounding the alarm.

"It's the spirits!" I quavered, pulling desperately on my oar.

My father shook his head. "No, they've landed a boat on the island and posted a lookout. They've seen us, so they're ringing the bell!"

I had never rowed so hard before, but the ship did not pursue us. After what seemed an age we made landfall at the Haven, pulled the boat ashore and staggered home.

My mother wept to see us. She had worried that we had come to some harm as we had not returned the day after Modranicht. My siblings Tola, Godric and Greta did not stir as Cadmon collapsed on my bed. I followed and in moments fell into a deep, exhausted sleep.

I awoke a few hours later, restless and feverish, recent events running through my dreams. I saw my father was getting little rest that night. Erlina wanted to know everything that had happened since we left the Haven. She sat in her nightwear, her long tresses hanging loose, feeding her husband bread and broth from the pot that always hung over a low fire in the centre of our hovel. They spoke in a quiet tone not to wake us. Mother sat hand on mouth, scarcely able to believe what she was hearing.

When I awoke again, Galen lay fast asleep in my mother's arms.

7

Changing Lives

The Haven, Winter 589 AD

I AROSE IN the wintry morning light, threw back the covers and crawled out of bed. My father was already up and about, lighting a fire for smoking some fish. It was good to get back to a routine after the events of the past few days. We also had little option. As the seasons came round, we maintained Earl Sighart's hunting hides in the woods nearby, provided cartage for the harvest, cut deer-fences for the earl's herd and carried messages between his two homesteads, Ratteburg and Eastringe. When the earl's visitors landed at the Haven, we rowed them over to the manor house and tended Sighart's horses when his hunting parties came by for refreshment.

Our hamlet on the shore of the Haven comprised a small community of seven families and fifty people, several wood-and-thatch hovels, workshops, and storehouses. A dozen shrines to various deities dotted our communal enclosure, which was surrounded by high, sharpened poles to protect against forest animals and intruders.

Tola, at seven years of age, was two years younger than me, her long plaited hair as black as midnight, taking after my father. Lively, surprising, full of fun, she helped Mama with spinning and weaving, making clothes, cooking, bread making and looking after our two younger siblings. Greta was two and Godric about to turn six.

I walked over to my father at the fish-smoking shed. "You all right after last night, son?" I nodded, about to speak when we heard Godric shout, running towards us from the woods.

"The pigs have run away to the woods, Papa!" he panted out of breath. Galen put a comforting arm around his heaving shoulders. Godric pointed back down the path, beyond the thatched roofs of several hovels, the swine enclosure, and the sheep pen, to open scrubby ground where the goats grazed, then past some winter hawthorn and into a stand of coppiced beech. Beyond that lay alder and silver-grey birch trees and still further, towering ash and oaks where a thick carpet of dead brown leaves and ferns covered the woodland floor.

Godric pointed to the swine gate. "The gate wasn't closed proper, Papa, so I closed it, and I counted the pigs. I think two were gone, so I went to find them."

"And what did you find?" he coaxed. "Did you find the pigs?"

"I didn't see them, Pa."

My father thought for a moment, stroking his chin.

He said, "Go and tell Mama to look out for the pigs … also, go tell your aunt!" he called after Godric's retreating back; "Then the whole world will know!"

The footpath to the settlement at Eastringe began at our wooden quay on the edge of the Haven, then passed through our hamlet and into the woods for about three miles before coming to Eastringe, a village clustered around one of the king's many royal halls. Close by there was also a shrine to Wodin, on a hill alongside an old Roman road that led from the fort at Ratteburg to the coast. Sandwic Haven supplied fresh fish for the royal table during visits from the king and his retinue of councillors and warriors, which is how I once saw our late King Eormenric.

The Haven was a large bay, scoured out by the ocean tides from the east and the waters of the River Stour from the west. We lined a stretch of the Haven's shoreline with planks laid between poles. The earth behind was firmly packed and smoothed to form a quay for landing our catch and for passing trade in other goods for market.

Cadmon emerged from our hovel, rubbing his eyes, followed by Tola pulling on her shoes, a thick woollen shawl protecting her from the cold. Galen said, "Tola, go with the boys down to the quay, and if you see a big ship with a sail, you come and tell me right away."

Tola and Cadmon came down to the quay where I was shooing away some herring gulls flapping around my nets. They regrouped further away, waiting until I turned my back. I tied my knee-length shirt flaps between my legs, tucked them in tightly, tightened my belt and reluctantly entered the cold water. Cadmon stretched and yawned, watching me mending the nets, his thoughts distracted by events of the previous night. I also needed time to turn over in my mind all that had taken place over the last few days.

Tola found a place on the grass bank near to the gate and sat down to watch for a ship coming from the Channel. Time passed, and the mouth of the Haven gradually disappeared behind dull, grey rain.

At first, Tola did not notice the ship approaching as its slave crew pulled slowly and stealthily on the oars, the dark mainsail scarcely moving in the light, offshore breeze. The skipper carefully worked the tillers back and forth to keep the ship clear of the reeds, steering close to the shore. A large carved head and neck of a white swan loomed over the stern, coming into view as the ship turned and the prow slid quietly towards the quay. Moments later the oars came clear of the water, and the boat scraped against the planks of the quay. Two men lept on to the landing place and ran towards us.

Tola screamed a warning and began running towards Cadmon on the bank, as I hauled myself out of the water. Without a pause in his stride, the first of the raiders grabbed Tola, screaming with fright, wriggling with all her power to free herself. He tucked her under his hairy arm and ran back to the ship. "Tola! Tola! I'm coming!" I yelled, but her captor bundled her over to another member of the crew, and I stabbed at his upper leg from behind with my belt knife. He howled in pain then turned with a snarl, grabbing my wrists and with a heave flung me into the hold of the ship. Half dazed, I could not stop the third crewmember tying me with rope to a bench, and he did the same to Tola.

Another member of the crew ran down the landing place. He was the skipper we had first noticed two days earlier, shouting orders at anchorage in Raculf. Cadmon rushed at him, growling and snarling like a lion cub, but another crewmember was close behind. Together they dragged Cadmon kicking to the ground, giving a stunning blow to the side of his head. Carrying Cadmon between them, they clambered on board the ship, pulled the ropes free of the poles on the quay and pushed away from the shore. The crew dug their oars hard into the cold, swirling water. It was all over in moments.

Too late, Galen appeared in the gateway, a fishing spear in his grasp, running fast from our compound, yet there was nothing he could do as the bull-necked skipper yelled at his crew. "Pull hard!" Cracking the bullwhip, the gap between shore and boat increased with every stroke. Slowly, the sounds of shouts and voices on the quay grew fainter and fainter, until finally, they faded away altogether.

Tola wailed loudly for Mama as one of the crew dragged us into the prow of the ship, our hands and feet manacled to a bench. The wind sprang up, the mainsail snapped sharply, and the vessel lurched forward. In a state of shock, I looked back to the quay. Thoughts flashed through my mind of home, family and my future—then in a moment, all I had ever known was gone. We were captives on a raider's ship, and no one would come to our rescue.

Cadmon groaned in pain at our feet. Tola strained her eyes towards the vanishing shore, her dark tresses whipping across her face in the wind, her tears wet and salty.

Two figures sat motionless on the rough wooden bench in front of us. The shorter of the two turned around and leered, lifting his manacled hands. The colossal figure at his right hand half turned his head, and I saw the long, scraggly beard and bloodshot eyes before I recognised his unmistakable, overpowering odour. Hrothgar sat beside his son Falk, the pair of them now thrust into exile and heading somewhere over the bleak horizon.

I looked away, my heart too sick to rejoice at their misfortune in the face of our own.

The reeds whispered in the wind as the ship drew further from the shore. Above us, I heard the high-pitched screech of a lone gull following behind in that cheerless dawn, until it too caught the wind and vanished from sight.

I looked up at the grey sky as the three Fates, the Wyrd sisters, began taking shape in the clouds. They sat still at their loom, no longer bothering to weave my fate. Instead, I saw my life dangling at the end of a short, breaking thread.

8

OUR STORY

Rome, May 589 AD

AT THE END of the period of afternoon rest on our second day in the monastery, we gathered again in Prior Pretiosus's study. The abbot, together with Petrus and Augustinus, was eager to learn how we had journeyed to Rome from Sandwic Haven. Abba Gregorius nodded encouragingly. "Please, we are ready to hear your story!"

I sifted through the sequence of events that followed our capture at the Haven. Cadmon also added his own comments as I told our story. I began describing the long, dangerous and exhausting journey that brought us to Rome.

The first day of our capture came back to me vividly. Felix and his crew took us by stealth at the Haven. We put up something of a fight, but they had caught us by surprise. They were too quick and too strong for us. Felix wasted no time sailing down the coast. About noontime we came to a river estuary between two white cliffs.

Cadmon added, "This was a haven called Dofras—I went there in my father's longboat in autumn last year. There's an old Roman fort on the shore, like the forts at Ratteburg where I live, and Raculf where the king lived. There were two lighthouses on the cliffs at Dofras that showed the way into the harbour—and also give warning if there's danger or if there are pirates on the coast."

Here there was a wide river estuary, about a mile across. We sailed up river, past a massive old timber wall that sheltered ships tied up along the riverbank. Steep grassy hills rose high on either side of the river, and all the livestock were now sheletered in barns and enclosures for the duration of winter. Felix steered towards some long sheds on the riverbank. Souk jumped ashore to moor the ship. I looked desperately up and down the river for someone—anyone—to come to our aid. Some men were working not far away along the water's edge, and I knew this would be our last chance for escape; so did Felix. He yelled to Souk to fetch the chains, and sneered at us.

"Can't have you thinking of escaping now, can we?" Souk chained us to the benches, and Felix began to examine the three of us more closely. He saw Bertha's coin hanging around my neck, and said, "So, what have we got here?"

I said, "It's mine! Given me by Queen Bertha! It's dedicated to the gods!"

Falk looked over his shoulder with contempt as Felix ripped the leather cord from my neck. He said, "You keep your gods, and I'll keep your coin!"

With my amulet gone, Felix also took away something of who I was.

From that afternoon into the evening Felix, Souk and Anaxos were busy preparing for our next voyage. The slaves hurried to load barrels of foodstuffs and fresh water. Felix worked without resting in case someone had raised the alarm at the Haven. I thought, surely they'll come looking for us? My father must have given the alert by now! But I said nothing that might upset Tola. Still tearful, she fell asleep on my chest, my arm around her thin shoulders, holding her close. I was relieved she had come out that morning with a thick shawl that gave her some warmth.

Abba Gregorius, following my story intently, leaned forward in his chair. "Did a ship come looking for you?"

Cadmon cut in, shaking his head. "No, my father and his ship were still at Raculf. It would take nearly a day just to get a message there from the Haven."

Gregorius nodded. "Of Course. Alric, do go on."

I recalled that at dawn, a light offshore wind blew and Felix set sail on the tide. The waves had dropped a little too, and the slaves rowed hard with the heavy oars. Cadmon and I also shared an oar; we too were now slaves. We crossed the ocean before darkness fell, and came to a large trading place. It was also on an estuary, but I didn't know the name.

As Petrus translated he added, "I think that may have been Bononia, where the Roman fleet anchored in old times; or perhaps more likely, a little further south—at Quentovicus, that trading emporium? Neither is very far from the coast of Britannia, I'm told. But it must have been a good ship even to attempt a crossing in mid-winter!"

It was.

Felix's merchant ship, as I later learned, was built in the shipyards of Massilia and had a large single mast, and sometimes a smaller sail was rigged above the prow. Two paddles, attached left and right at the stern, provided steering, and the benches allowed for twelve oarsmen. Cargo lay stowed beneath our feet—wood, iron and charcoal, woollen cloth from the royal weavers at Raculf, and also skins of beer. Merchandise filled the hull, protected from the weather beneath heavy, flaxen sheets; but those of us who pulled the oars had no protection at all. Only my sister was released from her chains. Perhaps Felix had a daughter her age? But that didn't explain what happened later.

After we crossed over, we entered another wide estuary. Upstream was a hilly ridge with a small castle and a hamlet a mile or so inland. Wooden piers extended far out in the river, so that at low tide the ships could load and unload at any time, day or night. The next morning, Felix was busy trading and dealing, and cleaning out his storehouse for the next leg of his journey.

Rows of traders' sheds lined this part of the river estuary, thatched roofs overhanging to the ground. Felix's storehouse had a wide double door facing the landing stage and here we unloaded his cargo. Some scraps of food were thrown at us like animals, and we slept on a damp floor. Our three captors took shifts staying awake during the night, so we had no chance of escape. They followed this routine at every trading port we came to. At night we lay manacled to one of the pillars, Tola squeezed between Cadmon and me to keep her warm.

All this while, Hrothgar never spoke a word—and I had not heard him speak since his humiliation at Raculf. He snored disgustingly all night, his odour the kind of nauseating, waxy smell coming from a maggot-ridden sheepskin. Yet somehow, our revulsion of him helped us to keep struggling on.

Cadmon spoke of the difficulty we faced in communicating with one other. "Felix yelled shuddup every time we said anything, and Souk used his bullwhip on us even when we'd done nothing wrong." Everyone flinched as Cadmon described, in vivid detail, the thin leather tail cutting into soft flesh on our exposed backs, necks and cheeks. Souk's face remains forever etched in my memory—perhaps in his twenties, his long, dark matted hair falling across his stubbled face, mouth fixed in a permanent snarl, eyes narrow, always watchful beneath his dark, resentful brow.

Abba Gregorius asked, "And what about Anaxos, the Greek you mentioned? How did he behave towards you?"

Cadmon thought for a moment and said, "Well, Anaxos never actually did anything bad to us – in fact, he was almost good to us."

For my part, I never fully understood where Anaxos the navigator fitted in. Felix showed enormous respect for him, treating him as a father. Perhaps he was his father! Or Anaxos owned the boat? Or did he finance their enterprise? Or was he a retired skipper who couldn't stay away from the sea? Whatever the reason, Anaxos had very little directly to do with us, or any of the slaves, and he didn't share in Felix or Souk's brutal punishment. Nor did he speak to us, but when he occasionally glanced our way, his expression was often reassuring. Once, as we prepared to leave the ship, Anaxos helped take off our chains. He unlocked mine and patted me on the shoulder, like a guardian with his ward—something Felix and Souk would not have done in a thousand years.

As we sat in the prior's study, the afternoon sun began dipping, casting its golden light on the limewashed walls. A small spider briefly caught in the glare scuttled into the rafters.

"And where did you sail to after that?" Gregorius asked.

We recounted how we sailed down the coast to another river mouth. After a few miles upstream, we came to a large settlement. Felix called it Rotomagus.

"Ah!" The prior snapped his fingers, looking up from his notes with a smile. "It's a city on the River Sequana!"

I nodded. It was on the riverbank, behind a high wall. Rotomagus was a milestone on our long journey. What little we could see above the city walls revealed several large buildings and palaces of dressed stone. I had not seen anything like these before, neither at the Roman fort at Ratteburg nor Raculf. We stayed there a few days. Felix talked with some warlords who were exiled from our kingdom by King Eormenric years ago. They mostly came from the Isle of Tanet. When the talking was over, Felix gave Hrothgar and Falk to these men, and they gave Felix a large purse of gold in exchange. He roared his head off after the warlords rowed away with Hrothgar and Falk. "The idiots paid me twice! Once by Ethelbert to take him, and now by the Tanet warlords to get him back!"

I was relieved we were finally rid of Hrothgar; throughout the journey he had said not a word, brooding like a dormant volcano. Cadmon and I had brought about his downfall, and he would not forget that. Hrothgar had also seemed resigned to his fate, or perhaps indifferent to it—as he was to us, mere vermin beneath his feet. Falk glared at us with undisguised malevolence, seeing in Cadmon and me the instruments of his fall from grace.

A brief discussion ensued between the four monks, and the prior broke off to fetch a jug of water, together with six tumblers. Augustinus poured and handed them around.

After Rotomagus, our sea journey continued south for some days, sailing in the manner of the Greeks, always seeking open waters but keeping just in sight of the land. Then we entered another estuary and shipped oars at a trading station on the Frankish coast.

I had come to the hardest part of our story. Gregorius looked at me and said, "You haven't said very much about your sister, Alric." I still found this too raw; I gestured to Cadmon to continue.

Cadmon took a deep breath and said bluntly, "Felix sold Tola at the next slave market we came to. We didn't hear the name of this place, and Felix didn't tell us, but it was half a mile from us and one of the largest slave markets."

"And what happened there?" Abba Gregorius shifted forward attentively, his hands clasped together.

Cadmon said, "While we were moving cargo to and from the ship, Felix took Tola to an old woman whose hovel was nearby."

I remembered every detail of what followed. The woman washed away weeks of filth from my sister's hair, face and body; combed lice from her scalp put fresh clothes on her and brushed her long, raven-black hair until it gleamed in the sunshine. All the while Tola sat composed, enjoying the unexpected attention.

Cadmon said, "When the woman finished, Felix and Souk went to collect Tola and led her away to the slave market, near the town. It was a terrible thing and we—Alric—took it very, very badly."

Gregorius turned to me. "Yes, of course; this must have been a most dreadful moment for you, Alric."

I nodded, staring at the terracotta floor, reliving the sight of Tola turning towards us at the moment she fully realised the purpose of all her grooming. She screamed a fearful cry, kicking and struggling to break free, but Felix clamped a hand over her mouth, picked her up and carried her away. I remembered that Cadmon had gripped my shoulder as I cried "Tola, Tola! I will find you, I promise! I will come for you, I Promise!" But I had said something like that once before; my promises were worthless. Cadmon kept me in his grip until Tola finally disappeared from our view. She was all alone now, a slave to people she did not know, with no hope that she would ever see us—let alone home—again. And I, her older brother, had utterly, miserably failed to protect her.

Cadmon and I did receive one unexpected act of kindness, though. The old woman who had bathed Tola, seeing our distress, came out of her hovel with a basket. She looked to Anaxos, who stood watch in the prow of the ship. He nodded, and she uncovered a few small loaves of bread; then pressing a loaf into each of our hands, she turned and hurried back to her home. Our strength and calm somehow returned for a while, but I soon plunged into black despair that lasted for days as the ship continued south, drawing us further and further away from my little sister, and even further from home. I felt bone-weary with this life, our prospects very grim indeed. What did I have to live for? More months, perhaps years, like this, then an early grave? And I was not yet ten years old!

I had said to Cadmon that I'd rather drown than go on living like this. But he said, "No! I do want to live. Every day my arms grow stronger pulling on the oars and carrying Felix's cargo on my back. So do you. We'll bide our time and be ready when any chance comes. But come it will!"

Abba said, "Then what happened? Did a chance come?" Even the prior had stopped scribing.

I shook my head. A wind sprang up and Anaxos set course westwards for us, and we sailed out of sight of land and passed a huge, rocky peninsula. Prior Pretiosus, who in his earlier years sailed merchant's vessels, said, "That may have been Cabo Finisterra. It's on the coast of Galicia."

The names meant nothing to me, but just as the sea-gods had been against us on our last day at the Haven, so the Fates began to spin their threads once more and drew us, unsuspecting, into a treacherous and fearful storm.

The winds grew to gale force, and Anaxos lowered the mainsail to prevent it rending, while Souk tied down the cargo.

On this part of our journey, the waves sometimes towered twenty, perhaps thirty feet, tossing our tiny ship about like a piece of flotsam. I hung over the side retching, oars shipped, while the vessel was driven before the wind. After a few days the slave seated in front of me lost his mind, howling and throwing himself frantically about to escape his chains. Souk crawled forward, slapped the slave's face hard, and released his leg irons. Then he pushed him overboard into the foaming sea. I can still see his head disappearing beneath the waves, bobbing up once, twice and then we saw him no more. Souk crawled his way back to his master, madness on his grinning face.

The abbot leaned back, shaking his head in disbelief, his hands covering his eyes.

"Go on," he said at last. "Go on; we must hear your tale to the end."

Looking back, how Felix managed to grip his steering paddles for hours on end remains a mystery to me. Again and again, he turned the ship into the oncoming waves, the prow rising to impossible heights before plunging headlong into seething foam below. Pulling desperately on the oars to steady our drift, we could not see what lay behind us in the prow, but terrifying waves arose all about like mountains, and I felt, Now we are truly lost!

I stared at Felix and Souk, not caring anymore whether I lived or drowned. Now it was vengeance that came uppermost in my mind for all that Felix had stolen from us. I vowed, "You have taken away my life. You have stolen the life of my sister! Now I want to see you lose yours!" I thirsted to see his face as he sank beneath the waves, the fear, the hopelessness, and above all, the naked terror in his eyes.

Anaxos had lashed himself to the mast, his face turned to the storm, shouting into the wind as the ship was forced up and up and up until only the chains held us to the benches. I stared at our navigator, his grey hair streaming, his broad moustache quivering in the gale, mouth wide open—not in fear, but exulting in the storm, his weathered face as bright as Greek fire!

At that same time, I saw what I thought was a trick of the light, or perhaps I had lost my mind—two figures walking on the sea, white like ghosts. There are many tales of apparitions at sea, sent to tempt sailors to leave their ship and drown in the waters. But not like this one. I slowly recognised the taller of the two as Queen Bertha. She was holding Tola's hand and coming towards us on the water. Were they both dead? I stretched out my hand towards them. They did not beckon me to follow, but each waved, as if in a greeting.

Yet the even more remarkable thing was that the queen, holding Tola with her right hand, had a coin on a chain, in her left, holding it up for me to see. I switched my gaze to Felix at the stern of the ship. I could not see my coin hanging around his neck on his gold chain.

I looked back at the two figures on the sea; the coin was still there, but the two images were turning away and began to disappear. I waved until I could see them no more; and when I looked again, I could see my gold amulet hanging around Felix's neck. This strange episode began to revive my spirits and signalled a turning point in my despair for it said to me, Tola is not alone!

The vessel ran and ran for three days. The wind fell, but our seasickness only worsened, and the ship rose and fell in giant swells after the storm. Then Cadmon saw whales breaking through the waves a little distance from our craft. Anaxos saw them too. He shouted, 'There is our sign! We follow the whales!' And he was right! Felix let out a roar of relief. A coastline came slowly into view. After a few more days a great rock rose out of the sea on our nearside.

Brother Petrus said to the prior, "That would be one of the Pillars of Hercules?" Pretiosus nodded. In his mind's eye, he was with us every step, retracing our route, living our experience. I recalled my shaking legs giving way beneath me, as I stumbled on to dry land for the first time in more than seven days. I fervently kissed the firm earth, clutching for my gold amulet that was no longer there.

Cadmon said in a tone of wonder, "We survived!" His face had suddenly changed. "We went through all that, and we were still alive!"

I realised then, as we sat in Prior Pretiosus' study, that two very different stories emerged from our account of the journey. One was my tale—of loss, grief, despair, hopelessness, and revenge. The other, Cadmon's story of courage, an iron will to survive and the triumph over all that had befallen us. His tale brought forth admiration; mine, only sympathy.

I felt ashamed, but the abbot said, "Your courage is certainly extraordinary, both of you, despite your loss of nearly everything." He looked at me. "You have overcome all this, and now you are here, as a blessing to our monastery!" He smiled warmly as he said this. Cadmon's expression told me he wasn't so sure what being 'a blessing' might mean. Abba Gregorius urged me to continue.

We sailed into thc warm waters of a different ocean, bright blue; and there were waves, but no tide. Augustinus said, "Yes—you sailed into Mare Nostrum—'Our Sea,' as we Romans modestly call it."

After some days, we came to a substantial port called Carthago. The port was a garrisoned Roman city on the North African coast, built on a spur of land overlooking the sea. Felix steered the ship beneath the city walls to a mooring in the ancient merchants' haven. Further in, a naval dock contained a fleet of three-deck warships, Triremes, swaying at anchor. The first signs of spring also came at Carthago, and with these came warmer days.

Then we set sail once again—to Catania, I think.

"Yes," Gregorius confirmed, "it's in Sicilia; my family once had several estates there."

We put ashore for a few days as we waited out another storm, then we set sail north, through a bay whose name I do not know.

"Golfo di Napoli. It's on the western seaboard of Italia," the abbot said.

I concluded the story of our journey. Four days ago we came to port—we heard Felix call it Ostia—at the mouth of the river that passes by this city. From there, teams of oxen hauled the ship upriver to where we moored the ship two nights ago.

Abba Gregorius leaned back in his chair."And so you came to Rome!"

We all sat in a reflective silence.

Abba said, "That's an extraordinary story, Alric and Cadmon, quite extraordinary! While I can't hold out much hope that you will soon return home, I can promise we will do our best to help you feel at home here, and find your way in life. I will also make every effort to find your sister, Alric."

A bell tolled for evening prayer, and the abbot rose to his feet.

"Come, boys; it is time to bring all we have heard to the Almighty in prayer. Tomorrow Brother Petrus will acquaint you with our monastery—and particularly the library for your grammar lessons!"

9

DEPARTURE DEFERRED

Rome, August 589 AD

CADMON POUTED. "HOW long have we been here now? It feels like years!"

The days following our arrival at the monastery stretched into weeks and the weeks into months, as the freshness of spring gave way to a hot, sticky summer. The daily regimen of the monastery meant rising in the dark for the first prayers of the new day in the oratory in the grounds, nearby the town house. We returned for prayers six more times until night prayer then lay down to sleep in our shared cell. We ate breakfast and a midday meal in the refectory and helped with the day-to-day needs of the monastery; cleaning, kitchen duty, and laundry. We had no idle moment, and shared no idle conversation, except for mutters and whispers in our cell at bedtime. Aside from chanting the daily offices, the days passed as silently as ships in the night.

In our first month, we understood very little of the language while Brother Petrus instructed us in the basics of Latin vocabulary and the alphabet. He showed us how to scratch letters into words on a wax tablet with a thin metal stylus, and we began to learn by heart all one hundred and fifty Psalms that the brothers chanted each week in the oratory. Most afternoons we met in a study at the entrance to the monastery's large library, the Bibliotheca Agapito behind the San Andreas oratory. Brother Petrus, our Grammaticus, wore a friendly smile on his pale, slightly pink face as he began our afternoon session. To alleviate the tedium of our grammar lessons, we tried diversions, such as asking Petrus about his life and the uncertainties facing Rome.

He parried, "Boys, things may come and go, but one thing is certain, you can rely on it. For grammar, you have come, and to grammar, you must now turn!" Then, pointing with his cane, "Open your tablets and write down the following words." We groaned, opened our wax-coated wooden writing boards, and gripped our styluses with clumsy fingers, sitting up, poised for him to speak. "Mensa, mensa, mensam," he said, pacing the room and we launched into another two-hour stint of exquisite grammatical torture.

In these early days, we were the two youngest in the monastery. Clementus, a year or two older than Cadmon, shared our small cell above the kitchen. His family lived on the monastery estate, and his father had formerly served Gordianus, head of the household until his passing; now he worked for the son, Abba Gregorius.

Clementus had entered the monastery to be educated as a postulant, seeking the life of a monk. Men and boys came to the monastery of San Andreas from all backgrounds, including as freed slaves like us. Women were not permitted to live in the monastery, or even to enter it. Most husbands, wives, sons, and daughters lived and worked on the monastery estate. Boys and young men who entered the monastery, like Cadmon and me, were trained in reading, writing, and grammar; and we were glad to have Clementus in our cell, not least because he made a significant difference to our spoken Latin.

One night as we settled down, Cadmon said in a low voice, "Alric, I don't know how much longer I can take all this." I knew what he meant. Cadmon showed little interest in his studies, seemed hard to teach and was restless and disappointing to Petrus who rewarded our mistakes with painful raps on the knuckles.

"What about you, Clementus?" Cadmon asked.

Clementus rolled on his back and thought for a few moments. "Well, when I turn eighteen years of age, I expect to take final vows as a monk and join the brothers here. The choice is mine, but my parents certainly believe that having a son as a monk is better than being a soldier in the army."

Cadmon exploded. "No, Clementus, no! I was born into a nobleman's family and brought up to be a warrior! This life of books and learning is not for me! I must use my sword for honour in battle and make my fortune back home, with my people."

Clementus lay quiet at the outburst. Cadmon sat up, his back against the wall, releasing a deep sigh. He said in our Saxon tongue so Clementus wouldn't understand, "We need to find a way back home."

"Well, at least we are safe here," I argued, "and Abba and his monks are generous to us – remember what it was like with Felix! Anyway, I'm not a warrior. I'm not the son of an alderman, but the son of a churl, just a peasant fisherman, so I welcome the teaching."

Cadmon ignored my barb and went on as though I hadn't spoken. "I've been thinking about this a lot. We can go to the coast, to a seaport; maybe the one we came from up to Rome, find a ship and work our way home. We're experienced sailors now, Alric. We know how to crew a ship!"

"How would we get away with this? Just walk out of the monastery? They'll be looking for us in no time."

"I have a plan. You know that place – Jerusalem?" I nodded; the Bible readings in the oratory often mentioned Jerusalem, and so did the Church Fathers, whose writings were read aloud during the evening meals.

"We can put it around that we want to go to Jerusalem! Everyone wants to go there, to see the places where Christ lived."

"Yes, and where he was also crucified," I added. I didn't particularly like the idea, but Cadmon came back to it again a few days later.

"Look, I've sown some seeds among a few people. Tomorrow, we slip away after the midday meal. I'll say we are going down to the Porta Metronia, to put them off our trail." This gate in the southern wall lay the closest to the monastery. It led into the open country, once the nearest source of food beyond the city, but now it was better known as the gateway into Rome for farmers and their labourers fleeing from Langobard warriors.

I felt annoyed that Cadmon hadn't discussed this with me first.

"And then go where?" I demanded.

He smiled at his own twelve-year-old cunning. "We go north instead! Throw them off the scent, leave through another gate, say the Porta Pinciana. We won't carry anything with us, just a bit of bread and cheese in our pockets, or it will look suspicious. We just keep on walking. No one will notice."

I didn't feel any warmer towards the idea, but nor did I want to stay behind alone, and Cadmon grew ever more desperate not to lose his dwindling chance to be a great warrior—or any warrior for that matter. Greatness, fame, and wealth were his goals in life. He also had a score to settle with his older brother Derian, Cadmon's rival for Earl Sighart's affections, and eventually, for his title and estate.

Wasting no time, Cadmon put his plan into action the following afternoon. The day burned hot beneath a hazy sky. Perspiring monks crept into the shade praying for a breeze, and monastery cats flopped like black pools on the tiled floor.

We slipped away at the hour of rest after the midday meal, leaving behind the shaded courtyard and strolling unhurriedly down the steps to the street below. I expected at any moment to hear someone call out to us, but the only sounds we heard were two voices drifting over the monastery wall, near the oratory. I recognised one as belonging to John the Deacon, a monk and close friend of the abbot.

"Are there new troubles now occupying your mind, Abba? Even though you always carry many burdens, you seem more burdened than usual."

I heard Gregorius give a weary sigh. "My sorrows increase whenever I think of the holy lives of those who have departed this life, leaving us a difficult if inspiring example to follow."

"Oh? Which lives have you found especially inspiring?"

Before we heard his reply, we reached the piazza and started up the narrow street. Walking up the valley towards the Colosseum, we casually picked some fruit from the trees, trying not to draw attention to ourselves. We passed beneath the arches of the Aqua Claudia as it crossed the narrow street to the Palatine Hill; nervously looking back to see if anyone had noticed us leave. When all seemed clear, we walked on more swiftly as monks are meant to do, and skirted the Colosseum heading for the slopes of the Esquiline Hill.

We followed a path upwards through open fields, passing by the ruins of the Baths of Trajan. As this was still the hora sexta, the midday hour of rest, very few people were out in the blazing afternoon heat. Sleeping farm labourers sprawled in the shade of trees or beneath their carts. A few glanced up as we hurried by, too drowsy to show interest in young boys in monks' habits. The path meandered further uphill to the left and right, taking us past farm buildings. In the distance, near the brow of a hill, rose the imposing ruins of Diocletian's Baths, and ahead of us were a few streets of town houses, similar to our monastery, but in various stages of decay. We noticed some poor souls living in lean-to shelters, propped against the walls of some abandoned villas.

Cadmon's plan was simple: we keep walking in a northeasterly direction until we reach the city wall. However, walking directly to our goal proved difficult. The roads twisted and turned in every direction, except the one we wanted. Now the rest hour had ended there were more people around. Some older boys, sitting in the deep shade of a tree, noticed our corn-yellow hair, hanging down to our shoulders.

"Are you a monk?" one called out to us as we hastened by. "You don't look like a monk; your hair is too long!" As we were not postulants, our hair remained uncut.

Another joined in, "You look like those Langobards that burned down our farm!"

The first boy said, "You've come to spy on us, that's what you're doing!" They were standing up now, picking up stones to throw at us. Cadmon grabbed my arm.

"We'd better run; this is getting nasty!"

A farmer emerged from the house and shouted at the boys. "Leave them alone! We don't want trouble with the monks!"

"But they're not monks!" whined one, pointing at us.

The man looked hard in our direction and snapped, "Enough! Hitch the cart and get back to work!"

We hurried on without looking back, pulling our hoods over our heads so that we wouldn't have another encounter like that one. We came to a wide-open space in front of the Baths of Diocletian, standing on a slope below the brow of a hill. The baths were magnificent, even in ruin, their high arches resembling the dry bones of a dragon's rib cage, exposed to the ravages of sun and rain. We passed through a gateway in the old Republican Wall, and there before us rose the Pincian Hill.

Heading towards the low summit of the Pinciana, a path took us towards the Aqua Sallustiana, a stream trickling down through the valley. We paused in the shade of a tree, taking long swigs of water from our flasks. The heat had become unbearable—even in our light summer habits, sweat dampened our backs. The ruins of a large family house stood nearby, but this time not occupied by homeless farm labourers. Through the iron gateway leading into the yard, we could see dozens of amphorae stacked in the open courtyard around a wine press. We paused for a few moments, watching the men work. Some were drawing water from the nearby stream; others siphoned wine into clay amphorae before diluting the contents with water after the Roman manner.

As we passed the open gate, the supervisor saw us approaching and, glancing at our monks' habits, called out to us. "You've come for the cognidium?"

Cadmon and I stared at each other.

The supervisor continued, "I think I told your cellarer we will deliver tomorrow, it's not ready yet." Taking a cue from our puzzled expressions, he asked, "Aren't you from San Andreas? The wine for your abbot – we'll deliver it tomorrow!"

Cadmon cut in before I could speak. "Yes, thank you," he said smoothly, "we'll tell him when we return!" We hurried on before he could ask any further questions, and approached the stream, named after the overgrown Gardens of Sallust from which the Sallustiana stream flowed. I looked to the left and right. "Which way now?"

Cadmon pursed his lips, looking up towards the Gardens and back downstream again in the direction of the Campus Martius.

Just then a goat came meandering aimlessly down the narrow valley, its brown coat in very shabby condition. The beast seemed confused. It paused awhile, looked about, shaking its head and turned to the stream for a long draught of water in the scorching, humid heat of the day. The goat lurched towards the shade of a low-hanging fig tree and collapsed in its shade, ignoring both the fruit and the grass.

"This way," Cadmon said, with all the confidence of an experienced guide, although neither of us had ever passed this way before. We crossed the stream and ascended the southern slope of the Pincian Hill, looking for a gate that would lead to open countryside north of Rome. From the top of the Pincian, the Aurelian Wall now appeared further away than we had thought. The landscape was a small part of what the locals called the disabitato, the uninhabited place. However, it was not a wilderness; farmers who had fled the countryside now worked every inch of the land for something to eat. A few wealthy families still occupied some of the remaining villas with their formal gardens.

We passed market gardens, stone quarries, walled enclosures for livestock, olive groves and vineyards in neat rows, trees, and furrowed fields. Two substantial farms answered to the city Prefect, their crops of wheat and barley supplying the city with food when other sources—from the Campania, Sicily and North Africa—failed to reach this hungry city.

We began to descend the hill, passing between rows of fruit trees leading to open pasture, and followed farm tracks until we reached the Aurelian Wall. A city gate lay open to our left. With our hearts beating faster, we made our way towards its twin arches.

We held back some distance from the gate and watched the comings and goings. Most new arrivals to Rome came fearing for their lives, fleeing their villages and towns to the north.

I glanced nervously at Cadmon. "Do we still want to go through with this?"

"Yes," he said, nodding vigorously, his resolve strong.

"Let's go then. It's now or never!"

We walked quickly to the gate. I held my breath, my heart pounding. But the soldiers took no notice of two young monks; their attention occupied registering a new influx of people coming through the arches of the gate.

We slipped past and found a track to our left, following the wall, until at last, we stood outside the Flaminian Gate, the main entrance into the city from the north. In the near distance, I saw the upper reaches of the River Tiber and also a low, rocky hill surrounded by a grove of trees. We rested in its merciful shade on the low hillside, looking down at the yellow-green river. Nearby, cicada beetles scratched away at a high-pitched tune while we ate some of the bread we had squirreled from the midday meal, washing it down with water. We emptied our pockets. Together, all the food we had left comprised a few olives and the grapes and figs we had picked earlier.

More than two hours had passed since we slipped out of the monastery. "Petrus must have noticed we're gone by now," I said. "They'll start looking for us soon."

I looked about; there was a cave not far from us, and we went over for a closer look. The mouth of the cave gave entrance to a catacomb, an ancient burial-place of the dead. We entered with some trepidation.

"We could hide here for a day or two until they stop looking for us," Cadmon whispered, "but I don't fancy going much further into the cave."

I said, "Let's bring some stones and build a wall over the mouth. No one will see us then, and we can hide out for as long as we need to."

The hillside was deserted, and only a few passers-by travelled the Via Flaminia, a hundred or so paces below us. We set about gathering loose rocks strewn about the hill and closed most of the mouth of the cave.

As time slowly passed in the gloom, I began to wonder what was happening back at San Andreas. By now it was well past the hour for our afternoon lessons. Our schoolmaster Petrus would search for us and then—do what? Report us to the prior? Get a search underway? With all the exaggeration that fear awakens, I pictured the entire community, monks and lay brothers alike, pouring out into the city and countryside in hot pursuit. But that was ridiculous—two runaway boys were hardly of such importance. Prior Pretiosus would send one of the younger, fitter monks—someone like Brother Rufinian, who was a skilled rider—with perhaps one companion, or two at most. And if our plan worked, they would not turn north, but go down to the Metronian Gate and the Latin Way. I hoped they would soon abandon their search.

Turning to Cadmon, I said, “We’ll run out of food and water before long. We should have gone straight out of the gate to Ostia to find a ship. Now we have to go back, through Rome! They’ll be looking for us by now.”

“We can go up the road and cross the river, then go down to Basilica San Petri, follow the river round to Trans Tiberim and cross the river to the quay, then wait for a ship to come.”

“That could take days, Cadmon! Someone will spot us waiting there! Look, we’re already running out of food and water!”

Before he could reply, we heard the sound of horses coming along the road. Cadmon put a finger to his lips, and we crept towards a gap we had left at the entrance to the cave, and peered outside.

We froze as we recognised the two riders, hardly able to breathe as we peered between the stones we had placed over the entrance to the catacomb. Brother Rufinian and another monk, John the Benedictine, were dismounting under nearby trees, drinking from their flasks. I could see and hear them, sitting not twenty paces from our hideout. After a short rest, the two monks rose and moved to untie their horses. They came a little closer to our hideout, and we were able to hear snatches of their conversation.

"I’m afraid they’ve given us the slip, brother,” said Rufinian, reaching for his reins.

“Well, we’ve done the best we can.” Brother John sounded exasperated. "Every gate from south to north, and not a soldier on guard who remembers two young rascals in monks’ habits! Perhaps they’re still in the city?” He swung into the saddle, and we sighed as he dug his heels into the horse’s flanks, flicking the reins. But his horse would not move. Nor would Rufinian’s. No matter how hard they tried, cajoled and shouted, the horses would not budge from the spot. Puzzled, John dismounted, shaking his head and looked around, his eye resting on the caves dotting the hill. “There’s a mystery here, my brother!” He glanced around. "We are at the crypt of martyrs and the horses will not move! I think we should take a closer look and see what's what."

We shrank back into the darkness and waited. A few moments later we saw two heads outlined against the blue evening sky. Brother Rufinian said, "These stones look newly placed to me, but these martyrs have slumbered here for centuries! Do you perhaps think, Brother John, that the dead come out and walk about in the moonlight, then return before dawn and put these stones back in place?"

John said, "Yes, brother, I'm sure that's what happens; and I think I can see one of them stirring there in the dark right now!"

We gave a yell and scrambled out, pulling the rocks and stones away in our haste to be out of this awesome place. The two monks stood back, roaring with laughter as we tumbled on to the grassy hillside.

"So, you two have come here to venerate the martyrs, have you? Your piety is truly beyond your years! Come, I'm sure the prior will want to commend you personally!"

Cadmon and I looked shamefaced at each other, saying not a word.

"Boys, the evening is upon us. Climb up behind me, Alric; and you behind brother John, Cadmon, and we'll bring you home!"

We returned to the monastery in time for the evening meal. Everyone glanced at us as we entered, and we were thankful that the meal was always taken in silence. I hardly heard the reading from the works of San Ignatius that evening. Afterwards the prior beckoned us to his office. My legs trembled as we followed him. What would happen to us next? What punishment would we receive? Would they send us away? Would this be the end for us? I kicked myself for listening to Cadmon. Never, never, never again!

Prior Pretiosus sat down and looked at Cadmon and me standing in front of his desk. We could not read his expression, but he certainly wasn't smiling.

"Well, you two have led us quite a dance this afternoon! What were you thinking of?"

Cadmon mumbled something about us wanting to go to Jerusalem, but the prior knew we were lying. He sighed.

"Well, if you take the road to the north, the east or west, the Langobards will seize you; they will make you work on their farms or in their households. You will be a slave for the rest of your life, which will not be very long, that I can assure you.

"If you go south, you might be able to reach Ostia, but no one will give you passage on a ship without payment, unless, again, they seize you as a slave. Either way, you will not achieve what you most seek; to return home."

I squirmed, biting my lip. The prior's face was stern as he spoke calmly but firmly.

"Look at your arms. Do you see the brand marks of a slave anywhere? No. You don't have any stigmata, because, instead of branding you, Abba adopted you into his family, into this monastic community. You can choose, boys, when you reach sixteen years of age, to make your first vows and stay, or to leave as free men to pursue another life. That will be your choice. But in the meantime, you are under Abba as father of this house, and under me as your guardian."

Pretiosus looked at Cadmon then at me for a moment. His face softened a little. "We'll put today's episode behind us now, shall we? No more running away!" Then in a more conciliatory tone, "Much as I would wish it could be otherwise for both of you, it is highly unlikely that you will ever see your homes or families again. Don't cling to what is past, boys. Build a new life here. Make this your home. And give thanks to God for each day he gives you, as it comes. You never know what tomorrow brings."

The strange miracle of the horses refusing to budge, and the sobering words of our prior, made a powerful impression on both of us; well, certainly on me. After Compline that evening I expected some words of contrition from Cadmon. Instead, as we flopped on to our beds, he finally spoke.

"I'm going to have a horse like that one day," he said. "Or perhaps two," and rolled over, falling instantly asleep.

10

Cloaca Maxima

Rome, Autumn 589 AD

WE BEGAN TO adjust to the monastery's daily routine.

Outside the monastery, however, life was less predictable as Langobard dukes tightened their stranglehold on the Duchy of Rome. By early September, the steady stream of people seeking refuge in the city had turned into a flood. Rome's population swelled to thirty-five thousand and grew daily. All new arrivals registered at the city gates, and officials directed people to reception houses and insulae apartments, clustered around the Field of Mars. Most people arrived destitute, displaced from farms and homesteads. Abandoning their sole means of livelihood for fear of their lives, they came disoriented and fearful. I could understand their shock, entering Rome unprepared for this new way of living, particularly as most of these reception houses were apartment blocks, five or even seven storeys high.

Our monastery on the Caelian Hill became increasingly drawn into food distribution to the poor. Five of the city's six welfare and food distribution centres clustered close to where most people lived—in District XI—including the Forum Boarium, one of one of the most overcrowded areas in Rome. At the Lateran Palace, the Administrator General of Accounts kept a record of everything that was handed out to people listed on the register. On the first day of the month the poor, elderly and destitute in each of the city's regions came to distribution centres for their wheat-dole; and, in season, received a dole of wine, cheese, vegetables, bacon, meat, fish, and oil.

Abba Gregorius, drawing on his personal resources, sent a dish each day to those in need who were of high rank and too proud to beg for charity. Most of these lived in villas on the slopes of the Seven Hills of Rome, and we delivered meals to their doors with the words, "A present from San Petro!"

"My parents," Gregorius once said, "chose to return here out of a deep sense of loyalty to this Holy City. Others also chose to return to Rome, after that mad dog King Totila abandoned this city in ruins. So it is right that we now honour these poor and destitute who have chosen to return." Abba saw to it that the cooked dishes he sent were delivered before he sat down for a midday meal. Many said that the whole of Rome, in one way or another, experienced the kindness of this man.

On one occasion it was Cadmon's turn to carry one of Abba's meals to the house of a woman on the Aventine Hill. Her villa overlooked the Circus Maximus and had a grand view of decaying imperial palaces on the Palatine Hill.

"Couldn't believe my eyes," Cadmon said later that night, as we returned to our cubicle for rest. "When I handed the dish to the slave at the door, the owner herself came out, asking from whom it was sent. She lifted the silver lid, sniffed at it, and marched inside!"

"I'll wager she ate it all when she got inside, though," I said, rolling on to my side. "But anyway, what's so remarkable about that?"

"Well, listen to this. The slave who opened the door was Edoma—the slave Felix sold to that woman just before we came up for auction. Remember? Well, this was the woman who bought Edoma! I'm even more grateful for Abba Gregorius!"

So was I. Nor was this the last we heard of Edoma.

My food-distribution activities took a different turn. One morning Prior Pretiosus called me. "Alric, you're serving with Martinus in the triclinium over lunch – twelve very important guests; with Abba, thirteen in all. And let him know when his guests begin to arrive, so he can be there to welcome them. Martinus will show you what to do."

The triclinium was an outdoor dining room next to San Andreas Oratory. We arranged four couches around a large marble dining table for twelve guests, and an additional seat for Abba as their host. We threw a heavy cloth over the tabletop and brought out from the kitchen storeroom Samian tableware of fired clay and also silver cutlery, used only for these midday dinner occasions.

We hurried back and forth between kitchen and dining room, passing beneath patches of shade and light from cypress trees under a bright midday sun. We carried out jugs of water drawn from the well in the atrium and placed thirteen mugs on the table; then carefully laid out wine glasses, together with three flagons of fine white wine.

We laid out the gustatio, the first course of eggs and salad and arranged these in dishes around the table. Finished at last, we stood back and looked at our table setting, and I thought about the king's hall in Raculf where noblemen ate at the king's table.

"Who are these important guests?"

Martinus glanced towards the stairs. "You'll see. Now quickly, call Abba! I can see some people coming up the street!"

I hurried back into the monastery and across the atrium. This would not be our cool interior courtyard for very much longer; plans were in hand to build a church dedicated to San Andreas over this space. For our monks displaced from this area, and also for visitors and pilgrims to the monastery, new cells were nearly completed in the courtyard near the kitchen.

I skirted around the well and into a peaceful courtyard-garden that lay open to the sky. Eight small cells led off this courtyard on two of its sides. Abba Gregorius's small room occupied the far right corner, a curtain partially drawn across the doorway, allowing him some privacy.

I exclaimed, "Abba! Your guests are coming!"

"Deo Gratia!" he said, rising to his feet. A dove sitting on his shoulder stretched its wings and flew out the window. "One of my little friends," he gestured. "That's where my best thoughts come from!" and hurried out to greet his new arrivals.

I dashed back to the outdoor dining room and at last saw who these important guests were. The abbot invited twelve heads of families in the city to dine with him, a different group each day. Abba called this open loggia at the entrance to the triclinium, "the dining room of the poor." The twelve weren't from Rome's noble families but were drawn instead from the most recent arrivals in the city—and the poorest —the ill-clad, confused and destitute, washed up on the streets of Rome by a restless tide of war.

Abba Gregorius greeted his guests wearing his usual coarse monastic garment, looking very much at home among his guests. He had long since laid aside his patrician street garments of a red toga, worn over glowing silk and adorned with precious jewels. I watched amazed as he greeted each one like a long-lost friend, ushering them personally to their seats.

Using wine sourced from Abba Gregorius's family estate, I poured glasses of mulsum, an expensive chilled white wine, sweetened with honey and herbs and diluted with water.

Before the meal began, Abba rose to his feet and prayed. "Thank you, O Lord, for calling us to your table, set in the wilderness of these present times. Bless what you have laid before us."

He raised his glass.

"Now, let us all drink a toast to the King of kings!"

Martinus and I fetched a main course of fish from the kitchen, sauce and flat round bread that we cut into slices. Meanwhile, our abbot engaged his guests in easy conversation, asking after their welfare and their families, what skills they brought with them, how they were finding life in Rome and offering suggestions for how each could best use their talents for the benefit of their families and the welfare of the city. Idleness, he said, is the devil's tool that eats away like a canker and affords too much time to brood over the losses of the past.

We brought out the dessert of pastries, fresh fruit, and nuts, while an animated conversation ran back and forth around the table. However, for some, living on the edge, the food was both too much and too rich. Finally, the meal drew to a close. Abba Gregorius rose and prayed once more, before personally bidding farewell to each guest. Everyone left with a linen table napkin, filled with leftovers for their families, living in cramped apartment blocks in Trans Tiberim and on the Campus Martius.

Somehow, they seemed to walk a little taller when they left than when they first arrived.

As I busied myself clearing away, Abba said, "Alric, when you've finished, could you come back for a few moments?"

I feared he might raise my attempted escape with Cadmon, but when I returned, he merely asked me to walk with him for a while in the cool shade of the trees, in front of the oratory and triclinium. After a little while, he broke the silence.

"Brother Petrus speaks well of the progress you've made with grammar, Alric!" He smiled down. His words both pleased and surprised me; our schoolmaster had never said this to Cadmon or me, but after nearly five months in Rome I could now speak and understand enough Latin to hold at least a simple conversation.

"Are you more settled here with us now?" Abba made this only oblique reference to our abortive attempt at escape.

"Yes, Abba. Everyone is very kind, and I am learning many things I've not known before—many things that are very different from home."

"You mention your home, Alric. We offer prayers daily for you and Cadmon, your sister Tola—and for both your families, so far away on a distant shore. We pray that they will be kept safe. Perhaps, God willing, you may one day be reunited with them."

"Thank you, Abba," I said to this painful and increasingly remote possibility.

"We give thanks to our God who spared you from harm and brought you to our shores here in Rome. You have enriched our community very much in these last few months."

I wasn't sure what he meant, or what I should say in reply, but I nodded as we continued walking, thinking that I had little to thank our gods for, back home on the Haven. I thought of my mother, Erlina, making her offerings for us on our household shrine to our ancestors; and my father, making offerings of fish to the god of the waters, over which we had travelled for several cold, wet, back-breaking months. Not one of the gods had come to our rescue, not one lifted a finger, or even noticed our plight before we came to Rome.

"Tell me Alric, in your homeland, are there Christians who worship as we do, or does everyone worship a god at a shrine?"

"The queen is a Christian," I said, "but I've only seen her twice. Once, on the day of my birth – she gave me a gold coin that Felix took from me – and also at Raculf when Prince Ethelbert fought Hrothgar for the crown."

"So your people worship pagan gods in the Kingdom of Cantia?"

"Well, Abba, there are many gods and also spirits with their shrines, but the chief god is Wodin. His shrine is near Eastringe, not far from my home."

"And what happens at the shrine?"

"Every year the chief men of the kingdom come in their ships from all over to this shrine set on a hill. The chief priest makes a sacrifice and sprinkles the blood for good fortune for the king and his kingdom, and the king's men make their oaths there."

"You have seen this?"

"No, Abba, but Cadmon has. He told me what happens there because his father is one of the king's aldermen."

"So, what good fortune do they seek from Wodin?"

"Well, they ask for favours in battle, or for a good harvest on their estates, or sometimes for health when pestilence strikes their animals. They also give thanks if there are any favours they have received in the past year."

Abba nodded, gesturing me to continue.

"Many people also consult with a wéofodthane, a priest, for omens before getting married, or planting a new crop and so on, to know how this might turn out."

"The same was true in pagan Rome," Abba confided. "Usually with the entrails of birds. While there may be some power in their names, they are not true gods."

I thought about this as we walked on together.

Abba said, "You know I once served as Prefect of Rome?" I had; Petrus had mentioned this to Cadmon and me.

"In ancient days, but not now, the appointment ceremony for a Prefect would not take place until a pagan augur, or priest, sacrificed a bird and read its entrails for an omen. It seems your people have much in common with pagan Rome!"

I agreed.

"And what of your shrines? Did you have a shrine?"

"My family has a shrine, for Neorth, the god of the sea."

"And what do you do at this shrine?"

"We make a fish-offering so that the spirits of the water will let us catch their fish. The farmers also have their shrines, to make a grain offering for the spirits of the field before ploughing. When we take a journey through the woods, we offer a dish of acorns fallen on the ground, so that no harm befalls us when we pass through."

"And your gods, Wodin and so on, do they decide what happens to you?"

"No, Abba, we are much too small for them to take any notice of us! What we want from the gods are good fortune, health, and good luck. So we make sacrifices to please them. We all wear amulets to ward off evil spirits, and there is one on our houses too."

Like everyone else in the Kingdom of Cantia, I believed in a hierarchy of unseen powers, in much the same way that we submitted to earthly powers under our king. What we desired most was gaining the favour of the gods in the heavens; and here on earth, the goodwill of the elves, spirits, and ghosts. This belief demanded rituals and sacrifices to bring benefits to us, or our whole community.

I said, "What happens to us is not in the hands of the gods but in the hands of the Wyrdae, the three Fates who spin our future for good or ill."

Intrigued, Abba raised an eyebrow that said, "Go on."

"They use thread from Frigga, the wife of Wodin; and on the day of our birth they set up a loom in the sky to weave our fate. I used to think this is how Cadmon and I came to be here—because of what the Fates had spun for us, but now I'm not so sure."

Abba agreed, fanning himself occasionally in the heat with his linen napkin from the midday meal. We circled slowly past the loggia again, the afternoon sun creeping towards the back wall of the dining room.

"Alric, I believe that God saw your desperate plight at the hands of evil men and brought you here, out of danger. He has a purpose for you, a purpose for which I believe you will serve him all your life."

We were silent for a long while I digested what Abba had said; a purpose for my life? What purpose?

Abba said, "And when someone dies? What of their spirit?"

"Well, warriors who die with honour in battle and with their weapon in their hands are welcomed by Wodin in the great mead-hall in the heavens. Some warriors might go to the mead-hall of the goddess Freo, and it is much the same for them. Those of us who are not warriors pass over to the Great Beyond, because the mead-halls are not for the likes of churls."

I remembered supper in the king's mead-hall at Raculf, when my father and I sat at the back of the hall, a long way from the king's table.

"There is no place in the great mead-hall for little people like us. We have no opportunity—nor any skill—for showing valour in battle. Life is short, and when we die, our lives are gone. Perhaps some people will still remember us, but the bards do not usually sing odes about churls!"

Abba Gregorius picked up on what I'd said. "Ah, so that's what makes Cadmon so restless here? He wants to be a warrior, so he can join his ancestors one day, as a man who has died gloriously in battle?"

"Yes exactly, Abba. He is the son of a warrior, and if he does not find a war band to join soon, he will not learn the skills of a warrior. This concern weighs heavily on him."

"God prepares a place for every soul at the great banquet in His Kingdom, Alric—whether rich or poor, slave or free, men or women—and yes, warrior and peasant farmer alike."

While I struggled with this thought, he said, "And your father is not a warrior?"

"No! We are fishermen!"

Abba's face lit up with delight. "Now that is a truly noble profession! The Apostle San Petrus, whose tomb is here in Rome, was also a fisherman! He also 'fished for men' as Our Lord commanded him. Even here, in Rome itself! Perhaps one day, Alric, you will also become a fisherman for the souls of men?"

I remembered Queen Bertha had said something similar to my mother at my birth, but before I could reply a messenger from the Lateran Palace arrived. As Abba had been Papal Envoy to the Imperial Court in Constantinople, it was not unusual for Pope Pelagius to seek his advice on matters concerning the imperial court.

Abba read the note and sighed.

"The Pope summons me, and I cannot refuse!" He added, "We must continue this discussion some other time."

I was sad that our conversation had ended, and looked forward to speaking with him another time; but as fate, or the will of God, would have it, we never had the opportunity to talk in this way again. Still, his gentle probing was not merely for interest; it had a purpose that would only become clear much later. Soon, very different and unexpected paths opened for both of us.

I returned to the kitchen, hungry for the midday meal I had missed while serving Abba's guests, but the prior intercepted me as I passed his office, a scroll tied with ribbon in his hand. "Alric, I need you to deliver this urgently to the Prefect's Office. If you hurry, you'll be back in time for your afternoon lesson!"

With that to look forward to, and with a growling stomach, I hastened towards the Colosseum, gorging myself on wild figs and olives I picked on the way. Hurrying through the Forum Romanum, I soon plunged into the now-familiar narrow streets of the Campus Martius to reach the colonnades of the Septa Julia. The round bulk of the pagan Pantheon rose high above the walls of the Septa's arcade as I hastened across the courtyard, accompanied by the usual mixed feelings on my journeys to this place. On the one hand, a great sense of relief that Abba Gregorius had freed me from slavery; on the other, a shiver of fear as I recalled the journey from home under Felix and his brutal henchman. Some wounds run deep and don't always heal.

I handed over the scroll to the Prefect's Office and worked my way past the throng around the fountain. My stomach had begun to ache with all the fruit I'd stuffed myself, my bowels loosening with every step. I hurried towards a public latrine a few streets away, not far from the river. As I entered, I could dimly see a dozen or so customers of both genders, some talking loudly to their neighbours while others sat silent, deep in thought. Shafts of light from the doorway and the high windows partially lit up the room.

At the entrance, I snatched up a sharpened stick, speared one of the fresh sponges on the brick table in the centre and hurried to a place on the long benches. With a groan and an explosion worthy of Vesuvius, I relieved the contents of my stomach into the waiting trench below, flushed away by the Aqua Virgo overspill of the Septa Julia fountain. This public latrine once had another use—as the last Republican Senate House; and on this spot, members of the Roman Senate murdered Julius Caesar. Because of the disgrace of this event, Caesar's successor, Augustus, demolished the building and erected this lavatory over it.

Men and women came and went as I pondered these great things. My thoughts were suddenly interrupted as three men, talking loudly, entered the latrine and sat down together along the back wall, facing the entrance. I recognised their voices at once; my stomach seized in a spasm, my mouth went dry, and my heart thumped in panic.

After six months, the slave-traders were back in Rome! Souk made a joke about Roman women, Anaxos ignored him and asked Felix a question, and then Souk replied before the skipper could answer. I sat side-on to my captors, in a dark corner near the entrance. My gold coin, still hanging around Felix's neck, shone in the gloom.

No one paid any attention to me as, with trembling hands, I stealthily pulled down the hood of my cowl to hide my face, reached into the keyhole beneath the seat with my sponge-stick, wiped my backside and rinsed the sponge in a small trench that ran in front of the bench. I stood up, tossing my stick and sponge on to the used pile on the table and turned towards the bright, sunlit entrance.

"Why, a monk, I see!"Felix's basso voice rang out as he noticed my retreating figure, merely a dark outline against the light. "I wonder if he knows some young friends who might like to say a few prayers for us?" As I slipped into the street, I heard Souk say, "Do you think it's him? I'm sure it's him! Come on!"

Pushing into the crowded narrow street, I turned left into an alley leading towards the old Theatre of Marcellus and the Forum Boarium. With perhaps fifty-paces head start, I began running, dodging and weaving my way through the crowd. I glanced over my shoulder as I turned a corner. The three were in hot pursuit, shoving people out of the way, forging a path through the crowd and closing the gap with every pace.

I burst into the Forum Boarium, thinking to reach the safety of San Maria in Cosmedin, but in a panic, I turned instead towards the nearby Arch of Janus. As I passed beneath its arch, a young urchin, watching me running frantically from my pursuers, grabbed my arm and pulled me towards a heavy metal cover directly below the arch.

"Come! Quickly!" he said, and together we dragged the iron lid aside, exposing a tunnel beneath. The young lad pointed down into the darkness, and I saw metal rungs leading down into the abyss below.

"Go!" he commanded and without a second thought, I half-slid down iron ladder embedded in the cold brick wall. The light from above suddenly disappeared as the boy followed behind, heaving and pulling the heavy cover back into place with an echoing clunk.

After a few moments, my eyes adjusted and below I saw a flickering torchlight. My rescuer called down, “Keep going!” I gingerly climbed downwards and further into the tunnel, to the burning torch held in a metal ring. Below that ran a narrow walkway, only just clear of the stinking sewage.

“What's your name?” I gasped, out of breath.

“Theodore,” he said.

“Alric,” I said. “Thank you, Theodore, you’ve saved my life! If they’d caught me, I’d be a slave again.”

“I saw them chasing you. These are bad men; they have come a few times now, always bringing slaves. I have seen you too. You bring food to people in the apartments here.”

I nodded, and we listened in silence for a while, waiting for the danger in the street above us to pass.“What are you doing down here?” I asked, amazed that any human being would risk their life in a place like this.

“My father and mother are dead, so I live where I can, sometimes down here.”

“Where are we?” I asked my newfound friend. He pointed. By the flickering light, I could see a large brick tunnel leading into the darkness beneath an arched ceiling.

“This is the Cloaca Maxima,” he said, “the great sewer of Rome!”

Theodore looked up as we heard the metal cover, scraping overhead. He whispered urgently, “It is not safe for you to return up there. Come, we’ll find another way!”

Theodore grabbed the flaming torch, and we continued across an iron catwalk, down a rusty ladder and into a sewer that looked like a vaulted brick oratory. We pressed on. Sometimes I tied my monastic habit around my waist as we passed along narrow, slippery walkways. Theodore moved quickly, and every so often I found myself plunged into darkness as he turned a corner, or dropped out of sight. He returned when I called out, my voice echoing on the brick walls, then we continued a little slower for a while until I called out again.

I could tell we were going uphill. The terrible smell became even worse, but still, we pressed on, following the twists and turns along the Cloaca tunnel, until Theodore called back that we were beneath the Forum Romanum. By now the arched roof of the tunnel ran only inches above our heads and ended abruptly in a spacious chamber with brick arches. I stared in amazement at the sight illuminated by Theodore's blazing torch.

On the dry, raised floor of the chamber stood a marble shrine, built on a circular marble plinth and perhaps six or seven feet across. A rusting iron balustrade ran around the edge of the plinth, holding up an ancient marble rim. In the centre stood identical, near life-sized marble statues of two women, facing each other. One held a marble flower in her left hand. Two low pillars, with a bird perching on them, supported each figure. Several silver coins, sparkling in the torchlight, were scattered about on the floor of the shrine.

"What is this?" I exclaimed in awe.

"I don't know," whispered Theodore, afraid to raise his voice. "We are below the Via Sacra. The Cloaca begins not very far from here."

I reached through the balustrade and picked up one of the coins, trying to read the inscription. On one side I saw a word embossed, surrounding a woman's covered head. On the other, an image of the shrine before us, inscribed with the same word. I could make no sense of it.

"I'll ask my teacher what this means," I said, as I put the coin in my pocket. Theodore looked hesitant. "Who knows what curse might fall upon anyone who steals one of these coins?"

"I'll bring it back, I promise," I said, but he gave me a doubtful look.

The chamber was a dead-end, so we retraced our steps a little way until we found another tunnel, branching away to our right. How to get out? Theodore pointed to the rungs of an iron ladder embedded in the wall. "You go that way; I'll go back the way we came."

I clasped his hand to say goodbye. "Thank you for saving my life, Theodore! I won't forget you!" I reached out my arm to take hold of a rung of the ladder. My foot slipped, and in a moment I found myself floundering in the effluent, gurgling through the Cloaca Maxima.

I thrashed helplessly around in the filthy water and instantly found myself washed by the eddy against an arch of the tunnel. Theodore stood by, ready to assist, but after a few moments to regain my breath, I slowly dragged myself out of the water, soaking wet and smelling atrocious. The heavy iron cover proved hard to shift, but little by little I pushed and slid it slowly to one side. As I came up through the hole, it took a moment or two to recognise where I was.

The remains of the Basilica Aemelia were close by, a ruin with grass growing through its stone floor. Even closer to me stood a small group of onlookers, astonished as I emerged, soaked with effluent. Without a word, I closed the heavy cover, wished them a good day, and hurried back to the monastery.

I arrived as Cadmon returned from repairing a wall in the monastery grounds. Although we still shared a cell, I saw less and less of him as the days went by. Cadmon worked with the farm labourers on the estate, carrying heavy loads and mending the estate walls—to strengthen himself, he said. His woollen habit proved far too hot for such manual work, so he now mostly wore those despised barbarian leggings and a shirt that he took off while working on the wall. Cadmon's growing physique had slowly turned brown in the sun. Young girls from the estate came by on their way to the milking shed, gawping and giggling at his sweaty, muscular torso. This eventually reached the ears of the prior, so his shirt went back on and the girls who milked the goats went by another way.

Cadmon doubled up laughing when he caught sight of me. "So, now you are a sewer rat! I always suspected that!" Prior Pretiosus entered the outer courtyard, shaking his head at the sorry sight. I told him what happened. "Felix is back in Rome; the sewer is how I managed to escape."

"I will inform Abba of this! Meanwhile, go and get yourself washed down. Throw your habit on the fire and draw fresh clothes from the laundry room." The launderer shook his head when I told him, and snatched up my habit. "This is too good to throw away," he muttered, heading towards the washroom, my odorous garment dangling on the end of a pole. By the time I had dowsed myself under the water pump and washed off the filth clinging to my sandals, our launderer had returned with fresh clothes and a towel. I dressed and went to my cubicle for a short while.

Abba Gregorius sent for me immediately on his return. The dove was there again in his cubicle, sitting on his shoulder. I stood still, so as not to drive it away.

"Alric," he said in concern, putting down his quill, "I am deeply sorry you have been troubled again by this slave master and his crew. What he has done is an offence to Roman law, as well as to your person as a freeman under guardianship. I am writing a letter to the City Prefect and also to the Captain of the Vigiles. If this detestable man should so much as set a toe on Rome's soil again, he and his henchmen will be arrested, his cargo confiscated, his ship seized, and all his slaves set free."

I stammered my thanks.

"Do not fear, my son," Abba said, half waving acknowledgment, half gesturing towards the curtained door of his cell.

Augustinus set off once again on my behalf to alert the Vigiles, but the ship had already slipped its mooring and departed for the coast.

Arriving at the library just in time for our afternoon lesson, I gave Brother Petrus a full account while Cadmon listened. I started with the effects of my hasty lunch, my escape from Felix and finally falling into the foul muck of the sewer. I handed Petrus the coin from the shrine as my tale unfolded; he wiped the grimy coin and rubbed it to shine. Petrus turned it over in his hand and studied it carefully, spelling out the inscription "Cloacinae". He motioned us to look closer.

"See these flowers? And the birds? These were well-known symbols for the pagan goddess, Venus. The shrine you saw is the Shrine of Venus Cloacina."

"Why was it there, in the sewer?"

"In pagan times, Venus Cloacina stood for both the goddess of purity and also the goddess of the sewer. That's why there are two women on this coin, one for each attribute, purity, and filth. You could say, the two sides of human nature."

He looked meaningfully at Cadmon and me.

"So, that makes it a Christian symbol then?" Cadmon asked, wearing an innocent face; "because we are all born with sin in our natures, we have within us both good and bad."

Our Grammaticus handed the coin back to me, looking hard at Cadmon to see whether he was fooling about, cloaked beneath a guise of innocence.

"No, I don't think so, Cadmon. We do have both natures struggling within us, and which one wins depends on which one we feed. But remember, these are pagan, not Christian symbols. There is nothing to suggest it comes from a Christian source. Just another piece of pagan Rome."

The news of my misfortune swiftly spread, and by evening prayers everyone in the monastery knew. Some smiled in my direction as we lined up for the oratory, others winked as they pulled up their noses. This was going to take some living down.

I lay awake for some time that night, the day's events churning over and over in my head. That Felix was back was deeply troubling. Had Rome become an unsafe place for me again?

Cadmon, sensing what I was thinking, reached out in the dark.

"Don't worry, Alric. You won't see Felix back here again. He has too much to lose."

I thought, If only that were t rue!

11

TIBERIUS'S FLOOD

Rome, November 589 AD

POPE PELAGIUS II, Bishop Of Rome, arrived to lay the foundation stone for our new monastery church on the last day of November 589, the Feast Day of San Andreas the Apostle. The church, like our oratory in the grounds, was to be dedicated to his name. Abba Gregorius presented a relic from San Andreas's arm, which he had brought from Constantinople five years earlier.

For several days beforehand the monastery hummed with activity. Laying a foundation stone was a prestigious event, clergy and acolytes arriving from monasteries and ancient basilicas all over Rome. The pope, a native of the city but also of Germanic stock, was nearing his seventieth year. His most significant gift to Rome, only recently completed, was a basilica and monastery outside the city wall, near the Appian Way, and dedicated to San Laurentius the Martyr.

Pope Pelagius, arriving on horseback from the Lateran Palace with a full retinue, cut a strikingly handsome figure. By his side rode a priest with piercing eyes, holding the rank of an archdeacon, serving as the pope's assistant at the Lateran. Together with Abba Gregorius, he was one of the Seven Deacons of Rome and widely expected to succeed Pelagius to the Throne of San Petri. The archdeacon's gaze swept over the throng to where all our monks stood on the monastery steps. His lip curled in disdain at the sight of our rough, woollen habits. I thought this was strange – our monastery abounded with learned men, some even from noble families and some were skilled physicians. But then, renouncing a secular life of rank and power did not seem to sit comfortably with many of Rome's clergy.

I had also noticed this look before, from those of higher station than I—on Hrothgar's face for sure, and sometimes on the faces of our own Saxon warriors, particularly the younger ones who most wanted to make a distinction between the sons of earls and the sons of churls. Even Cadmon could show something of this, but he wore differences much more lightly after our experience together on the high seas. However, a face on which I had not seen this superior look was on Abba Gregorius himself—except for the time he had confronted the slaver Felix. Abba was unquestionably the most educated man in Rome at this time, of the highest rank in noble birth, yet he chose to wear the humble cloth of a monk. Wearing my own, I straightened my shoulders and thrust out my chin, feeling a new sense of pride rising in my chest.

At last, after much bowing and introduction, the ceremony began. The well in the atrium had already been sealed over. A wooden cross, set in place by two builders on the floor of the atrium, indicated where the altar would eventually stand. The pope sprinkled the cross and the foundation stone with holy water. The stone bore an engraving made using a knife rather than a chisel, with crosses etched on each of the four sides. The pope pronounced a blessing over the stone and said a prayer of protection for all craftsmen involved in the building work. Then he led the Litany of the Saints, beseeching the Triune God, the Blessed Virgin Mary, angels, martyrs and the saints, for protection and support. We sang Psalm 126, beginning with the verse, "Unless the Lord build the house, they that build it labour in vain." Two of the builders lowered the stone into place, accompanied by another prayer and again the pope sprinkled holy water.

Afterwards, Pelagius exhorted everyone present to contribute to the construction and furnishing of the new church in any way they could. Finally, he dismissed us with a blessing and feasting began in the outdoor dining room and overflowed into the gardens.

After an hour or so the time came for Pelagius to depart. He looked up at the sky as the first drops of rain began to fall, and mounted his horse in the piazza below the monastery. Together with his retinue, the pope turned homeward towards the Lateran.

We had no intimation that we might never see Pelagius again.

The rains continued for days without respite, and rivers of water beat against our schoolmaster's window in the library. Cadmon had his own explanation for this unrelenting rainfall.

"It's an ancient pagan legend," he said to Brother Petrus and me, as we sat in the study. "King Tiberinus drowned in the River Tiber, yes? So, to console him, Jupiter made Tiberinus god of the river! Now, because Tiberinus spends all his time drinking with his friends among the gods, when he feels the need, he gets up and relieves himself into the Tiber—for days and days. That's where all this rain comes from!"

For us on the receiving end, King Tiberinus had now kept up his marathon for several weeks, and the churning yellow-green waters of the Tiber were close to bursting their banks. Our tutor had a less dramatic explanation.

"It's simpler than that, Cadmon. When it rains for a long time in the mountains to the north of Rome—and at the same time there is a great cloudburst above the city—the rainwater flows from many small streams into the Tiber. The water level keeps rising until floods devastate Rome. Can you agree with that, Cadmon?"

Cadmon pulled a face; for him, the first story had more appeal. Either way, day after day rain fell without respite, the Tiber swelled and its overspill spread swiftly into the marshy, low-lying, heavily overcrowded Campus Martius.

One morning in December, a short while after the dedication of our new church, Cadmon, Clementus and I filled a donkey cart with sacks of grain and crossed over the bridge to the district of Trans Tiberim. Half a century earlier the Roman general Belisarius had replaced the windmills on the ridge of the Janiculum Hill with less vulnerable floating mills on the Tiber.

We stopped briefly on the bridge, overlooking the mills moored between Tiber Island and the riverbank. The mills were already hard at work and grain carts, lined up on both banks, waited their turn. Without milled flour to bake bread —the city's staple food—Rome would be on its knees in a matter of weeks. The heavy rains over Rome had eased slightly, but not so further upstream. The river swirling past Tiber Island was still rising as we unloaded the first of our wheat sacks. Working in pairs, we gingerly climbed down the slippery path, carrying a heavy load between us and crossed a narrow footbridge to one of the floating mills. After returning with the milled flour, I rested on the donkey cart while Clementus took the next load with Cadmon.

I studied the mill below me. A stout shaft extended from the floating millhouse to a smaller boat anchored in the river. A large waterwheel was fixed to this shaft, between the boat and the mill, churning furiously in the foaming waters. Inside the mill the shaft from the waterwheel turned a millstone, shaped like a giant coin with a hole in its centre. This stone fitted on top of another flat stone and together they ground the grain into flour.

Back in the mill a few minutes later, I watched as the miller's son climbed a ladder and emptied our grain into a hopper, feeding the coarse grain into the hole at the centre of the upper millstone. The grain was ground into flour, and captured in a tray beneath. The air was thick inside the mill-house, every surface white with flour. Marius the miller and his son as assistant looked as white as ghosts. We refilled our sack from the tray below the millstones, tied the neck and carried it carefully across the narrow bridge, and up the slippery steps to the cart waiting at the top of the bank.

As the morning wore on, the fast-flowing river began rocking the floating mill ever more wildly, making the task increasingly difficult. Clementus and I carried our last sack of grain to the mill as a surge in the river drove an uprooted tree trunk into the back of the mill-house, throwing the upper millstone on to the wooden floor and smashing through the planks. Water surged up from the river below. The miller yelled, "Get out! Get out! It's breaking up!" We left our precious grain swirling in the water and, staggering like drunks, scrambled for our lives towards the door of the heaving watermill.

Outside, the narrow wooden bridge to the riverbank bucked and twisted. I gripped the guide ropes, crawling on my knees to reach the bank. The steps were slippery, but at least the bank wasn't moving. As others emerged behind me, the ropes that held the mill to the shore began to pull loose, until, with a loud snap, the footbridge ripped away from the mooring. The millhouse broke free, swept away by the raging water. We watched in horror as it smashed into another floating mill further downstream, finally coming to rest jammed beneath an arch of the bridge.

We crawled up the steps to reach the road, soaking wet, legs trembling with shock and exertion. Cadmon, above me, leaned over the parapet. "I've never seen anything like this before! Look!" He pointed downriver. "Another one's pulled away!" Crowds were beginning to line the riverbank alongside us, and also on Tiber Island. "We must go now," Clementus said, covering the sacks. Wet and trembling, we hurried back to San Andreas, our beast of burden leading the way.

As we crossed over the bridge to the Forum Boarium, we saw the Geto district on the bank of the Tiber beginning to submerge beneath rising waters. Downstream of us, more water spewed out of the Cloaca Maxima. With a great sense of relief we crossed the Forum Boarium and returned to the monastery, unloading our precious sacks, the flour still dry, into the kitchen storeroom.

Abba Gregorius and our prior stood talking with Martinus in the now empty and forlorn atrium, where the building work for our new church had come to a standstill soon after the rains began. Abba beckoned to us as we came in.

"Martinus has returned from the Prefect's Office bearing bad news."

Martinus nodded. "The Tiber's begun overflowing on the Campus Martius—at the bend of the Tiber, near the Flaminian Gate. The Pantheon's already knee deep in water, and also the Septa." This was not good news, as the Septa Julia was the only reliable source of clean water for thousands of people living in that district.

Gregorius turned to the three of us, sodden and bedraggled.

"How was it at the mills? You look as though you've been dragged out of the Tiber!"

"We have, Abba!" Clementus said. "Some of the water mills have broken loose in the flood. The Geto is also beginning to flood now."

"And the Boarium?"

"It can't hold out for much longer," Cadmon said. We all nodded.

Gregorius thought for a moment.

"The food centres will flood next," he said decisively, "We'll lose all the dole grain stored there. Quickly! Back to the Boarium and get the flour sacks moved out of reach of the water!"

The four of us, now including Martinus, hurried back past the Circus Maximus to the Boarium. Saving the grain was vital, as Rome depended on this monthly dole. I asked Martinus, who had been in the monastery longer than me, "How does this dole business work?"

Only slightly out of breath, he said, "Alric, it's like this. Everyone arriving in Rome registers at whatever city gate they come to. This record is sent to the Lateran Palace. A book is kept there that shows the names of persons of every age and profession, both men and women, who receive aid—the amounts to be given to them and the dates when due. That is how the City Prefect and the Bishop of Rome know the needs of the city's population—and also how many people are living in the city."

We arrived at the Forum Boarium where some of Rome's centuries-old, patched-up, high-rise insulae were nearing collapse. This included apartments on both sides of the river, opposite Tiber Island, as well as around the crumbling Theatre of Marcellus and the Capitoline Hill.

Martinus said, "Nearly all of Rome's welfare centres are near here. Most of the food is doled out by these welfare centres, so that hunger doesn't turn into starvation."

The granaries of the imperial warehouses had collapsed a long time before. It fell to these welfare centres to store nearly all of the city's grain supply, and it was towards these that we now hurried.

"Four of the five centres are here, in this one small area, Alric. There's also another, a little further out, along the Via Del Corso, right at the edge of the Campus Martius. It's on the street that runs straight to the Flaminian Gate."

The Church in Rome had become a source of supply for the whole city. Lay officials of the Papal civil service, responsible to the Guardian of the Church in Rome, supervised all five centres.

"So," Martinus finished, "on the first day of every month, food is given out to the poor and needy. That, in a nutshell, is how Rome survives."

We arrived at the first of these welfare centres on the Forum Boarium. The marketplace was nearly empty as the last frantic stallholders—a man and his wife, and their frightened dog barking at the rising tide—threw what they could into their cart as the water swept towards them.

I saw our floating mill still blocking the arches of the Pons Aemelia. Through the bare winter trees on the riverbank we could see the floodwaters overwhelming the low-lying Geto, spilling into its narrow, crowded streets and on towards us in the Forum Boarium. Shops and workshops were mostly at street level, where artisans ran their businesses; but after only a few hours, the rising waters had brought a thick oily layer of foul-smelling mud, and nearly everyone was closed for business.

We entered the porch of the church of San Maria in Cosmedin, the foul water from the Tiber already ankle-deep as we entered the lobby. This building was the former Market Inspector's office on the Forum Boarium, but the cattle market had long since gone, and with it the inspector. The arches of the church facing on to the square, were bricked-in to create a large distribution hall. The free flour dole was called "step bread", given out from the steps of the porch to people on the register. They took their rations to the bakers, who turned the flour into flat, round bread. But now, even the bakeries were flooding.

Some helpers had already arrived at San Maria, moving heavy sacks of milled flour to an upper level. Cadmon led the way for our small party, swinging a heavy load of flour on to his shoulders and staggering up a flight of stairs. We worked together for a while, then the overseer sent us on to San Giorgio in Velabro, a hundred paces away towards the Palatine. In this short space of time, the swirling, muddy water had risen to our calves. We splashed on, our robes pulled up and tucked under our belts. Around us, frightened voices cried out as men, women and children began fleeing to higher ground. The circular temple of Hercules Victor close to the Tiber was submerging, its columns reflected in the dark, rippling water. Near the bridge, firemen of the Vigiles made a futile effort to pump the water back into the river. "Where there is a need, there go the Vigiles!" I said under my breath.

We splashed on towards the Arch of Janus, standing heavy and squat above the Cloaca Maxima sewer, where it snaked beneath the three welfare centres we were now struggling to reach. Floodwaters rampaging through the Cloaca below began pushing sewage up into the streets above, gurgling through the metal covers and drains all along our route, further raising the level of the water and stench around us. Just beyond the Arch of Janus, I stumbled on the uneven surface of the street. Several hands grabbed my habit and arms, hauling me out of the water. Two of these belonged to Theodore, who had rescued me from Felix.

"Come with us," I said, as I searched in my pocket to give the silver coin back to Theodore.

"The sewer is full with rainwater," he said sadly, looking at the coin. "It will be a while before I can return there. Maybe this is why there is so much water now." His reproach for removing a sacred coin from the sewer lay heavily on me. I made no reply, aware of my feelings of guilt for what misfortune I might have brought upon my rescuer.

An hour later, we finished working at San Giorgio and splashed on towards three more centres, San Teodoro, San Maria Antiqua and San Maria in Via Lata. At each place our urgent task was lifting sack after sack of dry grain and milled flour out of reach of the rising waters. It was exhausting work. Only Cadmon, like a fast-growing young bull, never seemed to flag. By late afternoon we had moved tons of grain out of reach of the water in four of the welfare centres serving this area.

The thin line held that day; but for how much longer?

As we left San Maria in Via Lata, I said to Theodore, "Where are you living now?" He shrugged and waved in the general direction of the insula apartments in the Geto. "You can't live there! The ground floor level is already under water! Come back with us to the monastery, Theodore. Please!"

It was nearly nightfall. The sky darkened further as a million starlings returned to the city, sweeping back and forth in a dazzling display over the Palatine Hill, desperate to escape waiting birds of prey. By the time we returned to San Andreas, the birds were settling, squabbling for a perch in the branches of the monastery's evergreens. Even the incessant rains had failed to wash away their thick guano, accumulating beneath the trees, and we slid and slipped our way up the steps to the courtyard above. With our sandals left in the courtyard, we joined the procession barefoot and entered the garden oratory for prayers. Like Noah of old, we prayed fervently for an end to the rain.

After supper Theodore became the fourth member of our small cell, and the sound of snoring coming from exhausted bodies rattled our thin wooden door to its hinges.

Before the week was over, floodwaters in the low-lying areas of the Campus Martius had risen as high as third-floor apartments in the Geto. Along the southern edge, entire blocks began collapsing into the streets and the river. By the end of the following week the rising water and the falling rain had swamped even the churches' granaries, sweeping away thousands of bushels of wheat. Our thin line separating hunger from starvation had finally broken.

The rains continued unabated until the end of December. Then one afternoon early in the New Year Cadmon looked out of Brother Petrus's study window at a blue, winter sky. He said, "King Tiberius seems to have pulled up his britches and gone back to his quaffing companions in the great hall of the gods—wouldn't you say, Grammaticus?"

12

PERILOUS PLAGUE

Rome, January 590 AD

THEODORE DID NOT settle well into the routine or the discipline of the monastery. Fending for himself in the sewers and alleyways of Rome had made him increasingly feral. He remained on good terms with me, Cadmon and Clementus, but rubbed up against our tutor, and also the prior. Theodore refused to hear anyone speak to him about his soul, nor would he listen to anything that the monks considered virtuous. Instead, his angry words were scornful and he laughed and swore in a way more suited to a blacksmith's forge than a monastery. In short, Theodore vowed never to adopt the habit of a holy life.

Once the floods began to recede Theodore's outbursts drove him from the monastery. Some time later, Remus, Captain of the Night Guard, found him in dire straits in an empty apartment. Theodore was sweating profusely with the symptoms of fever. Remus brought him back to the monastery and our physician Justin took him straight to the sanatorium. Over the next few days, in the last week of December, his fever worsened.

A small group of us, Clementus, Martinus and I prayed at Theodore's bedside. Nothing seemed to help him, and we thought he had breathed his last; then Theodore sat bolt upright and stared wildly around him. He cried out to us, "Go away! Leave me! A dragon's come to take me, but he can't while you're still here!"

He was damp with sweat, the strands of hair sticking to his face, eyes wild with terror. Trembling uncontrollably, Theodore cried out again, "He's already swallowed my head! Why do you make me suffer more? Stop praying! Let my torment stop! He must do with me what he must do!" We knelt down, scared witless, with no time to call the prior to our aid.

Martinus called out, "Theodore, what do you mean? Sign yourself with the sign of the cross!"

Theodore's screams rose even more as he thrashed about in horrific pain. "I want to sign myself, but I can't!" he wailed. "I am tied down by the dragon's coils!" All we could do was prostrate ourselves on the hard tiled floor and redouble our prayers.

After what seemed an age, Theodore cried out again.

"Thank God," he panted, "the dragon has gone! He couldn't withstand your prayers!"

His breathing was laboured, but the wildness had gone from his eyes. He lay on the pillow, totally wrung out, but in his right mind at last.

"Pray for me," he begged, "pray for my sins! I'm ready to let go my evil ways and leave behind my life in the world."

We heard the sound of footsteps hurrying down the corridor and Prior Pretiosus burst into the room, taking in the situation at a glance.

He said, "Abba heard your cries, Theodore! He has prayed for your soul. And now, thanks be to God, I see that you are in your right mind again!" He grasped Theodore's hand.

So much for our prayers, I thought, but I was glad Theodore had begun to make a recovery. After only a few days, he rejoined our cell. At Theodore's first meal in the refectory after his ordeal, Abba Gregorius welcomed him back into the fold. "My son, I know that you have now turned to God with your whole heart!"

I was shaken by what had taken place, but also deeply moved. Theodore's dramatic conversion was a turning point for me too. While I was praying for Theodore on the sanatorium floor, I had seen Wyrd and her sisters at their spinning wheel again. Then, before they could spin, a hand took the thread of my life and held it fast. Here was something more remarkable than anything I had seen before. The power that the Wyrdae held over my life was finally broken, and I saw the Saxon gods fading, the future somehow in another's hands.

Theodore was baptised at the font in the monastery oratory a short time afterwards. I stood beside him, not as a friend or supporter, but as his fellow candidate.

At the time that Theodore's ordeal reached its end, Cadmon awoke from a dream in the middle of the night. He shook me until my eyes opened and whispered, "I saw the four horsemen of the Apocalypse on a hill, Alric. Waiting to visit death on the city!"

"You've had a bad dream, Cadmon," I yawned. "The reading over supper was about horses, remember? It's not often a horse gets a mention, let alone four! Maybe that's why you had this dream. You like horses. Go back to sleep."

"No, Alric! It's a warning! Dark forces are gathering against us. This rain has served to open the city's gates!" Cadmon's dream, or our worst nightmare, soon came to pass.

The very next day the plague, like a stowaway, crept into Rome on a ship from Egypt, where this pestilence had already taken hold. It was soon given a name, ingruinaria, after it broke out in Rome early in January. There was no treatment for the plague. In crowded and unsanitary high-rise apartments, men, women and children experienced agonisingly painful carbuncles in the neck, armpits and groin. Some swellings were the size of hens' eggs, leading to blackening fingers and nails as living flesh rotted and putrefied. Victims falling to the grim reaper multiplied daily; fewer than half survived.

That was the plague's first week.

By the end of the second, the plague had swept through apartment blocks closest to the river, and there were reports of dead rats in great numbers flushed out of the Cloaca sewer. The disease followed an invisible path left by infected fleas and dying rats, running through the apartments of the poor as well as the villas of the rich, showing neither favour nor mercy. A sight I had never seen before soon became commonplace—stretcher-bearers daily carrying scores of victims outside the city wall for burial.

Hunger, then famine, soon followed in the Holy City. While some grain remained for the garrison defending the city, food supplies, already depleted by the floods, were now exhausted and produce would not come from Rome's farms before the summer harvest. Rome was no longer a safe haven; in coming to this city, we had sailed into the very jaws of hell. All that held us together in these dark days was the disciplined rhythm of prayers in the oratory.

Abba took the only practical step available. Under his orders and the watchful eye of Prior Pretiosus, the monastery took great care not to offer any invitation to vermin. We kept our small supply of food sealed, and the storerooms thoroughly swept and scrubbed daily.

Then, to everyone's dispair, the contagion slipped under the door of the Lateran Palace and into the Pontiff's own private chambers.

Pope Pelagius's first symptoms began to appear some days after his celebration of Epiphany on January 6th. He awoke with a fever, his muscles ached and he could not keep down his food. The most skilled physicians in Rome were called to his bedside, among them Copiosus, our physician from San Andreas. The Pope's headaches and abdominal pains became unbearable. Exhausted, he could scarcely move from his pool of sweat. On the seventh day of February, after a horrific night of diarrhoea, he died in agony, his physicians and chamberlain helpless at his bedside.

The following morning Abba Gregorius prayed for Pelagius's soul, and a few days later his body was taken from the Lateran Palace and buried in the Basilica San Petri. As the basilica lay outside the city walls, burial was permitted under Justinian's Law.

Following an ancient tradition for the Bishops of Rome, Pelagius was carried in relays on the Via Papale, the Papal Way between the Lateran Palace and Basilica San Petri. The Papal Gentlemen from Rome's noble families were the first to bear his body as the procession wound through the narrow streets of the Campus Martius. This was usually the most crowded part of Rome, but as we processed we found the streets eerily empty. A brooding silence hung over the city as all business came to a standstill. A few people scuttled by, furtive and wary, eyes averted, avoiding any contact with strangers.

In contrast to these empty public spaces in Rome, panic-stricken citizens crammed into church basilicas, and these too became centres for the spread of the pestilence. Even so, these citizens now made up the greater part of the mourners following Pelagius's funeral procession, wailing and lamenting the pope's passing, and fearful of what might lie ahead for Rome.

The great basilica came into view, Cadmon and my first glimpse of San Petri's imposing edifice. An Egyptian obelisk dominated the centre of the square, once the centrepiece of Nero's Circus, and a lasting reminder of the place where the Apostle had been crucified, upside down. Behind the obelisk, colonnades of pillars surrounded a courtyard that led to the gleaming white marble exterior of the basilica. We climbed the long flight of steps and passed beneath huge doors before being swallowed by a mass of people cramming into the courtyard.

The sight overwhelmed me, and I recalled the words spoken by Princess Bertha to my mother at Ratteburg fort, on the day of my birth, "May the Almighty bring him one day to the place of the great Fisher of Men." At that moment the meaning of Bertha's cryptic saying was finally revealed; her prayer for me had come to pass!

My eyes shining, I turned to Cadmon processing beside me, but he was looking the other way, into the throng that pressed close by our procession.

A pretty young girl waved shyly at him, her cheeks reddening. I groaned, my moment gone as Cadmon turned to me with a triumphant look in his eyes and a grin on his face.

Cadmon was taller than many of us in the procession, handsome and broad-shouldered, his golden hair loose on his shoulders. This young boy, once hunted by his older brother, was steadily growing into a swaggering, self-confident woman-hunter himself. Even in the midst of death, the thrusting cycle of life went on.

No sooner was Pope Pelagius laid to rest than speculation ran rife through Rome about who would succeed him. A three-day pause always followed after the funeral of a pope before a new election began, allowing Rome's nobility time to participate together with the clergy. In the second week of February, the great men of the city gathered to elect a successor to the Bishop of Rome. It was clear to everyone that a decision was critically important and needed soon, to stem the growing tide of panic; but also, to give fresh direction to the desperate citizens of Rome.

The clergy of the Diocese of Rome formed the electoral body for the new bishop and proposed candidates from their number. The name of Pelagius's archdeacon at the Lateran came forward, but attracted little support outside his narrow circle among the city's nobility. What Rome needed now was not an insider bureaucrat, but a man who could hold everyone together with a strong and unwavering hand.

No monk had ever served as pope before, but despite this, Gregorius's name was submitted to the people. His credentials included serving a term as Prefect of Rome, the most senior civil servant in the city, and also as Pope Pelagius's private secretary, so that Gregorius knew how to deal with affairs of both church and state. In addition, he had served for a number of years as the Pelagius's Legate to the Imperial Court in Constantinople, and he spoke on firstname terms with all the imperial family and aristocracy in the city. In terms of both experience and reputation, Abba Gregorius was second to none.

Instead of casting votes, the bishops of Rome were selected by consensus. Gregorius was the unanimous choice; his election following this tradition that was once common amongst Roman troops when they chose their emperors.

Shortly after Abba's election, Cadmon and I sat in our tutor's study. Cadmon again shared his dream of the four horsemen. Petrus said with characteristic sarcasm, "You are remarkably prescient of these events, Cadmon! Quite remarkable—even though Rome has lost its pope, and now we have lost our abbot! Superficially, this does not appear to leave us in a good place. But what do you make of all this, Alric?"

I said, a touch gloomily and with a little melodrama, "These riders of death want to destroy Rome once and for all. But instead, they've entered a trap they have not foreseen!" Pctrus ceased pacing up and down in his usual manner and sat with us at his desk. "Go on," he said.

"These horsemen have revealed their intentions by taking the life of our pope, but they could not foresee that another would arise who would turn the fortunes of Rome for the good, even in these End Times. These events are only the beginning, but I can also see doors opening that once were tightly shut. Instead of destroying us, they will hand the advantage to us. We aren't seeing the beginning of the end; it's the beginning of the coming Kingdom!"

Brother Petrus looked at me steadily, his eyelids half closed, lips pursed as he reflected on my words. "Falling into traps, revealings, destructions, doors opening, doors closing, an End Time! Well, Alric, you are quite the prophet it seems! We shall have to wait and see how all this turns out, shan't we?"

He rose to his feet. "Now! Open your writing tablets and let us begin, while we wait and see what unfolds!"

We did not have long to wait.

While Gregorius awaited confirmation from the Emperor, he refused to occupy the papal apartments within the Lateran Palace. He moved instead into modest accommodation behind the Lateran, with an aspect over the Basilica San Iohannes in Laterano.

Although we were overflowing with people, after Abba's departure our monastery felt not so much empty as bereft. Gregorius appointed an aristocrat by the name of Marinianus as Abbot of San Andreas. Marinianus was in every respect a man of noble birth. In appearance, his long face was smooth, complexion ruddy and his friendly eyes a shining pale green. By nature, he was kindly, courteous and gentle, making few demands on others and ruling with a sensitive hand. He was also a close friend and confidant of our new Pope, and one of Gregorius's trusted inner circle.

Meanwhile, all around us, the plague continued unabated. Something had to be done. Gregorius acted swiftly. He ascended the pulpit of San Iohannes in Laterano and began preaching to a vast congregation of silent, despairing, yet expectant people. He did not mince his words as he took his flock into his confidence and shared what he saw.

"Behold, all the people are smitten with the sword of God's wrath and men are laid low in sudden destruction. There is no interval of weakness before death, for this death leaves no time for the slow process of decay. Before the sufferer can turn to the Almighty in penitential mourning, he is gone. Think in what plight that man will appear before the strict Judge, as one who has had no time to bewail his evil deeds."

Gregorius preached in this vein for some time. He was the last in the tradition of great Roman orators, and it showed. This was not a time for polite listening. Some beat their breasts and sobbed in penitence, their dispairing hearts thirsty for hope. Gregorius spoke his final exhortation to this frightened assembly in a conciliatory and calm voice of authority.

"Let us then, each one of us, flee for refuge in penitential mourning, while we have time to weep before the blow falls. Let us summon up before the mind's eye the sins we have committed. Let us bewail what things we have done amiss; let us come before His face with confession and as the prophet admonishes us, let us lift up our hearts to God and heighten the earnestness of our prayers by the merit of good works. He surely gives us confidence in our fear, he who cries to us by His prophet: 'I have no pleasure in the death of a sinner, but that the wicked turn from his way and live.' Let no one despair for the greatness of his iniquities."

Bishop Gregorius ended with an exhortation to make a special act of contrition, so that the wrath of God, seen in this deadly pestilence, might be turned away. He proclaimed a processional litany to pray for an end to the plague.

A few days later, in answer to the call, bishop and people processed solemnly through the near-empty streets of the city, coming from the four great monastic basilicas and the three titular churches from the earliest years of Christian Rome. The city had once been famous for its Seven Hills and great monuments to the glory of Rome. Now, in their place, stood the seven great monastic basilicas of San Petri, San Pauli and San Laurentii—all outside the city walls, and San Iohannes in Laterano within, together with three great titular churches from the early years of Christian Rome under Emperor Constantine—San Maria Maggiore, San Croce in Gerusalemme and San Sebastian.

The spectacle of religious processions had long replaced Rome's bloodthirsty circuses of centuries past. Now, to bring an end to the plague, from these latter-day seven 'hills of Rome' the people, priests, monks and nuns streamed out in seven separate processions to meet at the bridge leading to Emperor Hadrian's fortress-like Mausoleum.

It was another dismal morning as we processed with heavy hearts under lowering skies pelting with rain. Intermittent groans and shrieks, coming from inside insula apartments, broke the unnatural quiet of the streets, as did the subdued, distant chanting of Misereres, mercies for the burial of the dead. So many were dying in Rome that burying each body separately was now impossible. Night after night, the incessant rumble of wagons carried corpses away from the city to be flung without ceremony into deep pits dug outside the city walls. Pope Pelagius was among the fortunate few to have received a proper burial.

San Andreas's monastery, of course, turned out in force following behind Bishop Gregorius, as we knew how to sing the processional litany. Even at a distance one could tell a monk from a priest, and not because of their tonsure, as priests were also tonsured; nor because of their habit, as many dressed similarly. The difference is the pace. A monk's stride in the street is faster and more urgent, just short of a run, showing there is no time to waste in these Last Days. On this last day, however, we set off walking slowly and in step, in tune with the sentiment, at one with the cry repeated over and over again:

Kyrie Eleison – Lord have mercy,
For your Holy City is holy no more,
And we have surely sinned.

We processed in pairs, shuffling forward at a funereal pace in open sandals, bending into the freezing wind. Behind us came clergy from the Lateran, not happy with their position further back in the line. The three youngest in our monastery took turns carrying the heavy processional cross; Clementus, Theodore and me. We walked a few paces ahead of Bishop Gregorius, proud at the privilege and fearful of the plague, as death raged all around us. Some in the procession died even as we walked and lamented through Rome's misery-ridden streets. I was shaking like a leaf, feeling exposed, away from the relative security of the monastery. My eyes darted to the right and left, looking for vermin in our path, and fearing contact with the crowd behind.

At last, we reached the bridge leading across to Emperor Hadrian's Mausoleum. Clementus stopped, and the procession came to a standstill. Now it was my turn. I drew beside Clementus to take the cross, while he and Theodore stepped back a pace or two behind. I faced the bridge and waited, briefly glancing up at the heavy silver crucifix studded with precious stones. Then I saw the sky lighten as a watery sun struggled to emerge from behind shifting clouds, and the shape of a man's arm began to appear in the swirling cloud. Then came the likeness of a sword, and a head began to take shape, revealing a stern face and pursed lips. All the while a cold wind whistled through the bridge, carrying with it a high-pitched sound like voices singing; but where they came from, or what they sang, I could not tell.

As if in response to the vision in the clouds, Bishop Gregorius stepped ahead of me, his bishop's crook raised as though warding off a mighty blow. Kneeling down on the cobblestones, he interceded with the Almighty for the plague to pass us by. While I stared over the top of his mitre at the procession waiting for us on the opposite bank, he cried out,

The inhabitants are taken away;
They fall, not one by one, but all together.
Houses are left empty; parents see their children buried,
Their heirs go before them to the grave.

When his intercession had ceased, Gregorius our Pontifex, the "bridge-builder" of the Church in Rome, raised his eyes to the stormy heavens. I followed his gaze up into the clouds. This huge apparition had formed into a shape on the far bank of the Tiber, above the mausoleum. From the gasps and whimpered cries rising behind me, I knew I was not alone in seeing the figure emerging, his right hand grasping the flaming sword of judgment. This, surely, was our moment of crisis, a judgment for us or against us. Would we be permitted to pass, or would we be struck down where we stood? I was rooted to the spot in the grip of fearsome trembling and great awe.

A chorus of voices coming from the procession behind us now punctured the air as a thousand tongues cried out,

Mary, Mother of God, have mercy on us!

The angel's face had now taken full shape, lips grim, eyes stern and piercing, weighing up the very thoughts of our hearts. I had stopped breathing—what was breath to me now? In a moment I would surely be cast lifeless to the ground. Cries and wailing from the procession gradually fell away, like a dying wind. All the while that strange sound of singing continued. Across the river, the procession coming from Basilica San Petri also stood frozen in this moment of engulfing crisis.

A great silence followed, the moment stretching into eternity. Would we live, or would we die, right here at the foot of this bridge? The vision of the Fates, sitting motionless before their loom, swam briefly before my eyes, yet my life no longer hung on a breaking thread but was held tight in my own hand, and at that moment, my soul cried out, "I choose to live!"

Many others must have chosen the same, for the figure in the cloud slowly drew back his arm and the sword of judgment returned to its scabbard. The clouds swirled, a small patch of blue sky broke through, and in a moment, the ethereal messenger was gone.

"The plague is over!" cried the Bishop of Rome. "Let us cross!"

The Lateran choir began a quavering hymn of praise and thanksgiving as Gregorius set one foot on the bridge, then the other, and like an exodus we all crossed over to the other side.

The plague was indeed over and with this respite, hope returned to Rome. Emperor Mauricius finally ratified Gregorius's election as Bishop of Rome later in the summer. To such a humble man as Gregorius, the Emperor's decision came as an unwelcome shock, yet he finally consented, was carried off to the Basilica San Petri and elevated to the pontifical office on September 3rd, in the Year of Our Lord, 590.

By what seemed coincidence, an unusual guest arrived at our monastery in late August, making a pilgrimage to the holy sites and places in and around Rome. In itself, this was far from unusual. The relics of the apostles and martyrs made Rome the undisputed Holy City of the Roman world. Pilgrims came to Rome in search of holy shrines of the martyrs to pray and intercede with the Almighty to grant a request.

Our new guest was Agilulf, a Frankish deacon and confidant of the aging Bishop Gregorius of Turones on the River Liger in Francia. Deacon Agilulf I guessed was in his late thirties. His hair was short and tonsured in the Roman manner and he wore a loose, pleated tunic that fell below his knees, tied at the waist with a cord. He fastened his black cloak in the centre of his chest with a brooch that bore the arms of San Mauricio, patron saint of Turones's newly rebuilt cathedral.

Agilulf accepted our hospitality at San Andreas, as did others. The Lateran Palace itself was overflowing with bishops from Italia, Sicilia, North Africa and Constantinople. Like many pilgrims, he stayed on for Gregorius's enthronement in September. However, Deacon Agilulf brought with him a letter from the Bishop of Turones, and gave it to Pope Gregorius at their first meeting.

I was not aware of the letter's existence for another six years, let alone its contents; nor did I know anything of the conversation that followed between Pope Gregorius and the deacon from Turones. When we did finally learn of it, the letter's contents were a revelation, another closed door opening, a turning point that would change the course of our lives.

13

SIEGE

Rome, July 592 AD

IN THE SUMMER of 592, after three chaotic years, we witnessed a crucial event that, like waves lashing a waterlogged ship on the high seas, possessed all the potential to thrust Rome into extinction.

At this time Cadmon and I had just entered our fourth year at San Andreas's monastery. After many months of work by builders, carpenters and masons, our basilica was finally completed and a date set in July for Pope Gregorius to consecrate the new church. This engagement was his first return to his beloved monastery since his election as Bishop of Rome, but his guiding hand seemed to touch every stage of the work.

Gregorius arrived on horseback at noon, under a clear blue sky. Although his garb remained the poorest monkish habit, he was very particular that his steed was of the finest, as befitted the highest-ranking bishop in the Roman world. A prestigious group, comprising the Seven Deacons of the Roman Church and officials of the papal palace, escorted him up the stairs from the piazza. So did Valentinus, who served as abbot of the Pope's small Lateran community, his new family; and also Laurentius, Gregorius's prior at the Lateran.

I searched for the steely-eyed archdeacon who had accompanied Pope Pelagius on his visitation, but I could not see him amongst the guests. Gregorius dismounted his white thoroughbred on the piazza. After greeting him warmly, Abbot Marinianus escorted Gregorius to robe in the garden oratory. The whole monastery community lined the stairs to greet the pope. With crook in hand, he nodded and smiled his greeting to each one of us. It was a warm and memorable moment, warmer even than the sun, as we sweltered beneath its merciless gaze.

Many of the pope's entourage from the Lateran had yet to set foot inside the monastery. They saw as they ascended the marble stairs, the original open courtyard enclosed by a columned portico on all four sides. Ahead lay a new marble and lime mortar façade and a large central doorway giving entrance to the new church. Three windows stared down, and above these, a semi-circular window, capped by an oculus—a watchful eye that brooded night and day over the courtyard, and the Palatine Hill beyond.

Our newly constructed house of prayer now covered the former atrium and the cloistered rear garden. In the next hour, this whole area would become the focal point of the monastery's life, as the interior of the church was far more spacious than our small garden oratory. A supporting framework of rigid wooden beams supported the roof. Two rows of columns held the roof-work in place. Arches framed both ends of the nave, resting on stone columns reused from the former atrium.

A marble altar occupied the semi-circular apse at the end of the nave. The outer walls of the church were without windows. Two murals of the pope's parents, Gordianus and Sylvia, painted decades earlier, remained on the southwest wall inside the church.

What also remained was Abba Gregorius's former cell, once the end room in the former cloistered garden, but now leading off from the far southwest corner of the church. It was a place to which we hoped he would return for writing and contemplation, away from the affairs of the Lateran. It was a measure of the pressures of his papal office that in the last two years that he had not found time to do so.

The floor of the church was a decorated mosaic pavement, in a style widely adopted in Constantinople, where Gregorius had served as papal legate. It was one of the few ideas from the East that the pope chose to use.

Gregorius was delighted, visibly moved by this transformation, and said as much in his opening greeting to the assembled congregation. According to custom, a deacon—in this case John, a close friend of Gregorius—waited alone inside the church, while the pope blessed the stoup of holy water and twelve lighted candles placed outside. He sprinkled holy water around the outside walls and knocked at the door with his episcopal crook. The Bishop sprinkled the exterior walls a second time and then a third, knocking on the door on each occasion. Finally, Gregorius entered and blessed another twelve candles inside the church, then fixed a cross in the centre of the church, and said a litany of prayers for the consecration of the church and altar.

All this took place while Cadmon and I were standing with the monks in the open courtyard at the top of the marble stairs. With the litany over, we all proceeded into the new church, including the abbots of all nearby monasteries in Rome and a congregation of guests, led by the prior and Abbot Marinianus. As the youngest member of the monastery, it fell to Theodore to carry the processional cross before the pope, followed closely by the papal deacon. As Theodore processed up the nave, seven candlesticks were carried before him, incense was burnt, and the choir chanted a psalm. A sudden, welcome coolness washed over us as we passed through the large entrance into the church.

With all finally consecrated, the church was formally recorded by the Lateran notaries as the Church of Sant'Andrea al Celio, of the Monasterium ad Clevum Scauri.

As Cadmon said later, "It was all very thorough."

The first celebration of Mass followed, then the Pope addressed the assembly. It was a joyous occasion for our community. I concentrated on the pope's words, scratching away with my stylus on a wax tablet, with three more in my habit pocket. I needed them all. The Bishop of Rome's homily was lengthy. He concluded with this exhortation:

"The Evangelist Mark tells us of a miracle Our Lord performed. They brought to him one who was both deaf and dumb and begged the Lord to lay his hands upon him. And then he said to the man, *Be opened*! And immediately his ears were opened, the string of his tongue was loosed, and he spoke plainly. He spoke plainly, my brethren. For he speaks plainly who, by obeying God first, does himself what he instructs others to do. So, in all that our minds dwells on, and in all our deeds within this church and without, let us pray that at all times we shall meditate by His inspiration and live by His aid alone. Amen."

Scarcely had Pope Gregorius finished speaking when we heard urgent footsteps running up to the church door. I turned and saw that the new arrival was a soldier. Gregorius, noting his urgency, motioned him to come forward. With considerable deference and helmet in hand, the soldier crossed the mosaic floor and whispered in the pontiff's ear. Gregorius's face was grave as he listened, then he straightened and pronounced a blessing and dismissal. Theodore led the pope down the nave aisle to the door, the monks and postulants of our monastery following close behind.

Those remaining in the church sat in confused silence for a moment, necks craning back towards the empty doorway.

Losing little time, Cadmon and I hurried down the steps to the piazza below, the church congregation streaming out behind us. In a few moments, the air filled with the excited chatter of the crowd, aware that something was afoot but not knowing what. We pressed towards the pope as a tall military figure, quickly identified by whispers in the crowd as Castorius, Commander of Rome's garrison, approached on horseback accompanied by his aide. The garrison commander leaped from his horse and bowed.

Addressing him by his familiar name, the pope said, "What is this I hear, Castus? Is it true?"

Castorius nodded. "Yes, Your Holiness! The Duke of Spoleto has taken Namentum and Fidenae and is now marching on Rome!" Both these small towns were close to the banks of the Tiber, only a short distance north of the city. "To be precise, the Duke has arrived at the Porta Flaminia and demands to meet with you without delay!"

"He comes alone?"

"No, Your Holiness. He comes with several thousand men! You must know that I have at my disposal a mere eight hundred."

Gregorius mounted his white thoroughbred and, with Castorius at his side, rode up the narrow path towards the Arch of Constantine. Cadmon and I raced behind on foot, half-running, half-walking, coming close enough to hear some of their conversation. The wax tablets lay heavy in my pockets, noisily clacking as we sped on.

"And your men, they are manning the gates? And the walls?"

"Not all, Your Excellency, there is a mutinous temper among them. This very morning the Theodosian Regiment refused to stand guard on the walls—they have received no wages from the Chartulary in Ravenna for these last two months. These are professional soldiers, Your Holiness. They will not fight unless paid. But our coffers are empty, and now we have mutinous soldiers within the city!"

"And what of your volunteer reserves, Castus?"

"We have no shortage of recruits, Your Holiness! The young men are eager for a chance for glory in battle, but hotheaded youngsters with bravado and no stability are undisciplined and unreliable. Morale remains a problem. Occasionally some desert the ranks for occupations they find more rewarding and less demanding, and others more from boredom than battle fatigue!"

Gregorius and Castorius swept on like a spearhead through Constantine's Triumphal Arch and onwards to the Arch of Titus. We entered the Forum Romanum, where most of the temples and buildings that had made Imperial Rome the centre of the world now stood as naked as skeletons. The meagre civic resources were not sufficient to maintain all the memorials of Rome's past glories.

Akakios, a Greek from Constantinople, came bustling down the steps from his headquarters on the Palatine. His function in Rome was to represent Romanus, who was the exarch, or governor of territories in Italia. Romanus, based in Ravenna and answerable to the emperor for his governorship, considered himself to be the emperor's sole representative in Italy, and therefore the pope's superior. Imperial officials like Akakios, when assigned to Rome, always occupied the Palatine Hill, commandeering the few imperial residences still maintained by the Curator of the Palace. Akakios exercised his duties from the prestigious Palace of Augustus.

Akakios naturally shared the Exarch's attitude, that Rome's finest hour had come and was now long gone; therefore his mission was to oversee the final burial of the city. "Akakios" apparently meant "innocent, not evil." His reputation in the city was so low that this irony made him the butt of many jokes in the city's taverns. His legation to Rome had arrived in the wake of Romanus's appointment to Ravenna. It was said Akakios hoarded supplies of corn and wine and exotic foodstuffs shipped directly by the Imperial Navy from Sicily. The silk sheets that nightly bore Akakios' enormous weight were snatched from palace beds in Syracuse, Sicilia's capital city. While Rome starved, Akakios's luxury apartments were never wanting for luxuries, or for prostitutes.

Every week his henchmen transported sacks of grain to the water mills anchored on the Tiber, rebuilt after the floods. Akakios always demanded to have his wheat milled without payment. In tune with attitudes prevailing in Constantinople, Akakios' main purpose lay not in the interests of the city but in feathering his own nest. At the same time, he attempted to frustrate any settlement with the Langobard dukes that might otherwise alleviate the miseries of Rome. Pope Gregorius well knew from his private sources that our imperial masters bullied, bribed and took without payment whatever they wanted from the Sicilian farmers. When it came to greed, there was little to choose between Langobard overlords and imperial officials.

Akakios reached the bottom of the Palatine steps, yelling, "Bring my horse, dammit! Bring me a horse!"

Akakios held the rank of Tribune, a minor military officer with civil powers appointed by the Exarch to take charge of a town and administer it as governor. He also notionally had oversight of the local militia and was therefore responsible for their pay, but his actual position and influence in Rome was negligible. Like all the imperial representatives on the Palatine, Akakios had a solid reputation for inefficiency and greed. With the exception perhaps of Felix, Souk, and Hrothgar, I had yet to meet a more odious person than Akakios. His small eyes beneath a dark forehead and thinning hair blazed with anger as Gregorius and Castorius passed swiftly by on the narrow pathway.

"What's going on here, Gregorius?" demanded Akakios. He never used the pope's title. Akakios was also compelled to speak to the pope in Latin, rather than his native Greek. Although Gregorius had formerly been papal legate to the Imperial Court in Constantinople for seven years, he chose not to learn even a sentence of the Greek tongue. However, as most officials, senators and imperial notables in Constantinople also spoke Latin, Gregorius did not need to learn the Greek language himself.

He replied to Akakios, "The Duke of Spoleto awaits us at the gates of Rome, Akakios. I go to hear his terms."

"I am the one to make any terms," he squeaked in a shrill voice, wobbling on his skittish beast, "and the Exarch will make no treaty with this Langobard scum! As Romanus's representative in Rome, I have no mandate for negotiating any treaty!"

"But as Bishop and Duke of the Duchy of Rome, Akakios, I do."

We skirted around the steep flank of the Capitoline Hill and the derelict Senate House in the Forum, passing by the remains of Trajan's markets. Pressing on beyond the Capitoline, the crowd behind us swelled at every turn in the road as the news spread. Cadmon and I still ran behind the horses at as fast as we could, sweat pouring from us like wild boars running from the hunter's lance.

I was dying of thirst. Ahead of us, a water trough stood on the side of the road. I swerved towards it and plunged my head into the water, drinking down huge gulps to quench my thirst. Cadmon did the same. In a few moments, we were back running behind the Bishop of Rome and the Garrison Commander. In front rode the pontiff's deacon, side-by-side with the commander's adjutant, making a path through the swelling crowds.

Castorius's military garrison lay on the sloping hillside above Trajan's markets, its high square lookout tower brooding over the city. We ran on, turning onto to the narrow cobbled thoroughfare of the Via Corso. The Prefect of Rome kept main thoroughfares like this clear of debris; whereas, in other parts of the city ancient winding streets lay beneath layers of earth and rubbish, making passage difficult.

We hurried on towards the Porta Flaminia. The city's population had swelled to nearly forty thousand in the past year, and Langobard overlords aggressively encroached on outlying areas of the Duchy of Rome. As most of the city's population lived on the Field of Mars, to the west of the Via Corso, the crowds behind us continued to swell. Shopkeepers on the narrow cobbled street slammed down shutters and bolted doors against this unpredictable throng.

The pace of the horses slowed almost to a walk in the narrow Via Corso. We could hear the Pontiff saying, "So, Akakios, how do you propose to defend the city if you will neither pay the troops nor parley with the Duke?" Gregorius, it was said, had never graced Akakios with any official title, refusing to recognise his claim as Governor of Rome. "I hear this morning that you have not paid the troops their wages for some considerable time. Their patience is at an end. As they are professional soldiers, they will not fight with pay. How do you answer this charge?"

Akakios waved his hand dismissively.

"We have had no funds from Ravenna to pay them – the roads are closed, the Imperial fleet is late in coming. They will have to wait."

"Oh? Was it not your shipment of luxuries from Sicilia that landed only a matter of days ago? Or did you perhaps fail to submit an invoice to the Imperial Paymaster when you last corresponded? And refresh my memory; was it not you who approved the removal of a cavalry detachment from Rome to Perugia? Could not Romanus have sent a detachment of cavalry from Ravenna? After all, it is scarcely further! Now here we are, without soldiers, defenceless, without a denarius in the coffers—and still, you refuse to negotiate for peace?"

We did not hear Akakios's reply as the goal came into view, the Porta Flaminia, the gateway to Ravenna on the Via Flaminia, stretching from Rome to the east coast of Italia. The Duke of Spoleto had come down this same north road. This city gate marked the low point of our failed attempt to escape the monastery, but I nudged that thought aside.

Crowds of onlookers, gathered on top of the city wall, stared out to the north. Pope Gregorius turned in his saddle towards Castorius.

"I see the crowds, Commander, but where are your men?"

"They are still in their barracks, your Holiness." He shook his head despairingly. "As I have said, they will not fight until they receive their pay." Akakios broke into a tirade of threats and abuse that I cannot record here.

Gregorius said to Castorius, "Commander, whether they will fight or not, order them all to come to the square at once." The Bishop of Rome dismounted and, with a mitre on his head and a crook in his hand, climbed swiftly up the steps to see what lay beyond the wall. Cadmon and I followed immediately behind. The tightly packed crowd of onlookers on the wall shuffled aside to make way for us.

The sun blazed down, now well past noon and the square inside the gates heaved with people. Hazy blue-brown hills met our gaze in the northwest. The Tiber flowed by to our left, its milky green waters curving around the Campus Martius. Directly ahead, in the middle ground, Duke Ariulf's army that had come to attack us was impossible to miss. A dense sea of helmets, shields, and spears had crossed the Milvian Bridge. Before us, only few hundred yards from the wall, Langobard warriors positioned themselves just beyond the range of our archers, leaning on their shields and spears, increasingly restless in the heat.

There was no way of escape from the city on this side. Duke Ariulf had moved detachments of his warriors around to other gates in the north wall, particularly the Porta Pinciana and Porta Salaria. The no man's land between the Langobards and us lay devoid of all life, shimmering under the scorching heat.

Pope Gregorius pointed beyond the Duke's line of cavalry to the centre of the camp, where the Duke's flags fluttered in the breeze. Cadmon, who, like me, had never seen such a sight before, gripped my shoulder painfully as he drank in the drama and the raw fear of the spectacle before us.

Belisarius, the great Roman general, had defended Rome half a century before. He said, "It has never been possible, even with several times ten thousand men, to guard Rome for a considerable length of time, because the city encompasses such a large territory; and also because Rome is not on the sea, the city is easily cut off from all supplies." That was plain enough as we looked out upon the hordes of warriors below.

Down in the square loud applause broke out, the crowds giving way as the first troop of soldiers marched into the square. With Akakios following behind like a dog at his heels, Gregorius descended the stairs and positioned himself between the soldiers and the gate.

He called out, "Gatekeeper, open the gate!"

Cries of disbelief rose in the square, but the pope's authority held sway. The two halves of the wooden gate swung slowly inwards, revealing a lowered portcullis beyond, now the only barrier between Rome and the Duke's warriors. Castorius's men stared ashen-faced at this vastly superior army from Spoleto. Cadmon said, "These Langobard warriors do not fight for pay; they come for the spoils, and they look ready to tear Rome apart!"

"Treason, Gregorius!" cried Akakios. "Treason! This is madness!"

For once, the soldiers murmured in agreement.

The pope turned back to the multitude of faces ringing the square. He raised his hand for silence. When the murmurs died away, His Holiness drew back his sleeve like the orator he was and addressed the soldiers directly.

"Men, I am informed today that you have received no wages from the Imperial Treasury for these last few months and this is the reason why you refuse to take up arms." A muted murmur arose from the troops and also from the watching crowd.

Bishop Gregorius motioned for silence.

"Since the emissary from Ravenna," he looked briefly towards Akakios, "has failed to fulfil his duty towards you, I give you my pledge that I shall pay the wages due to you before sunset today." The imperial soldiers glanced at each other in surprise at the sudden turn of events, as a roar of relief rose from the crowd.

"But," Gregorius emphasised, "you must be in no doubt that my one concern is for the welfare of the citizens of this Holy City. I speak of the men, the women and the children who daily suffer privations on every side, who bear their sufferings with fortitude, who do not lose courage, even in the face of flood, famine, and plague. Yet more people arrive by the hour, evicted from their farms and villages and cities by the very barbarians that you see before you this day."

He swept his arm towards the open gate. All eyes followed the pope's hand, spellbound, as he pointed through the arched gateway to the serried ranks of warriors camped beyond the narrow strip of earth, only an arrow shot from Rome.

Gregorius fixed his gaze on the troops.

"The fortitude that I have found among these people within this Holy City, I now expect of you—the courage to continue this seemingly impossible struggle, because your citizenship is greater than the city of Rome, greater than Constantinople, greater than the Roman Empire. You are citizens whose names are enrolled in the Kingdom of Our Lord himself, an eternal citizenship that neither life nor death can take from you! Now brace yourselves for whatever may follow; with courage, play your part!" The crowd roared. Gregorius waited for silence.

There followed a long pause, during which the pope signalled again to the gatekeeper to raise the portcullis. Aghast, with a quavering voice the gatekeeper pleaded, "Your Holiness! When the Duke arrived at the walls of the city this morning, he brutally killed captives and mutilated others like a barbarian!" But Gregorius signalled a second time to the gatekeeper.

Slowly the portcullis creaked upwards, everyone's attention riveted by the rattling chains until nothing but open ground stood between the Duke's camp and us. Langobard warriors began rising to their feet, shielding their eyes and looking towards the gaping entrance that had opened in the Aurelian Wall.

Pope Gregorius continued, "But if anyone among you lacks the courage to give heart and soul, life and limb for the people of this city, as befits a

Roman soldier, then that is the road back to Ravenna. You are free—to throw yourselves at the mercy of the Duke of Spoleto. Soldiers of the Empire, choose now!"

The crowd held its breath, the air crackling with unbearable tension. The soldiers stood like frozen statues. Even Akakios had lost his tongue. The pope's finger still pointed to the gateway. After what seemed an age, he let his hand fall, and in the collective sigh that escaped the lips of everyone in the crowded piazza, he spoke again.

"So be it. You have chosen the nobler way expected of every soldier in the service of the Holy City. Now, back to your stations, while I go to meet with the Duke of Spoleto!"

"No! No negotiating! That is the Exarch's command!" shouted Akakios, finally recovering his voice.

In the months before, the pope had appealed to Exarch Romanus to assist Naples against Langobard attack, but Romanus thought it better to remain in central Italy. He had also withdrawn a cavalry unit from Rome, severely weakening the city's defences. Romanus avoided any military contact with the Duke of Spoleto, yet at the same time forbade the Pontiff to make a peace treaty with the Langobards.

The time to be counted had come.

Gregorius turned to Akakios. "He who pays the piper calls the tune, Akakios! You know that better than most. This army is now Rome's army, answerable to the Bishop of Rome for the defence of this city. You have not only failed in your most basic duty to the Imperial Army, but you have also brought dishonour upon the Emperor by your disgraceful conduct that you visit upon all these citizens!" Akakios stood speechless, rooted to the spot.

"Now I give you the same choice. The road to Ravenna lies open for you, too. You will find that the distance measures much the same for a legate as it does for a soldier!"

Akakios went pale.

When he had recovered his voice, he stammered, "I will have you removed for this!" and turned on his heel. His bodyguards forced a way through the crowd back to the Palatine. The citizens clapped and shouted as the Exarch's representative in Rome struggled to make headway through the throng.

*

High on the wall, Cadmon grasped my arm. "Alric!" he said, his face flushed and eyes shining in a way I had not seen since we were last on the shores of the Haven. "I am a warrior, born and raised in a warrior's household. Enough is enough! I know what I must do!"

Before I could reply, below us, the Bishop of Rome turned to the commander Castorius and said, "Now, Castus, I need an awning and two chairs."

From our position on the wall, we saw the pope striding purposefully through the gate towards the line of waiting warriors. Four soldiers followed, carrying a large white awning, four poles and two chairs set in the shade, along with a table, goblets and a jug of water. Pope Gregorius took his seat, waved his escort back to the city, and awaited the Duke's arrival.

The price paid for this peace was a staggering annual ransom, as well as handing over the city of Perugia to Ariulf, the Duke of Spoleto. This was to the intense dissatisfaction of Romanus in Ravenna, and in the days that followed, yet more fugitives flooded into Rome.

There was also a personal price the pope had to pay. Overwhelmed by a deep sadness at all these events, he fell ill and took to his bed for several days.

Duke Ariulf's successes, however, were short-lived. Romanus's forces retook Roman fortifications and the city of Perugia, about halfway between Rome and Ravenna. This opened a narrow corridor between imperial and Langobard territories so that for a time the roads were freed from Langobard control.

In late November, as a bitter winter drew on, Romanus, at last, paid a visit to Rome. However, the Exarch did not bring wages with him to pay the arrears for his troops in Rome. Instead, he stripped bare the Prefect's Civic Treasury and after only a few days, returned to Ravenna. The Church's wealth in Rome, however, remained firmly in the tight fist of the Papal Treasurer.

What more could befall us? The mood in the monastery, as in the city, was sombre. But for Cadmon, out of this adversity, a door to his future had finally begun to open.

14

FOUR HORSEMEN

Rome, Autumn 593–Spring 594 AD

IT TOOK A while for Cadmon to talk his way out of the monastery and into the military. As Abbot Marinianus well knew, Cadmon, at around the age of fifteen, was too young for military service. He also hoped Cadmon might become a monk. Justinian's Law decreed no military man could forsake his post for a monastery so returning to San Andreas in later life would be out of the question. In any event, Cadmon's age could not be verified, as he did not arrive in Rome carrying documentation. He also looked physically mature, and his skill with a sword was an advantage in his selection. Persistence eventually bore fruit. Besides, the garrison was desperately short of men who could ride a horse. A supportive word from Pope Gregorius finally settled the matter.

In the autumn of the year 593, on Cadmon's last day at San Andreas, I walked him to the marble steps facing the palaces of the Palatine. I made a last feeble attempt to change his mind.

"Are you sure you want to do this, Cadmon? Think what you're leaving behind. And you're giving up the chance of learning to scribe!"

"I will have others to write what I dictate," he said with an arrogant curl of his lip. He soft-punched my shoulder. "You can write for me, Alric, I'll let you be my scribe!"

"Oh, so the same old master–churl thing then!"

"Why not? That's the way things are, Alric, that's the way things are meant to be!" He gave me one of his dazzling grins. Before I could shove him down the steps, Cadmon turned and skipped down to the piazza. I watched as he strutted up the track towards the Colosseum, with his few possessions slung in a sack over his shoulder, until he disappeared from view. He did not look back, his eyes fixed on the future opening before him, giving only the briefest wave of his hand.

One crisp winter's afternoon, a few months after Cadmon's enrolment, I went to see him at the barracks. I ascended a broad flight of stone steps leading to the garrison, a short distance behind Trajan's Forum. A high, square lookout-tower loomed to the right of the main gate, providing a spectacular and strategic view of Rome and the surrounding countryside. From here, so it was said, Emperor Nero had watched Rome burn. And from here, a lookout had given warning of the arrival of the Duke of Spoleto.

I passed two soldiers on guard and walked beneath the archway into a parade ground, surrounded on all four sides by stone pillars supporting dark brick arcades. The building rose a further two floors, and another arch led to stables at the rear. A fountain stood in the middle of the parade ground, an island surrounded by a carefully tended sandy floor. Water spouted into a circular trough from four copper horse-heads attached to a carved stone pillar, rising from the middle of the fountain. A dozen soldiers stood watching as a rider took his horse through its paces. Commander Castorius observed from the doorway to his headquarters, occasionally conferring with his officers. His voice boomed across the parade ground. "Keep your back straight when you're in the saddle, Cadmon! You're a cavalryman, not a farmer taking a nag to market!"

The onlookers cheered and shouted as his horse trotted in a full circle around the fountain, Cadmon running alongside, leaping on and off the leather saddle from the side, from the back, the front, even from beneath. No longer wearing a monk's habit, Cadmon was barely recognisable in his leather tunic, brown trousers, and cavalry boots. He wore no armour except for his brightly polished helmet, a plume of bleached white horsehair flowing from the top of its cone. He excelled as a horseman, as one would expect from a son raised in a high-status family where his father served as an adviser to the king.

"This is Belisarius," Cadmon said, patting the horse's neck. Belisarius turned his head, sniffed my rough woollen habit and snorted. I patted his flank. His coat was dark grey, except for a striking white patch down his nose. "Named after the general who broke a siege here in Rome. He's the biggest horse in the regiment. No one else could ride him," Cadmon grinned proudly, "so they let me try my hand. As you can see, I'm in the cavalry now."

Already, in just a few months, he had acquired a working Greek vocabulary, the language of the army, and introduced me to his squad gathered around him. “This is Alric,” Cadmon said. “He’s from the pope’s monastery.” The cavalrymen were on good terms with each other. Unlike the infantrymen who stood guard at the city gates and the Palatine Hill, they were not selected for their height and stout build but their horsemanship and their skills with bow, lance, and sword.

Cadmon spoke with a tinge of bitterness, “There’s only a dozen of us in the camp. The Exarch Romanus withdrew most of Rome’s cavalry—a hundred horses—only months before the Duke of Spoleto came to lay siege.”

One of his companions, young enough to be earnest, old enough to grow a beard, said, “Yes, very strange. Particularly as the cavalry are now more useful than the infantry, but” – he put a finger to his lips and looked towards the guards on the gate – “don’t say it too loudly around here!”

My time since arriving in the Holy City had passed through five hot summers before each turned into autumn, then winter, and rolled into another year. However, the monastery’s daily routine seemed designed to create resilience in these times of change. Our pallor and thin bodies marked us out us as monks, right across the city of Rome.

I found it strange not to see Cadmon around the monastery, or hear him snoring in the dead of night. I also felt a weight had lifted, a sense of release from a burden to do something about his constant restlessness, stemming from not entering the only life he cared for, the way of the warrior. I could now turn to my own needs and hopes for the future. While Cadmon loathed learning grammar, I found pleasure in my studies, and felt, at last, I had discovered something of my own.

My learning had begun to blossom, surprising both Brother Petrus and me. Abba had wanted to found a school of theological study in Rome and left this enterprise and the library in Petrus’s hands after his consecration. I found myself spending more and more hours in this Bibliotheca Agapito, reading and taking notes of words I did not understand to raise with Petrus later. Abba Gregorius had inherited this library from his distant uncle, Pope Agapitus. Housed in a small basilica behind San Andreas Oratory, the library held a significant collection of books by Christian writers.

Ostrogoth warriors had sacked the library when Rome fell to King Totila, several decades earlier. The barbarians, always looking for loot, found nothing of worth for themselves, so they threw a pile of books on to the mosaic floor of the vestibule and attempted to light a fire. Most of the volumes survived, but forty years later the faint whiff of smoke still clung to these pages. A scorch mark on the entrance floor bore testimony to these former, darker days.

One afternoon, I came across a two-centuries-old work by the theologian, Augustinus, from whom our Brother Augustinus took his name. The book, De Fine Saeculi, On the End of the World, was a response to Bishop Hesychius of Salona in the Roman Province of Dalmatia, asking Augustinus about Daniel's prophecies of the End Time.

Hesychius had posed the theologian a question. "If the end of the world is prophesied to be near and all nations had heard the Gospel, why has the end not happened yet?" The theologian wrote back, "The prophecy made of Christ through Solomon; 'He shall rule the sea,' must refer to the whole earth, with all its inhabitants, because the universe is surrounded by the Ocean."

I sat staring at these words. My people, the Cantwara, lived at the end of the sea, and yet we had not heard the Gospel preached to us! Surely Rome must send out missionary preachers?

Brother Petrus strode in, interrupting my thoughts, and announced, "Alric! I have noted your diligence and the good progress you've made in reading and writing. I do believe it will be to your advantage to learn the craft and skills of a scribe, take dictation, write up documents, and so forth." That came as a surprise, and I mumbled my interest. Petrus said, "Good! I'll write for you to meet with the Tutor of Scribes at the Lateran, and we'll take it from there."

A few weeks later, with mounting excitement, I found myself entering the vast reception hall of the Lateran Palace, gawping at its arches and decorated ceiling, tall windows, mosaic floor, and murals of the Apostle San Petrus, the Blessed Virgin and the Martyrs. The Bishop of Rome and notables of the city gathered here once a year to raise a glass on the Emperor's birthday—the only day in the year Akakios, the Exarch's legate, set foot in the Lateran.

A throng stood milling around, talking in hushed voices, although the dome above dampened most of the sound. Others stood around tables where officials sat taking down details. I joined one of these, and eventually, my turn came.

"What's your business?" demanded a dark-cloaked official.

I cleared my throat and said hesitantly, "I have come to see the assistant to the Notarius. My name is Alric; I am from San Andreas's Monastery. Brother Petrus has sent me with this note." I handed over my tutor's letter, neatly written on a page of parchment. He scanned it, passing it to an assistant standing behind him. "Take this to the Office of the Notarius. And you," he said brusquely to me, "wait over there." He pointed to a spot some yards away on the mosaic floor, and I hastened towards it.

I found that I was standing near a group of young priests, deeply engaged in discussion. They stood out from other visitors thronging the hall, coming from Napoli, Sicilia, Francia, Egypt, Constantinople and the coast of Africa. Clergy, like monks, wore their hair in a short Roman tonsure with a shaved crown. They also wore a small napkin, made of white, fringed saddlecloth, around the neck over a black cassock and white stockings ending in flat black slippers—all trappings inherited from the early days of the Imperial Senate. One or two wore an alb, a loose white tunic tied at the waist with a cord. Over the tunic, a brooch fastened a cloak in the centre of the chest. Laymen wore the pin on their right shoulder, leaving the sword arm free.

While I stood facing the official at the table waiting to be summoned, I began to notice the conversation behind me.

"It's despicable, the way he's treated the clergy since he was elected," said one. "He removed the archdeacon from his traditional place as Secretary to the Pope and appointed monks to senior posts within this palace!"

Someone else said, "He hasn't bothered to occupy the papal apartments in this palace either." Another responded, "No, he set up his apartments with his monks—next to the Benedictines! The palace is turning into a monastery!"

Another became aware of me standing close enough to hear. I dressed in the simple habit of a monk, but even without a tonsure, it was easy enough to mistake me for a postulant. The conversation changed swiftly to music and liturgy until a clerk appeared, motioning me to follow. Leaving behind the sound of murmuring in the reception hall, I followed one of the Lateran aides up a flight of stairs and along a balcony overlooking a spacious interior courtyard. We came to one of the rooms leading off the balcony.

This former reception room, now used as a scriptorium, was spacious with large shuttered windows facing west. Shelves lined nearly all of the walls, crammed with papyrus scrolls and ready for use. Each of the writing desks overflowed with pens, inkwells, and manuscripts. Some styluses were bone; others copper and iron. Horn inkwells rested in holes bored into desktops. Glass jars filled with copper, lead and arsenic minerals, to make green, red and yellow pigments, stood on the shelves. Rolls of papyrus and pale goatskin parchment filled row after row of shelves. Crescent-shaped knives used to scrape calfskin to make vellum, hung from a wall. Boxes of wax tablets bound together in multiples from two up to a dozen rested on the floor.

Writing words and sentences on a wax tablet using a stylus was as commonplace in the Lateran as in all the monasteries of Rome. Several scribes toiled at their desks. One stood up and came over as I entered. He was surprisingly young, perhaps in his early twenties, tall and dark-haired, an apron over his long robe.

"I'm Alexius," he said in a friendly greeting. "What can we do for you?"

"My tutor at San Andreas sent me here to learn how to scribe. I can write on a tablet, but I can't take notes very quickly on papyrus. Brother Petrus has sent me to learn the ways of the scribe."

Alexius read Petrus' letter and took me over to a vacant desk.

"Trying to write out the full words as someone speaks is very difficult, Alric. What you will need to do is to write down a siglum—a symbol—in place of the full word, because this is much quicker; and then later rewrite these into a full script on to papyrus. Watch this." Alexius sat down and reached for a clean wax slate and stylus. "Now, tell me what you did this morning."

"Well," I said, suddenly tongue-tied, "I got up early and went down to church for morning prayers, then we all went for breakfast." Alexius made quick, deft strokes with his stylus while I spoke. "Go on," he urged, "don't stop!"

When I finished, Alexius showed me the tablet—a jumble of marks cut into the wax, and he read back to me precisely what I had said.

"You see? The fewer symbols you use, the faster you can write them down."

Like sea bass on a fishing line, I swallowed the hook!

Alexius said, "Tiro, who was Cicero's scribe here in Rome a long time ago, invented this for all his master's legal documents. He used about four thousand symbols. Today, we use thirteen thousand, so you will have lots to learn!"

"Where do I start!" I said.

"I'm glad you are so enthusiastic, Alric!"

"No, more a cry for help!"

The months went by. I had not seen Cadmon since my first visit to the barracks when, one afternoon, I found myself sitting in the unexpected warmth of a December sun after the midday meal. A familiar clip-clop of hooves came down the path and into the piazza below. A rider, dressed in the full cavalry armour of the Eastern Empire, came into view. His helmet topped with a plume of bright feathers, his neck protected by chain mail, his chest, arms and thighs covered with lamellar armour. He carried a small round shield, and a short sword hung from his belt. Cadmon held his lance in one hand, a quiver slung over his shoulder, and his bow rested close to hand on his left side.

"Alric! Still dozing while there's real men's work to be done!"

Cadmon dismounted, and we embraced with much boyish punching and hand clasping.

"You've grown, Cadmon! Or is it just padding from the uniform?"

He laughed. "I'm one of the tallest in the garrison! But come with me," his voice low and conspiratorial, "I'm on a quest outside the city gates."

"I only have two hours, then lessons, as you may vaguely remember."

"We'll be back by then," he said in his confident, breezy manner and put a foot in the stirrup, swinging into his saddle. The memory of our previous ill-fated escapade outside the city wall flashed briefly through my mind, as Cadmon reached down and grasped my wrist. "I'll pull you up. Hold on!" The saddle was pommelled at the front and back for better grip, the stirrups providing additional stability; but as I discovered immediately, it only had room for one.

"What's the quest?" I asked, as his steed Belisarius swung around and trotted towards the Colosseum.

"Truffle-hunting!"

"Truffles?"

"Well," he said, raising his hand casually, "we soldiers need to find ways to boost our wages. Many people in Rome are very fond of truffles—particularly unseasonal ones—and these people are prepared to pay a good price for them!"

"Who are they?"

"Oh, this is for one of my wealthy patrons, who lives in one of the grand villas on the Aventine."

"What wealthy patrons?"

"Wealthy women, mostly widows. They are very grateful. Truffles are a delicacy very hard to find, so they pay well. Sometimes there's a little extra for the service. But not this one!"

I caught the innuendo.

"So you're moving up from the brothel meat then?"

"Well, a charming and discerning young officer like me needs to sample a wider range of sweet-meats in the marketplace, not just buy from one stall." After a moment he added, "You still remember Edoma? The slave, sold just before us, in the Septa Julia? Poor sod! Could have been us! I saw him at that woman's house." I shuddered at the mention of the slave market.

Cadmon said, "Well, she has wooden teeth! She only eats soft food, easy to chew. Loves truffles! And she can pay for them! She's not as poor as she makes out, apparently. You were there when she bought Edoma! Anyway, she thinks, because I'm in the garrison, I'm in favour of the Exarch Romanus! She doesn't remember I brought her food from Gregorius. She said, 'When he comes to Rome, they say he'll push this monkish pope off the Throne of San Petrus and give it to the archdeacon he kicked out of the Palace!' She was extremely bitter about it. Turns out though, he's her nephew!"

We trotted past the Colosseum and worked our way through winding streets until we reached the Via Tiburtina, then turned east. Looming high on the Esquiline Hill to the northwest stood the Basilica of San Maria Maggiore, dedicated to the Virgin Mary and one of the great basilicas defining Rome. There were few people about as we rode in the opposite direction from the populated Campus of Mars. The long, straight streets in this part of the city, once crowded with the business of Rome, now stood derelict, as did the taverns and workshops. Iron gates rusted on their hinges, and upstairs floors of apartments had collapsed into the streets. At the end of a long road, we finally came to a place on the city wall where two aqueducts crossed above the Porta Tiburtina—forming something of a triumphal arch—dedicated to Emperor Claudius. A few soldiers at the gatehouse greeted Cadmon with shouts and waved as we passed beneath the archway and I wondered what they made of a cavalryman carrying a monk on the back of his warhorse; for good luck?

A mile or so down the road, as we drew near to the Basilica and Shrine of San Laurentii Beyond the Walls, we came across wagons carrying produce to Rome, with a very familiar figure on horseback leading the way.

"Graciosus!" Cadmon called out; "It's a long time since I last set eyes on you! How fares it?" Graciosus was one of several lay brothers at San Andreas. Pope Gregorius had given over his own family lands—near to the twenty-fifth milestone on the Via Tiburtina—to the monastery, and we depended on its produce for much of our food. Graciosus was the Conductor, or Steward, of this rural Villa of Endowment, and now answerable to Abbot Marinianus for his stewardship of the estate.

Graciosus drew his horse alongside us, acknowledging me with a nod. "You find me much relieved, Cadmon! We have been on the road since daybreak. This is the last of the harvest before winter closes in, and you can never trust the Langobards. But what brings you out from the city?"

"Oh, we've come to pray at the shrine, of course!" Cadmon said, waving a gloved hand in the general direction of the basilica.

Graciosus raised his eyebrows. "Well then, let me not keep you from your prayers! I know how much you are in need of a blessing!"

We laughed, and Cadmon turned Belisarius towards the crowded piazza in front of the basilica, while Graciosus and the wagons continued the last stretch to the city gate. Although it was early December, the square was bustling with farmers and pilgrims in this thriving little settlement. Guides, custodians, food-sellers, traders and beggars all thronged the square, while priests and monks walked swiftly to and from the basilica's steps, going about their business.

Three centuries before, San Laurentius had been one of the Seven Deacons of Rome. He was put to death in the days of the pagan Emperor Valerian and suffered a particularly gruesome death, slowly roasted like a boar over hot coals until his last breath. Along with all holy men, women, and martyrs regarded as saints, pilgrims believed San Laurentius to be both in heaven and yet also on earth. His bones lay in an earthly tomb within the basilica, awaiting the trumpet call on the Last Day. In the meantime, relics of the martyr were said to offer a direct link to the heavenly places for penitent pilgrims seeking remission for their sins. In spite of these troubled times, ever-increasing numbers came from far and near to pray at the shrines of the many saints whose mortal remains encircled the city of Rome.

Emperor Constantine was the first to build an oratory over San Laurentius's shrine—which was on his estate—in memory of the martyr. Pope Pelagius II had only recently completed his new basilica over the shrine, tended by a cloistered monastic community. I looked forward to paying my respects there, but before we reached the basilica steps, Cadmon drew up and dismounted. I was relieved to be off Belisarius's back after an uncomfortable ride. "The basilica's over there," I pointed out hopefully.

"Ah yes, but first I must bargain with a merchant who sells such wonderful terfez!" We had stopped in front of a bearded man in a turban and flowing robes, sitting within the shelter of his tent, surrounded by sacks of pale-skinned, slightly rose-tinted and fleshy truffles. Cadmon greeted him effusively like a long-lost friend, accepting a truffle the merchant extracted from one of his sacks. "Try this one, sir! They have no smell of their own; they take in the flavours of spices because they come from the dry regions. Just perfect for that special someone?" Cadmon pulled a face. It was purely financial reward he had in mind.

I stood waiting outside the tent as a party of pilgrims, coming from the shrine, passed by. We greeted each other as they paused and purchased some sacred relics for protection on their journey. I wondered how useful they would be, as I knew they were neither relics from the Holy Land nor the tombs of martyrs but manufactured in the workshops of Trans Tiberim.

A tall, bearded, older man seemed to be the leader of the group. It turned out he hailed from Francia and spoke a dialect similar to my own tongue.

I asked, "Have you also prayed in the churches in Rome? The Lateran and San Maria Maggiore are very fine basilicas." But these Frankish pilgrims had no interest in the fading splendours of the Imperial past, nor in basilicas that had no relics of saints or martyrs.

"No, young sir, there is nothing for us in the city of Rome! The churches there have no martyrs' shrines and no relics for us to pray before. Do not the Scriptures warn that Rome is the Whore of Babylon, forsaken by God, paying heavily for her sins? See, all the catacombs and shrines of the martyrs lie outside the city wall! No, no, we do not need to enter Rome!"

Our Frankish pilgrim made the sign of the cross, grasped his stout staff and set off with his party. He was right, of course. Burying the dead within the walls of Rome was against the law; therefore the shrines of San Petrus the Apostle and San Pancras lay outside the city to the northwest, while San Paulus the Apostle lay beyond the Ostian Gate, close to the Tiber.

San Sebastianus and San Laurentius both lay to the east outside of the city walls, as did San Agnese to the northeast. The hillside tombs, where Cadmon and I had once hidden to escape from the monastery, lay north of the Flaminian Gate, also outside the city wall. In the surrounding countryside, many roads and lanes linked these countless martyrs together, surrounding the city like a fallen army awaiting the final trumpet call.

Cadmon completed his haggling, paid with coins from his money belt and handed me the sack of truffles. He said, "We'd best head back now, or you'll be late for your lesson," as he mounted Belisarius. He tied the sack to his saddle and hauled me up behind him, setting off in the direction of the city.

The Frankish pilgrims ahead of us had been reluctant even to enter the gates of Rome, but now a loud shout changed everything, as an apocalyptic assault came upon us, quite literally, on horseback.

The noise came from behind us, on the Via Tiburtina, where it passed the basilica. I twisted around to see the cause of this commotion. A few hundred paces away, a squad of four Langobard cavalrymen trotted casually towards Rome, emptying the road before them as panic-stricken travellers scrambled out of their way. Cadmon glanced back and yelled, "These are Langobards! Hold fast! We'll race them back to Rome!" He dug his knees into Belisarius's side, and we leaped forward, the crowds now scattering before us. I looked back again, my arms gripping Cadmon's belt. To our rear, the four horsemen had caught sight of us on horseback. They recognised Cadmon as a Roman cavalryman and began forcing their way past the crowded market, yelling as they mounted their pursuit.

"Here come your four horsemen of the Apocalypse, Cadmon!" I shouted into his ear.

"And here comes the fifth!" he shouted back, urging Belisarius to even greater efforts. Shouts arose from the crowd on the wall as we neared the city gate. Ahead, people coming in from the countryside were running towards the open archway of the Porta Tiburtina. On the wall, a lone archer drew his bow, and an arrow whizzed over our heads, then another and another, until his range and aim found the leading horseman. He yelled out, wounded, and broke off engagement while his three companions galloped swiftly past. A second archer joined in on the city wall, arrows flying over our heads thick and fast as we drew nearer, perhaps a hundred strides from the gate; and a second warrior came off his horse.

Belisarius galloped at full stretch. I could feel every drive of his powerful hind legs, every movement of the muscles of his flanks, his nostrils snorting; ears flattened as he galloped with all speed towards the entrance in the wall. The last of Gracious's wagons trundled just ahead of us on the road.

"I'll drop you here! Get off, now!" Cadmon shouted, slowing down just enough for me to flop on to a pile of vegetables in Gracious's last wagon. As Cadmon swung Belisarius around, his sack of truffles thudded on to my stomach.

Belisarius—bred for war, and forced to retreat with his backside exposed to danger—seemed utterly furious. He snorted, head lowered, charging forward in a frightening spectacle towards the Langobard pursuer.

I looked towards the gate. To be shut out during an attack meant certain death. The leading wagon from Gregorius's estate was entering as the gatekeeper began to shut the wooden doors.

I turned and looked back again down the road. Now I could understand why Cadmon never left barracks without full armour, his bow, lance, shield, and sword, ready for any eventuality. The few horsemen still stationed in Rome were expected to serve as both light and heavy cavalry, trained for skirmishing and hit-and-run skirmishes, but also as heavy horseback archers, ready to join in with infantry lancers whenever called upon.

The third Langobard horseman was off his horse, attending to his fallen comrade, with the fourth still coming at full gallop. I held my breath as Cadmon rose up in his stirrups, spear at the ready resting on his shoulder and yelling a battle cry more familiar in a Saxon shield-wall than the city wall of Rome.

"*Vyand dood! Vyand dood*!" – death to the enemy!

The front-running horseman—lightly armoured and riding hard with his lance poised in his right hand—hesitated for the briefest of moments, but that was sufficient. Cadmon launched his lance at the opponent's shield, forcing him to deflect the blow by raising his left arm, and Cadmon snatched up his own sword as Belisarius smashed into the oncoming horse's shoulder. The rider, without pommel or stirrup, was thrown sideways, his shield-arm flung high, fighting to regain his balance. With the Langobard's left underarm exposed, Cadmon thrust his sword into the warrior's tunic, completely unseating him from his horse, his lifeless body tumbling to the ground. Wheeling around, Cadmon leapt from Belisarius and knelt down beside the body, closing the warrior's lifeless fingers around his sword. This gesture, surprising to those watching from the wall, ensured his opponent would receive honourable reception in the mead-hall of his gods.

The last surviving trooper of this cavalry unit was now in a precarious position. Leaping into the saddle, he swung his horse around and fled back along the Via Tiburtina. Even as the surviving warrior belted back to King Agilulf's camp at the Flaminian Gate, terror-stricken pilgrims and traders from the Shrine of San Laurentius came racing towards Rome. The solid, towering city walls were the only refuge from these rampaging warriors, and who knew how many more might be coming down the road? Graciosus with his men, wagons, and me sprawled on the vegetables, passed safely through the gates of the Porta Tiburtina.

Cadmon caught up with his opponent's panicky horse, seized its reins and trotted at a leisurely pace back to the gate, all the while the crowds clapping and shouting for him, and his dream of possessing two horses, at last, came true. He tied the Langobard's horse behind Belisarius and left instructions for the warrior's armour to be stripped as spoil and returned to him at the barracks. The rest, the archers could keep. Cadmon pulled me up again behind his saddle.

The tall, bearded pilgrim and his companions were standing inside the gateway, recovering their breath after racing to the city for shelter. As we trotted past, I leaned down and said, "I'm glad to see you have made it safely, brother. You'll find San Maria Maggiore is that direction." I smiled as I pointed up the road.

"Self-righteous bastard!" said Cadmon.

"No," I said. "He's really a sincere man."

Cadmon laughed. "I'm talking about you, shit-head!" and spurred Belisarius and his captive horse to a canter back to the monastery. We rode in silence as the energy from the encounter ebbed away.

Mixed emotions began to rise in my breast as I thought of events on that wintry afternoon. I found myself immensely proud of my friend and his bravery at saving the day. He had, in one hour, risen from obscurity in the barracks to a hero of Rome, giving release to the pent-up frustration that everyone felt—fearful of the enemy, cooped up behind city walls. Cadmon gave us a feeling of release and hope. It may have been short-lived, but Cadmon, along with the archers on the wall, had given the barracks a big morale boost and that was no small thing in a fearful and demoralised city.

But at the same time I also thought how our paths had diverged; he the soldier, me the monkish scribe in training. The sword had proved mightier than the stylus. I felt a useless buffoon, riding on the back of Cadmon's horse like a child —or worse, a circus monkey, sprawled out like a drunk on the back of Gracious's farm wagon, and making no difference to anything. I was no soldier and not cut out for it. I was only a fisherman's son, learning a few new tricks. Pride and resentment were still wrestling within me as we arrived at the monastery.

I glanced up and saw the church oculus staring down disapprovingly at me from the new façade. My feelings turned to shame at my poor, bitter, pitiable self. This had been Cadmon's finest hour, and he deserved all the praise he got. And yet.

We were late returning, as I knew we would be, but I did not need to fear a reprimand from Abbot Marinianus. Tall and aristocratic as always, he stood on the steps of the monastery in conversation with Brother Petrus and a group of our monks. News of King Agilulf's arrival and Cadmon's foray at the city gates had spread like wildfire. Marinianus had already taken in hand preparations to receive some of those pilgrims who were at this moment flooding into Rome from all directions. He broke off his conversation as we arrived.

"Cadmon! I hear you are very much the lad of the hour! The talk of Rome, it seems!" He beamed. Cadmon winced at the combination of praise and put-down, by calling him "lad" instead of a man. I couldn't resist a smirk, but Cadmon somehow managed a charming smile as he bowed in the saddle.

"Ah, it is surely not I, but the Lord! For doth not the Psalmist say, 'He trains my hand for war? I pursued my enemies and overtook them. I thrust them through, so they were not able to rise. For thou didst gird me with strength for battle'?"

My jaw dropped. These were the opening words of the morning Psalm! I had no idea Cadmon, sitting opposite me for hour after hour and day after day in oratory, had memorised the Psalms of King David during times of prayer! Or perhaps he had chosen to remember only Warrior Psalms, encouraging him to take up arms?

The abbot's jaw fell even further. What was he to make of this confession, I thought, coming as it did from Cadmon's avowedly heathen lips? Had he experienced a Damascus Road conversion on the way or was he merely mocking the abbot?

"Yes, well," Marinianus recovered, "we praise the Lord in all things." He drew a deep breath and went on, "The information I have received is this: the Langobards are at the Flaminian Gate in great force, and the Langobard king, Agilulf, has come. It looks as though we are in for a long siege. You need to return to barracks at once, Cadmon."

"On my way," he said, turning his horse around.

"Don't forget your truffles." I threw the sack up to him.

"Truffles?" The abbot looked quizzical.

"Yes, a little gift for the ... Commander," I said. "He is apparently very partial to truffles."

"Is he, now? How strange," said Marinianus, "Who would have thought?"

Cadmon managed a scowl at me even as he smiled and waved farewell to Marinianus and the monks on the steps, and with his prize of battle in tow, sped towards the Colosseum.

At night prayer, with great depth of feeling, we chanted from the Prayer Book of King David:

O God! Barbarians have broken into your home,
Violated your holy place,
Left Jerusalem a pile of rubble!
They have served up the corpses of your servants, as carrion food for birds of prey,

Thrown out the bones of your holy people
For the wild animals to gnaw upon.

After breakfast in the refectory the following day, Abbot Marinianus made an announcement.

"First, I want to commend Cadmon, both trooper and former member of our community, for his bravery in taking on four of King Agilulf's horsemen single-handed outside the Porta Tiburtina."

A murmur of approval rose from the room, a few spoons rapping on the tables.

"His action saved the lives of many pilgrims and travellers, including Graciosus and his wagons bearing food for our monastery. I am sure that Commander Castorius will want to recognise Cadmon's bravery in the appropriate manner."

I learned from Cadmon that Rome, on the eve of King Agilulf's arrival, had fewer than eight hundred of the Emperor's soldiers in the garrison, and despite Cadmon's spectacular encounter, the garrison had no cavalry for harassing enemy positions outside of the walls.

Marinianus went on.

"However, I also bring you grave news of recent events. On the king's arrival before the walls of Rome and in full sight of men, women, and children, forty people fleeing for their lives were overtaken before they could reach the safety of our city. I am told they were forced by the king to choose between eating meat sacrificed to pagan gods and death. Those who refused were slaughtered like cattle."

A loud cry of despair and disgust rose from the room. Many of us regarded the Langobards as heartless persecutors, practised butchers; a nation without compassion. King Agilulf was no exception; he was the exemplar.

Marinianus raised his hand for silence. "This morning, King Agilulf slew a further four hundred people in similar manner. Their crime was a refusal to worship the head of a goat, which the Langobards had sacrificed to the devil. We pray for their souls," he managed to say, as another outburst of horror and sympathy poured forth.

The pope had witnessed these events from the city wall. So had Augustinus, who was my source for learning of the pope's lament; "King Agilulf has dealt us a blow. We see, with our own eyes, Roman citizens tied by the neck with ropes like dogs and taken to Francia for sale!"

"What's going on?" I asked Petrus. "I hear rumours of some settlement and other rumours of war! What's really happening?"

Brother Petrus sat down opposite me, rested his elbows on the apse table in the library where I worked, and focused his eyes on the bookshelves as he marshalled his thoughts. When he looked back, his usual ebullient self had given way to a much more sombre demeanour.

"Well, Alric, a full-blown Langobard siege has been averted; that I think you know. Rome has sued for peace, King Agilulf's warriors are withdrawing from the wall, and they are returning to Turin as I speak."

I said to my tutor, "Yes, Grammaticus; but why?"

"Simply because the pope has had no alternative but to sue for peace and sign a treaty acceptable to King Agilulf, compelling Rome to pay him the staggering sum of five hundred pounds weight of gold from the city's coffers!"

I was stunned by the size of the settlement. I stammered, "And that's the end of the matter then? No more sieges?"

"Not exactly, Alric. King Agilulf has vowed to return for another treaty in three years' time!"

"And the Exarch—Romanus; he is happy with this outcome?"

Brother Petrus gave a grim smile. "This is where the story becomes difficult, Alric. The Exarch's representative here in Rome, strongly opposed any settlement with the Langobards, as you would expect. At the same time, Romanus refused to provide any military support to relieve Rome from Agilulf's siege."

"You mean, without a treaty, either Rome starves, or our defences are broken—and the Langobards take what they want either way!" I glanced around at the books and manuscripts lining the shelves; these had become my friends! "And the barbarians will try to burn down this library a second time!" I wailed.

Brother Petrus nodded. "Precisely so, Alric, precisely so!"

What an absurd position Romanus had put the pope in! I said, "And what do you expect Romanus will do, now that we do have this treaty in place?"

"I think the Exarch will use this treaty against His Holiness when he informs the Emperor of these matters, to blacken his name at Court in Constantinople. Romanus will also want to increase his own powers over Rome by removing the last small measure of independence currently enjoyed by the Duchy of Rome. This Holy City is the centre of the Catholic world, Alric, and Pope Gregorius is frequently at odds with the

Patriarch of Constantinople, who desires to be the supreme ruler of the Church! It is a source of constant irritation to them that Rome has the relics of our two great apostles Petrus and Paulus! And apart from Romanus, many in Constantinople would be overjoyed to see Rome disappear entirely from the Empire's map!"

Petrus paused a few moments to compose himself. "I tell you this in confidence, Alric. When the treaty was signed, Pope Gregorius is said to have exclaimed, 'And all this slaughter and brutality that we witnessed outside the walls, came at the hands of a king who is married to a Catholic queen!' And Romanus has doubly blamed His Holiness—for signing a peace treaty, but also for saving Rome from destruction! Now he has fallen ill, and has already taken to his bed for several days."

A cold spring brought no relief from this harshest of winters. Even so, Cadmon's biblical Four Horsemen of the Apocalypse, with their noses a little bloodied from the skirmish outside the wall, had turned away from the city.

What this bought for Rome was time.

What this did for Cadmon—and for me—was to open another creaking door.

15

EARLY STIRRINGS

Rome, Spring 595 AD

ON A WARM DAY in early spring I found myself a year older but not a year wiser as I carried out the mundane task of taking bread flour to a nearby convent. Our small party loaded the sacks and set off for a nearby convent called San Quattro Coronati, the Four Crowns. We led six heavy-laden donkeys a short distance along the narrow Clivus Scauri alleyway to Porta Caelimontana, a brownstone gate from Rome's Republican days set in the ancient Republican Wall. Passing through this gateway, we stepped into what appeared to be open countryside, where fields and groves of fruit and olive trees extended all the way to the dark brick of the Aurelian wall.

We turned briefly in the direction of the Colosseum, passing beneath the Claudian aqueduct, then turned onto a small track between overgrown fields. The oratory of San Quattro Coronati was visible in the distance, and we soon passed through a wooden gate on to a path on the south side of the convent. The path ended near the entrance to the basilica of the Four Crowns where substantial building work was in progress. Without warning, events began to unfold that swiftly unravelled my well-ordered monastic life.

All this began in March when Emperor Mauricius sent a gift of thirty pounds weight of gold to Rome. This magnificent sum, of course, paled beside the five hundred pounds in gold that Rome paid to the king of the Langobards. Still, it was a welcome gift for Rome's priests, pilgrims and needy—including many women devoted to the religious life. They had fled from the hill country of Sabina, the Campania and the nearby town of Latium, recently fallen into the hands of the Langobards.

The pope begged his Mediterranean correspondents to send clothing for these women, living on the edge of desperation in Rome. Arriving destitute as they did, finding a suitable place for them to live proved extremely difficult. Tenements, crammed into the overpopulated districts of Rome, were unsuitable for anyone attempting to pursue a religious life.

On my frequent visits to the Lateran Palace, I began to notice the building work progressing at a pace in the middle distance, around a substantial urban villa.

"What's all the building work about?" I asked Brother Petrus. In small communities like ours, someone knows something about everything in Rome.

Petrus answered, "The villa's now a convent for nuns and lay sisters, who've fled from Langobard overlords. The oratory has been renamed San Quattro Coronati, after four martyrs put to death under Emperor Diocletian."

The convent would eventually comprise living quarters for both nuns and lay sisters, built around a second courtyard adjoining the existing oratory. Their arrival boosted the number of nuns living in Rome to more than three thousand; and as San Quattro Coronati stood midway between the Colosseum and the Lateran, this was deemed a safe and quiet location for the newcomers.

In earlier days of pagan Rome, this whole site had been given over to worshipping the spirits of the woods and springs. Vineyards and orchards gradually replaced the woods, leaving a small grove of trees as the last remnant of the ancient woodland. For the sisters, it felt as though they were living in idyllic, open countryside. However, they needed more than an attractive view; they also desperately needed food, but their orchard could not provide sufficiently for their needs. Once a week, our monastery gave support by taking sacks of milled bread flour for the nuns and lay sisters registered at San Quattro Coronati.

Some of the monasteries in Rome had become the natural habitat for destitute contadini—peasant farmers who had fled to Rome as their farms burned—as they possessed the agricultural skills for growing food for the monks, lay brothers, and their families. The same applied to some of the lay sisters at San Quattro Coronati, who worked the soil and tended the vines and fruit trees.

As we arrived on this fateful day, I greeted the first lay sister we came across as we led our beasts along the path around the orchard. Her back was to me, but she looked up, half-turned and smiled, and I felt as though a bolt of lightning had struck me from the clear blue sky. Had I not been holding on to the reins of the donkey, I would have been knocked off my feet. My mouth became suddenly dry as she greeted me with her clear, musical voice. If my life had seemed a little dull before, it was as bright as a Roman mural now; I was smitten!

"You have brought us some food!" she exclaimed in delight, as much a statement as a question, her huge brown eyes twinkling in a smile, her voice happy, even playful, as she glanced at our sacks of flour.

"From the monastery," I stammered.

She seemed nearly as tall as me, and perhaps about the same age. She had a beautiful cherubic face, her clear skin a dusky peach colour, a slim straight nose and a warm and ready smile. This beautiful creature stretched out her hand, touching my sleeve.

"How wonderful! You are so kind!" I glanced towards those behind me, to include them in her thanks. They grinned back, teeth bared like wolves, amused at my obvious discomfort.

"Come," she said, "I will show you the storeroom."

She beckoned to those behind me, her arms, I noticed, shapely and strong. She led us towards the buildings at the end of the path, skirting the edge of the orchard.

"You are from Rome?" she enquired tentatively as we walked this short distance, one small, beautiful hand on the donkey's neck as she glanced towards me, her eyes bright with curiosity.

"No, I have lived in Rome for only six years." I glanced at the white scarf tied around her head, her dark hair tucked beneath, a few wisps hanging loose on the soft skin of her neck.

"You are a monk, perhaps?" she asked, with a glance at my woollen habit. I could not tell which would please her more, yes or no. Her white blouse was covered by an embroidered bodice, her skirt down to her ankles, an apron over the front, a red brocade scarf tied loosely around her neck.

I managed another croak, "No, I'm a lay brother."

I cleared my throat nervously. "And you? Are you one of the sisters here?" Her body was shapely beneath her garments, her waist narrow. Silently, my heart shrieked, Say NO!

Her tinkle of laughter reassured me even before her reply. "No, I'm a farmer's daughter, brought up on the land. I am a lay sister here; I work in the orchard and the vineyard so we can grow some of our own food."

We made our way around to the kitchen door, tying the donkeys before unloading our cargo of flour.

"My name is Alric!" I said my pubescent voice breaking.

"Paulina," she replied in a low, slightly secretive voice, a moment before the cook peered out from the storeroom door.

I looked forward to seeing her again the next week, and the next. I noticed she always contrived to see me when I came, but my turn to bring food supplies was irregular and sometimes weeks went by before I saw her again.

Slowly, we were drawn into an unspoken conspiracy. We both knew that a young man from the monastery developing a friendship or even speaking with a young woman from a nunnery was forbidden unless it was strictly about the work in hand. I was afraid the monks and lay brothers who at various times accompanied me would report my interest to the prior.

Someone did.

Augustinus, recently appointed as our prior, gave a weary sigh as I sat in his office. "Alric, you know it is forbidden for a monk or even a lay brother as yourself to form an acquaintance with a young woman. You must be careful; the devil is ever near to inflame young passions and to lead you into unseemly lust."

"Yes, Prior," I said, feeling ashamed, miserable and alone. I promised to be watchful of my thoughts and actions. Yet I was helpless; our trysts continued. Over the following months, in the few moments of conversation we could snatch together, Paulina unfolded her story.

She was forced to flee from Capua, a now deserted swathe of countryside to the southwest of Rome. Her family had worked the land for generations, growing a grain called 'spelt,' but also cultivating vines, growing roses, preparing spices and making unguents for wounds and burns and the like. The Langobards had ravaged Capua the previous year, and her family was murdered or captured. Paulina fled to Rome, protected by some of her father's farm labourers. The nunnery at San Quattro Coronati took her in as one of several women skilled in working the land, while many of the nuns, from more genteel homes, were not. Also, it was considered unwise to have male farmhands working around the convent grounds.

Complicating matters further, my own body had begun changing in awkward ways for a while now; my cheeks were showing the wisps of a beard, and my voice gradually deepening. More alarming, lustful dreams began disturbing my nights; and when I was with Paulina, even for the brief moments we shared in each other's company, my heart beat fast as I struggled to keep my feelings to myself.

What made matters worse was the expectation of Abba Marinianus for when I reached the age of sixteen years. In May of this year, I would take my first postulant vows towards becoming a monk before making a life commitment at the age of eighteen. I had wanted this too, finding myself drawn to the monastic life. Also, I had now begun to acquire skills none of my family or ancestors ever had—and would have thought worthless when put beside farming, hunting, fishing for food, drinking, taking wives and raising families. Celibacy was neither understood nor practised amongst the Cantwara; nor did we live in communities separate from our womenfolk, something that was unheard of.

More and more, I began to chew over how strange this celibate life was. Yet I had thrown myself fully into the life of the monastery, and after several years I found the life congenial, and also I could read fluently and write on wax tablets and parchment. Paulina, however, was illiterate; I could not write to her about my thoughts and feelings. I was devoted to my studies and had memorised all one hundred and fifty Psalms and two of the Gospels. I toiled at Latin grammar and vocabulary, gradually gaining mastery. I had begun to learn how to prepare goatskin parchment for scribes in the Lateran Palace Scriptorium and how to mix ink and sharpen quills. I had thrown my energies into all these. Now with Paulina on my heart, I wasn't so sure. I found myself rising uncontrollably to the heights of joy and plunging to the depths of despair. I was in no position to seriously begin exploring a monastic vocation, and when the abbot eventually called me to his office, I begged for more time.

Marinianus was sympathetic. "No one will force you, Alric. It is no shame to be uncertain. I am content to leave this decision for a few months longer. Better no decision than a bad decision. We'll talk again and see how things stand with you."

I was enormously relieved and expressed my heartfelt thanks, leaving his office with a great, if temporary, sense of relief.

Soon after, I arrived at the Lateran one morning for my scribal lessons with Alexius, to find a crowd gathering outside the entrance to the Reception Hall. It appeared that, at the command of the Bishop of Rome, all the Lateran clergy were present to hear and learn from a specially invited preacher.

Ever since his arrival at the Lateran, Pope Gregorius had lamented, “It is difficult to find educated clergy who can read and preach the Gospel, which lies at the heart of their priestly ministry. And the deacons are mostly appointed for their fine singing voices, rather than for their remarkable knowledge of the Scriptures!”

The Pope searched for ways to improve the quality of the diaconate. He took the step of issuing a decree criticising deacons for being too concerned with demonstrating their skills in singing, and not enough on improving the quality of their preaching and works of charity. Some of his clergy were, in fact, illiterate, and had advanced only because of their voice or physical appearance. Not a few were more preoccupied with their secular affairs than their ecclesiastical duties. The pope’s answer to this woeful state of affairs was Equitius, the preaching Abbot of Valeria.

Equitius held such a zeal for saving souls that he travelled up and down the country where he could, visiting towns, villages, churches, even private houses, to stir hearts to a love of their heavenly country. However, this strange evangelist had never received a licence to preach. His growing fame had fanned the flames of jealousy amongst the Roman clergy. They petitioned the pope to summon Equitius to Rome to give an account of his teaching. Equitius was more than willing to do so, and as I approached the Lateran one morning, I saw Equitius standing there before them.

I stood on the steps for a while and listened along with everyone else. Abbot Equitius presented an unfashionable and rough appearance. His clothes were coarse and shabby, and he rode on the worst beast imaginable, with sheepskin for a saddle, and his leather bags hung stuffed with parchments of the Holy Scriptures. Equitius had drawn a large crowd to hear him, and this had not happened at the Lateran for some considerable time.

As he preached, his audience was noticeably divided. Some clergy jeered at his antics, others fell silent as they watched and listened, and perhaps still more, felt a sense of shame because a untutored person could speak with such power and conviction. I found myself deeply moved by Equitius, a simple, powerful, humble person whose words I could embrace.

Afterwards, as I pressed through the throng towards the steps of the Lateran, some of the younger clergy were even more vociferous and bold in their dislike of Pope Gregorius than I had overheard on my first visit to the Lateran.

“Where are his great works?” one demanded in a mocking voice. “Pope Pelagius built a basilica to San Laurentius! But what has he done? A mere canopy over the tomb of San Petrus! Well, you can just see that going down in the annals of Gifts of the Great Popes!”

What was hard for the old possessors of power, position and prestige to understand, in these increasingly desperate times, was that the Bishop of Rome was intent on the very survival of the Holy City. Survival meant finding funds for the growing numbers of destitute in Rome, the payment of subsidies to imperial troops, and not least, handing over very substantial sums to the Langobard King. There was no money to lavish on great works when even the most basic needs of Rome were so enormous.

Some of those most vocal, as Alexius my tutor informed me, came from the most privileged families in Rome and what the young priest on the steps had just spoken was nothing less than sedition. I was older now, a bit more self-confident, a lot more familiar with the Lateran and much more eloquent in Latin. Hot coals of anger flared in me at the injustice of their remarks. I turned on the young priest who had spoken.

"That's utter nonsense! There's no money for such projects now! His Holiness spends what he has on the poor in Rome! He pays the soldiers, he pays off the Langobards, and he pays for your food!"

They looked at me in astonishment, with a mixture of surprise and contempt.

"Who are you to lecture us? Are you a priest? No, you're a monk, you're one of his monks! Just remember this, he won't last forever, then when we have a new pope, you and foreigners like you will be thrown out!" He stepped closer. "Just wait!" he hissed in my face. "When Romanus returns, we'll see the pope deposed, then you and your kind will be driven from Rome!"

I snapped back, "And if that happens, without our pope, there will be no one to stop the Langobards taking Rome! And you may well find yourself at the wrong end of a sword, as you flee down the steps of this palace!"

With my anger still burning hot within me, I pushed past into the Lateran.

Augustinus sent for me the following day. I went in trepidation to his office. He leaned back in his chair, his fingers forming a steeple, while I stood fidgeting uncomfortably in front of his desk.

"That was a commanding performance you gave at the Lateran yesterday, Alric. I hear you managed even to put Equitius in the shade! We are remiss, not to have noticed your eloquence before!"

"What happened wasn't my fault," I blurted out.

"And why so?" he asked mildly. "What is your defence for such behaviour?"

Out tumbled what I had heard spoken against Pope Gregorius by some of the clergy, and comments from Cadmon concerning the patrician widow on the Aventine Hill; suspicions that hung over the woman's nephew—the archdeacon that Gregory had discharged from his service who had once enjoyed the status of secretary to Pope Pelagius II.

Augustinus sat silent for a while after I had finished speaking. At length, he asked, "Alric, have you talked to anyone else about what you've heard?"

"No, only Cadmon; and he wouldn't go about spreading this abroad."

"Then keep it so." He frowned in thought for a moment, then sat upright. "Leave this with me, Alric. Let me know at once if you hear or see anything else untoward. And let's tone down the oratory, shall we? It seems we have enough enemies at the Palace without inviting a few more!"

That afternoon I hastened to Cadmon's barracks to pour out my heart over Paulina. We sat in his room on the first floor with a view over the courtyard. Cadmon cleaned his kit while I rambled on.

"You do know," he said at last, in a conversational tone, putting his cleaning cloth aside, "that all nuns who are found guilty of copulation are severely punished and confined in even stricter houses? And if their accomplices are laymen, they are excommunicated. And if they are ecclesiastics, they are degraded and confined in monasteries for penance?"

"I'm in a monastery already, so that won't be much punishment!" I said. "But for me as a layperson, the excommunication would be more serious. You seem more the expert on this matter than me," I said mockingly. "Besides, neither of us is a monk – or a nun."

"Look, don't take what you feel for her now too seriously, Alric," he said in a conciliatory voice. "This is your first love. Only time can tell whether it will last."

I sat hunched forward on a stool, head in my hands, as miserable as a prisoner awaiting execution.

Cadmon, turning back to his task, spat on his cleaning cloth. "We can't always get what we want in life." He paused and looked away. I sensed his thoughts: the life he would never have amongst King Ethelbert's warriors, thanks to Felix and his crew; his father's estate he would never inherit; his place in the King's Guard he would never take.

"I'll give this more thought," Cadmon promised, "and we can speak of it again."

Two weeks later, I was back at San Quattro Coronati with more food for the sisters. Paulina and I had scarcely time to greet one another, when four cavalrymen clattered up the sloping cobbled street leading to the nunnery. I recognised Cadmon at once on Belisarius, the lead horse in his troop. My bosom friend dismounted, completely ignoring me and walked up to Paulina. Removing his helmet and cap so that his thick golden hair fell to his broad shoulders, he said with a bow, "Greetings, sister! Our horses are weary with thirst from our travels about the city walls. May we refresh our steeds from your water trough?"

He gave Paulina a most dazzling smile. I noted her reaction, girlish, flattered, charmed and charming, even flirtatious.

"Of course you may, sir! Anything for those who defend Rome from her enemies!" She turned on her heel and led the way to the water trough. The others dismounted and followed behind.

With my heart in my mouth, I could not believe what I was seeing! Her pretty head turned by my best friend to whom I had poured out my soul! And now he had chosen to come and try her for himself! Perhaps steal her away, make her one of his army whores! I felt anger and bitterness like a lump of lead in my heart. I turned away, leading the donkeys and our party towards the kitchen. Behind me, Paulina took each horse in turn, quite unnecessarily it seemed to me, even holding the reins while they drank. I could hear snatches of banter and laughter from outside through the kitchen door as we unloaded our supplies into the larder beside the kitchen.

Our task over, the last donkey now led the way to the path skirting the orchard. I followed the train and passed the water trough as Cadmon and his men mounted their horses, waving a cheery goodbye to Paulina and the bevy of farm girls who had gathered, promising to call by again. Paulina swung round, saw us heading back along the path and hastened after us. She plucked a flower from the field and pressed it into my hand, then after the swiftest and softest peck on my cheek, ran back to the kitchen, where the cook was calling the young women back to work in the fields.

My emotions alternately soared and plummeted as I made my way back to the monastery. I did not know what sense to make of what had happened. The following afternoon I hastened over to the barracks. Before I spoke to Cadmon, I sat in the Church of the Twelve Apostles that served the barracks, only a short distance away from the Via del Corso. The

Twelve Apostles was another ancient titular church, used by the military for General Narses's Greek soldiers after their victory over the Ostrogoths. The eastern icons, flickering candles and the lingering whiff of incense had a calming effect on me, but a few minutes later, when I entered Cadmon's room, my anger and not my heart poured out.

Cadmon listened patiently to my vitriolic tirade then said calmly, "How could I possibly advise you, as you had asked, without seeing this woman for myself? Yes, she is more stunning than even you have the vocabulary to say! I wish I had her myself! But I was merely an object of distraction, as were my troop, not an object of affection. You noticed how she ran after you to give you her gift? It is you she cares about, you miserable shit-head!"

The crisis passed. The cavalry did not return again for water. For Paulina and me, this episode only served to intensify our feelings for one another.

I did not expect to see Cadmon for a while after this, but I was mistaken. He knew when and where to find me—after the midday meal and in the Agapito Library, built within a high wall that we shared with the narrow Clivus Scauri alleyway. As usual, Cadmon had entered the monastery grounds from the side gate near to the library, leaving Belisarius grazing beneath the trees.

I sat in the library apse at a good-sized desk for spreading out books and manuscripts, flipping through a drama by Sophocles and translated into Latin. It was unusual to find a book by a pagan Greek philosopher in our library, but as I turned the remains of its charred pages some words leaped out at me: "One must wait until evening to see how splendid the day has been." My thoughts turned instantly to my sister. How was the day turning out for her now? How splendid would it be for Tola when her evening came? Would I be with her to see it? Similar thoughts began drifting to Paulina when Cadmon swept into the library, down the long aisle to my accustomed workplace, his mail clinking and cloak billowing behind.

I called out, "Cadmon! Good to see you—and so soon!"

Cadmon dragged up a chair with his foot, removed his helmet, dropped his gloves on the table and looked towards the entrance for anyone who might enter. We were the only people in the building, but he glanced around searchingly before he spoke. Leaning forward, he said in a low voice, "I'm on duty this afternoon, visiting some of the Aurelian gates for reports from the guards, so I'll come straight to the point. Do you remember the day we went out to the shrine of San Laurentius?"

"You mean looking for truffles?"

He ignored my jibe and went on, "You may also recollect that the Langobard patrol we ran into weren't behaving as though they expected to find any of our cavalry outside the gates. They were taken completely by surprise."

I had missed that little detail in the panic that followed, but I nodded as the events came back. Cadmon said, "Now, how would they have known there would be no patrol from our garrison outside the wall at that time?"

I shrugged, puzzled. "I've no idea. What do you think?"

"I think they had inside knowledge of the military situation in Rome—like the size of our cavalry, like the number of soldiers in the barracks, like the number of guards on the gates, like the timetable of our movements. Now, who could have told them?"

Cadmon fixed me with a hard stare but said nothing. I looked back, shocked.

"You don't think it was me!"

"You do visit the barracks. You see what's going on. And I've said confidential things to you."

"Cadmon, this is ridiculous! Why would I want to betray the very people who are guarding the city? Or these people who have been our salvation here? Are you insane?"

"You could unwittingly have told others. Who have you spoken to about the military affairs of Rome?"

"No one!" I cried, my voice rising.

"Not even Petrus? Or the prior?"

"Perhaps Petrus, but mostly he talks to me. Besides, who would he tell? What motive could he possibly have to betray the city into the hands of the heathen? I cannot believe you are asking me this!"

Cadmon stared at me for a long moment, then leaned back in his chair, his stern look dissolving into a broad smile.

"No, Alric, I don't think you have, nor anyone else here in the monastery. Forgive me if my questioning unsettled you. But the garrison commander is agitated and believes that we are under close observation from enemies within. Castorius believes that someone—or some party—has planted spies in our midst. He asked me to sound you out in case you know might know something."

With my feathers now slightly less ruffled, I said, "Like what?"

"Think back to our attempt to escape the city. Do you remember those wretches lining up to enter the city at the Flaminian Gate?"

"You don't think—but they were fleeing from the Langobards!"

"Perhaps some of them were spies – citizens of Spoleto perhaps, whose lives or families they spared in exchange for information."

I shook my head. "You have local auxiliaries in the city, young boys, perhaps some of them have been bribed to inform on the barracks."

"On the contrary. We hear the local gossip from the auxiliaries! That's how I know what's going on in Rome."

I said, "So, why ask me?"

"Because we know there is a conspiracy against Rome on the part of the Langobards—but it's not the only conspiracy, is it?"

"And what does that mean?"

"There are other enemies within."

"Who?"

"Akakios, for one. He is always looking for anything to discredit the pope in the eyes of Ravenna."

"Cadmon, how do you know this for sure?"

No one had entered the library since Cadmon's arrival, but he glanced around once more, lowering his voice to a whisper, his face only inches from mine.

"Sometimes, our soldiers from the barracks do guard duty on the Palatine. It earns them a little extra. Akakios's men tell them tales of what goes on up there. They whisper that some of the legate's entourage are spies and assassins—and the pope is on their list."

"What?"

"Romanus loathes the pope. If he can find a way to make it look like a Langobard assassination, or better still, an accident, he'll do it."

My head was swirling; I pressed my fists to my temples. "So what's in it for Romanus?"

"I thought that would be obvious to you! If Gregorius is forced out of the picture, Rome will fall. No one else can hold this city together. And besides, it would take at least a year to find another Bishop of Rome, once all the squabbling breaks out and the candidates are jostling for position. That gets rid of a big headache for the Exarch. He won't have to pretend he's defending the city. Rome's a nuisance; it costs men and money. Better for him to remove this thorn from his side."

I slumped in my chair. My picture of Rome, a city united under the banner of Pope Gregorius, turned out to be little more than a cesspit, like the Cloaca.

"Why are you telling me all this?"

"Time is short, but there's something you need to know. There's also a plot against the pope by some of his priests, particularly those who have not benefited from his appointment as Bishop of Rome."

My jaw dropped as Cadmon pressed on relentlessly.

"You remember the cold-eyed archdeacon when Pope Pelagius came to consecrate the new church?" He pointed beyond the library towards the church rising from the heart of the monastery. "And Edoma's owner, the woman who is the archdeacon's relative?"

I saw the direction Cadmon was taking with all this, and I added, "Also, the young priests I overheard in the Lateran Palace, and the argument I had when I defended the pope when Equitius preached outside the Lateran." Cadmon sat in silence, taking in what I had said.

"But all the same—"

Cadmon interrupted, raising his hand. "I'm telling you all this, my dear friend, because you are their enemy also. There seems to be every chance you might be caught up in any action they take—because the way I see things going, the Langobards, the Exarch and a faction amongst the clergy, may—wittingly or unwittingly—coalesce into co-conspirators. And you, Alric," he leaned forward again, tapping a finger on the table, "may find yourself caught right in the middle of it!"

I barely had time to close my incredulous mouth before the door to the library swung open and Brother Petrus came in looking for me, already late for my lesson. Cadmon's chair scraped as he rose, patting me on the shoulder. "You may not think so, Alric, but I care for this place too," and scooping up his helmet and gloves, swept towards the great door of the library. The two men exchanged brief greetings as Cadmon departed.

I sat rooted to my chair. It was unimaginable, no, unthinkable, diabolical and yet somehow credible for something so evil to be afoot. A new attempt, perhaps, by another squadron of Horsemen of the Apocalypse? But whom could I tell?

I looked up as Petrus reached my desk.

"You look like you've seen a ghost, Alric! No time for dreaming. Come! There's grammar to be done!"

"Yes, Grammaticus."

I sighed under the weight of Cadmon's revelations as I followed Brother Petrus to his study.

16

LATERAN PALACE

Rome, July 595 AD

AFTER PRIME ONE morning in July, Abba Marinianus, with sadness in his voice, announced he would be leaving us to become Bishop of Ravenna. A collective groan rose from the community. Marinianus was a well-loved abbot who had steadied the ship after Abba Gregorius's elevation to Pope five years earlier.

We also wondered how Marinianus would cope in Ravenna, where Romanus ruled the roost. The city at first developed as an outpost for Constantinople, conveniently situated on the northeast coast of Italia. Not least, we speculated on who might succeed Marinianus as abbot of our monastery.

A little while after breakfast, I slipped out to the library to return some books. A horse whinnied nearby, and I looked to see who had arrived. Belisarius stood loosely tethered under a tree in a small grove. He neighed softly when he saw me and dipped his head towards the ground, signalling to give him a treat. I patted his head with a few soothing words and looked around for something to give him.

"I see you're annoying my horse again," Cadmon drawled, coming up behind me. He had long since made the transition from boy to manhood, but he had lost none of his boyish charm or his thirst for new adventure.

"Just finding something for him, to make up for your obvious neglect! So, what brings you here so early in the morning? I'd expect you'd still be sleeping off another late night of wine, women, and song in the brothels."

"No," he replied coolly, "the abbot sent for me. He needs an escort to Ravenna. He expected a platoon of foot soldiers, but the Commander could only spare me."

"Just you? On your own?" I said in amazement.

"I am worth ten men," he said frostily, swinging into the saddle.

"Of course," I said, pandering to his monstrous ego. "When do you leave?"

"As soon as the pope makes the abbot a bishop. The church is in one hell of a mess in Ravenna. We leave next week, in fact."

Eight days later we gathered on the steps of the monastery as our abbot—now Bishop Marinianus—and his small entourage made their farewells. The small group rode north towards the Flaminian Gate, Cadmon riding before and half a dozen asses following behind. Cadmon turned and waved. "I'll be back in a month."

But the Fates, if they still meant something to him, had already begun weaving Cadmon another thread.

One hot and humid morning later in the month I hastened with Prior Augustinus to the Lateran Palace, unaware that this Year of Our Lord 595 would be a turning point, a make-or-break year—and not only for Pope Gregorius.

I glanced at Augustinus as we walked. It seemed obvious to me that he should be the person most likely to succeed the saintly Abbot Marinianus.

"The pope is worn out with many concerns," Augustinus confided as we drew near to the Lateran. "Romanus still provides no military support from Ravenna; his malice towards us is even worse than that of the Langobards," he said with some vehemence. "The judges who rule Corsica and Sardinia in Romanus's name are corrupt to the core, and the affairs of Rome are now so onerous that His Holiness is constantly driven to his bed. I fear we ask too much of him."

Our prior had not shared such confidences with me before, and I realised just how deep his concern must be. I found myself uncertain how to reply, but he continued with a sigh; "And now we've lost Abbot Marinianus to Ravenna, with no replacement in sight."

"This puts a heavy load on your shoulders," I said.

He nodded but made no further comment.

With Bishop Marinianus's departure, Augustinus took charge until the appointment of a new abbot, but no name had come forward. Any monk elevated to the position of abbot would need to be wise in judgment and of evident virtue. The holder of such a position would not only be 'a good monk,' but one trained in the Holy Scriptures and monastic lore, particularly the rule of his monastery; and not least, skilled in dealing with the souls of others.

Augustinus glanced up at the Lateran Palace as we approached. He said ruefully, "Much has changed in Rome since the death of Pope Pelagius, Alric."

For one thing, Pope Gregorius had overhauled the Lateran household soon after his election and banished the fussy and costly collection of pageboys that had danced in attendance around his predecessor. As most of these young boys came from notable Roman families, this action did not sit well with members of the upper echelons of Roman society. In their place in the Lateran came the most learned clerks and pious monks, far better suited to serving an austere pope.

We turned at the ancient octagonal Baptistry towards a guarded archway opposite the Lateran Basilica, passing through into a large courtyard, occupied by a community of monks of the Benedictine Order for the last fourteen years. Like many who had sought refuge in Rome, they had fled when the Langobards sacked and burned their Monte Cassino monastery southeast of Rome.

Several buildings, enjoying a full view of the Lateran Basilica's striking apse window, looked out over the courtyard. The entrance to our destination—a three-storey cloister—was at the far corner. In these papal apartments, Pope Gregorius shared his daily life with a familia of monks and a few clerics—much the same as he had done while Papal Legate in Constantinople. Some members of this community were drawn initially from San Andreas's monastery when Gregorius succeeded Pelagius as Pope.

Prior Laurentius met us at the door before taking us to an upstairs chamber. He had served abroad as Gregorius's Papal Legate to Emperor Mauricius and had served as prior of the pope's family at the Lateran for the past two years. Laurentius's competence and administrative skills in Constantinople were well known even before he arrived at the Lateran, but he had no personal experience of monastic life. He wore a severe 'I brook no nonsense' face, tight-lipped with probing eyes. I sensed very little warmth from him but had little doubt he was positioned to rise high in the Church in Rome. I wondered whether he might be would given the position of Abbot at San Andreas. That would place him above Augustinus, and later perhaps Laurentius might attain to a bishopric. However, the relationship between these two men seemed more formal than cordial.

I nervously took a seat beside Alexius, temporarily replacing a scribe who usually attended to the pope's correspondence. A curtained archway into the Papal Archives lay directly behind us. I unpacked my wax tablets, opened one on my knees and looked around the room. The chamber seemed less grand than I had expected, modestly furnished with simple drapes and chairs in red upholstery.

Several times a year this small group gathered as the pope's inner circle - in part a private cabinet and in some measure a personal senate - drawing together a cross-section of the institutions that held Rome together. Glancing around, I noted a mixture of Gregorius's advisers and close colleagues from the Lateran, San Andreas monastery, the Prefecture of Rome and the military garrison.

Augustinus had carefully briefed me before we joined the meeting. Some I knew by name and a few by sight. Paterius, the Papal Notary at the Lateran, eased his large frame into a small seat directly in front of Alexius and me. I had met Paterius many times in the Lateran during my tutorials with Alexius. A calm, quiet, avuncular figure, Paterius supervised a devoted group of scribes who prepared and issued documents for the Papal Chancery. The Chancery also held copies of all papal correspondence produced during his pontificate. Paterius turned to acknowledge us and said, "Now remember, Alric, you are only here to listen and take notes, not to speak!" He winked. I nodded.

Petrus the Deacon arrived, a life-long friend of the pope; and also a newcomer, Cardinal Fortunatus. Augustinus took his seat as Prior and acting Abbot of San Andreas. Copiosus, the pope's physician, was also in attendance; and the Prefect of the City of Rome, confusingly also called Gregorius. Castorius, Commander of the Rome garrison, took his seat, assured, businesslike, vigorous and spotless in his uniform. Lastly, the Archdeacon of Rome, a smiling, affable man, waved a greeting at everyone and sat down. As one of Rome's Seven Deacons, he belonged to the elite circle from which successive popes were drawn. He gave me an appraising look and nodded. The archdeacon held a position of trust as treasurer of the wealth of the Church in Rome, authorising payments and receiving revenues for distribution among the poor of the city.

His Holiness entered the room and greeted each one with a kiss on the cheek, still the openhearted monk, grateful each one could spare the time to come. He recognised me instantly, ruffled my long fair hair and said, "Alric! How you have grown! It seems an age since we first met!" He spoke as though we'd once had a chance meeting in the Septa Julia while pursuing our respective business affairs, rather than Gregorius as my redeemer sparing me from a wretched life of slavery.

We sat in the round, the atmosphere one of expectancy, eager to get on with the overwhelming task of saving Rome. The pope sat with his back to a tall window that looked out on the Aventine and Palatine hills, and also the distant Colosseum. The Aurelian Wall lay to the left of this view, and the Aqua Claudia to the right, its arches just visible, traversing the slopes of the Caelian Hill into the pines of the Palatine. In the far distance, the Janiculum Hill was bright in the morning sunshine, the dark brown Aurelian Wall snaking across its ridge. The circular roof of Basilica Rotondo Stefano stood out in the foreground, and close by, tenant farmers tended fields of olive trees, fruit, and vegetables.

It seemed an idyllic scene, but I wondered whether the pope sometimes looked at this view, glimpsed his old family home peaceful and inviting in the sunshine, and gave a heavy sigh.

Or perhaps he wept.

We all bowed our heads as Pope Gregorius prayed, and opened proceedings by touching on a concern held by many in the room.

"As you may be aware, my brothers, for many years now I have been afflicted with frequent pains in the bowels, and the powers of my stomach are so broken I always seem in poor health. As if one thorn in my side was insufficient, I think you know I also suffer from a constant succession of slow fevers sapping my energies."

Murmurs of sympathy and concern arose from the gathered company, and Copiosus the pope's physician, confirmed this with a brief nod. Gregorius certainly did not seem in good health. He had lost weight since I last saw him and his usually dark complexion was pallid. His extreme asceticism was widely known during his years as Abbot of San Andreas and his fasts so rigorous and prolonged as to seriously injure his health. Never wholly free from disease, Gregorius frequently suffered from fevers carried by the ubiquitous marsh mosquitoes.

The pope's diet mostly comprised raw vegetables and fruit. His aged mother Silvia sent vegetables to him daily on a silver dish, and Gregorius returned it to her every evening. As a widow, she lived a reclusive life of prayer in a modest dwelling near the Porta Ostiensis. Sylvia had renounced every luxury she once enjoyed, but she still kept this one piece of silver plate, the last prized possession of her former mansion. I thought fleetingly about my long-absent gold coin, but mostly I began to wonder, was it possible the pope's enemies within the Lateran were plotting his overthrow by poisoning his food? I stopped scribing, and Alexius gave my elbow a nudge to keep up.

"But this is part of the burden of my office," Pope Gregorius was saying. "I beseech your prayers that I may continue this path set before me."

As Bishop of Rome, Gregorius had not spent time away from the city since his inauguration, and now even within Rome only went about on official duties. In winter and summer, in the cold and heat, he remained at the Lateran, frequently prostrate with illness, but, as Alexius confided, always at work on the overwhelming mass of business and correspondence demanding his attention.

The pope took a small sip of cognidium, liquor helpful for his stomach and flavoured with a resin from Alexandria. "In Rome," he sighed, looking into the cup's contents, "the traders claim to sell a drink which they call cognidium, but never the real wine itself! Regretfully, I am obliged to resort to wine peddled by local suppliers when my usual source from Egypt cannot be replenished."

He consulted a parchment on the table beside him and said briskly, "Come; there is much work to be done! Now, as you are aware, certain holy women who are devoted to the religious life have suffered the capture and sacking of their towns and have fled to Rome for sanctuary. Some of these, so far as there is a place for them, have been accommodated in existing monasteries and houses for women. To this end, it seemed good for the Church in Rome to receive the gift of the blessed Ameliana's titular church, with all its properties, and to consecrate the oratory as the Cardinal Church of San Quattro Coronati."

This development was, of course, how I had come to meet Paulina.

The pope gestured towards the cardinal, "And I have appointed Cardinal Fortunatus to oversee this new community." There were nods all round at his appointment as a cardinal priest, but in my surprise, I dropped my wax tablet with a loud clatter on the floor. A few heads turned in my direction, but otherwise, no one took notice of my confusion. They mistook my red face for embarrassment, which it was, but also mixed with guilt over Paulina and our blossoming relationship. So far, I had not crossed paths with the cardinal on my brief visits to San Quattro.

I stared down at my wax tablet. Fortunatus shuffled his black slippers as he sat forward to speak, his white clerical hose just visible beneath his dark cassock. His eyes were bright and alert, his smile both nervous and genuine, a man of energy and competence.

"I am now at the basilica every day, Your Holiness, to celebrate the Mysteries and oversee the work of some fine builders and craftsmen from Spoleto." These workers had fled from their city and were now receiving protection and support, as were farmers and merchants from all over the Duchy of Rome. To murmurs of approval around the room, the Cardinal concluded, " There is good progress on both the oratory and the living quarters. I expect to see all the work completed next year before spring."

"Excellent! Excellent! However, we cannot accommodated everyone in this way," Gregorius warned. "These women lead a life of singular destitution, and it has been thought good that what might be spared from the relief set aside for the blind, maimed and feeble should also be distributed to them. This means not only the needy citizens of Rome but also strangers and pilgrims who arrive here, should receive the compassion of the Emperor, whose generosity has provided the money to support this relief."

"A considerate step," Augustinus nodded, with supportive murmurs from around the room. After another brief sip, the pope continued, speaking in a low voice.

"What I say now must, of course, not leave this room." Everyone leaned forward attentively. "Should Exarch Romanus be unwilling to consent to make a treaty, King Agilulf promises to conclude a separate peace with us. But such peace would come at the cost of ceding even more territory to him, as our coffers here are all but depleted. Also, our various islands and similar places would undoubtedly be ruined, if we were forced to conclude a new peace treaty on his terms. But, if Romanus accepts the offer of peace, we would have a period of quiet here in this city, and the forces of the Republic would be better prepared to oppose the Langobards, with the help of God."

The room remained silent as the implications of the pope's words sank in. A separate treaty without Romanus would amount, in the Exarch's view, to treason. Gregorius looked around at everyone in the room, his eyebrows raised in search of a response. Everyone nodded.

Gregorius turned from politician to servant of the Servants of God, a theme he had written and preached upon ever since his election as Bishop of Rome.

"Well then, my brothers; once again, we find ourselves in an intolerable position. What is clear is that the world groans like a man who is ancient of days. Do we not see the signs of these times? Read the Scriptures; nothing happening here is novel, all is foretold concerning these Last Days. Truly, we are living straight from the pages of Scripture, our remaining days dwindling to a short span. We see everything in our world destroyed, as foretold long ago. Cities have been sacked, fortresses razed to the ground, churches destroyed and no farmer inhabits the land. A human sword rages against the few who remain. These are the world's evils we have long been warned would come upon us."

The silence in the room was palpable. After a long moment, Pope Gregorius continued. "Our priests hold a sacred trust for preaching to the pagan and unconverted, and yet I do not believe they are in a fit state to fulfil such a charge. They prefer to fuss over music, their robes, their status, their position in processions; and all the while the Gospel is silenced."

This seemed to permit a major unspoken concern in the room to be raised. Augustinus spoke first, choosing his words carefully as he stepped into this difficult terrain.

"Equitius highlighted this, Your Holiness, when he preached here at the Lateran." He gestured briefly towards me, and I froze for a moment in the sudden glare of attention. "Alric had a strong difference of opinion with some younger clergy on the steps of the Palace after Equitius had preached. There is deep resentment amongst some, and not only among the younger clergy."

Paterius, the Papal Notary, spoke next. "I have also heard it rumoured, Your Holiness, that when you are no longer pope, shall we say, there are plans to destroy all your writings. However, rest assured, we are preparing for such an eventuality, and we are making copies of all your writings and sermons."

Petrus the Deacon said, "Some of the old families in Rome have not found the transition easy. They have certain expectations of what the priesthood entitles them to. Pope Pelagius's archdeacon felt disappointed when you terminated his services, but I don't think he is at the centre of a plot against you, Your Holiness. Yet, he may be the focus for their dissent."

Gregorius nodded. "I worked closely with him in those six months between my election and the Emperor's ratification. I found him both helpful and astute, but I did not need his services as a chamberlain, nor an overseer of my public duties."

Prior Laurentius now interjected; "But as the pope's archdeacon, he may well have expected to be the successor to Pelagius as Bishop of Rome."

The pope gave a great sigh and for a few moments, buried his head in his hands.

"Enemies without and enemies within! My brothers, as a monk, I feared to ascend to the Throne of our Great Apostle for precisely this! Not everyone accepts a monk as the Bishop of Rome. There is no precedent, and it is not the place of monks to take on the apostolic role rightly belonging to the priesthood. I begged the Emperor, you know this, but to no avail."

The pope looked around at each one in the room.

"Those Greeks in the Imperial City, it seems, no longer care and no longer seek the lost. Pagan beliefs are not dead and buried; they still worship the old deities. What is left but for the gentile nations to come into God's fold? Did not our Lord cry out, when the Greeks in Jerusalem came looking for him, 'Now has my hour come to be glorified'?"

I had stopped writing again, my stylus frozen on the wax slate, as the words of the great theologian San Augustinus from "On the End of the World" came flooding back to me. Night after night over the years I had lain awake, longing to return to the home of my birth, but it always seemed hopeless. The hope of returning had faded. Now a completely unexpected door had opened, and without either thought or hesitation, I burst out, "Did not the great San Augustinus write that the end would only come when all nations have heard the Gospel of Our Lord? But my people the Cantwara have not yet heard it! Perhaps that is why the end has not yet come? Surely missionary preachers must be sent to them for the end to take place?"

The Notarius looked over his shoulder in alarm. Alexius put a restraining hand on my arm, and everyone looked at me as the room fell into a shocked silence. I had violated our agreement. I had presumed to speak when that was not my place. What would my punishment be? Thrown out of the Lateran? Cast away from the monastery? I lowered my head and waited for the storm. A horrendous silence continued for several long moments.

At last, His Holiness spoke in a voice all the more powerful for its quiet tone.

"Truly, my bretheren, out of the mouths of babes," he said. "Out of the mouth of babes! Did not Isaiah say, 'He will not grow faint or be crushed until he has established justice upon the earth, and the coastlands wait for his teaching'? Alric, you and Cadmon are both from the coastlands, are you not?"

I looked up in surprise, and nodded.

"And yet, as you say, no one has come!"

His gaze shifted from me to the letter on his table.

"A deacon of Turones, one Agilulf, brought this letter to me," he held it up, "five years ago, on the eve of my elevation to the Apostolic See." I recalled Agilulf's time with us at San Andreas, arriving in Rome from Francia after a long and arduous journey.

His Holiness continued, "Brethren, in this letter, sent by the Bishop of Turones, I read that Alric's people, the Cantwara, eagerly desired to be converted to the Christian faith. That came at the request of their Catholic queen, and with the support of her pagan lord. However, the Frankish bishops have neglected to respond to their entreaties, and in so doing have hindered the coming of Our Lord in these last and darkest days. Are we not in dire straits, because we have not fulfilled what these pagan peoples so earnestly desire, bringing the Gospel to the shores of the Kingdom of the Cantwara? It surely now falls to us to fulfil this desire they have so earnestly expressed!" Everyone sat in stunned silence while his words sank in.

"We will send," he said emphatically, "a mission from Rome to the Kingdom of the Cantwara!"

I stayed behind after others had gone, both recovering from shock but also comparing notes with Alexius in the papal archives next to the meeting room. I found myself in a state of ecstatic turmoil after the pope's words. Could this be possible? Would it happen? Would he change his mind? I found it hard to concentrate.

It had been a long meeting, and our line-by-line comparison seemed to take an age. Alexius was far more skilled than I but complimentary about how I had managed to scribe for such a difficult meeting. By the end, we agreed what was said.

"I have never heard the like of this meeting before, Alric! I hope and pray that this mission comes to pass for you!" I thanked Alexius from the depths of my heart and went down to the entrance. Augustinus was deep in conversation with Laurentius at the doorway into the garden. We bade farewell and set off in the noonday heat, the sky bleached of all colour and bright enough to hurt my eyes. We walked together for a while in reflective silence, my mind still whirling over what had taken place.

"When do you think this will happen?" I asked. "Who will His Holiness send?"

"Steady on, Alric! It could be months yet, and there will be much to prepare. Let's wait and see, shall we?"

Augustinus was silent for a few moments and then said, "I know you had a conversation with Abbot Marinianus regarding your period as a postulant. In the light of what we've heard today, I suggest we postpone further discussion until it is clear whether or not this expedition will come to fruition. Are you content with that?"

I thought over his proposal. I was in no less turmoil than I had been after my conversation with our former abbot. "Thank you," I said, "that is a very kind thought. And I accept."

We walked briskly on, my thoughts turning to my conversation with Cadmon in the monastery library some months ago.

"I have something to ask you."

Augustinus raised an enquiring eyebrow, inviting me to continue.

"Do you remember that Cadmon came to see me before he travelled to Ravenna?"

Augustinus nodded.

"Cadmon said there are spies everywhere in Rome, and it was very likely there may be a plot against His Holiness by some of his younger clergy - and perhaps even their families. There may be spies - even assassins - in the Lateran! You can see how ill he has become!"

Augustinus remained silent as we continued along the road to the monastery, then sighed as he made up his mind and glanced at me.

"Alric, I'm not sure about assassins, but the Langobards and Akakios are not the only ones who have spies," he said with half a laugh. I looked sharply at our prior. "Now you've raised it, I tell you this in the strictest confidence." I nodded agreement.

"You recall the archdeacon who sat opposite you in the meeting this morning?" I nodded, recalling the man with a friendly smile I had warmed to. "He is the Treasurer of the Church of Rome; he also has his own 'informants,' shall we say."

"And the Prefect?" I asked.

"The same."

"His Holiness?"

Augustinus paused. "Shall we just say that His Holiness is kept informed. That, Alric, is how the Bishop of Rome knows what is *really* happening in the city!"

I rattled through the list. "And the Garrison Commander?"

"Castorius would be failing in his duty if he did not have his own sources of military intelligence affecting Rome! So, I think we would know if there was a plot afoot to do away with the Pope."

"And you?" I asked impertinently. "Do you have spies?"

A broad smile appeared on the prior's face.

"Welcome, Alric! You are my first recruit!"

17

LEAVE-TAKING

Rome, May 596 AD

I HAD EXPECTED to hear soon of plans for the mission as the pope had declared, but months dragged by without further news. Then nearly a year had passed.

Augustinus said, "His Holiness is greatly distracted by his dealings with the Emperor and the Exarch of Ravenna, Alric—and also by his bishops on the mainland and in Sicily and Sardinia. Not least, he must cope with his poor state of health, so he is unable to give his full attention to the mission at this time."

My frustrations were partially alleviated—but also stoked—by my agonisingly fleeting meetings with Paulina. Our passion grew and restraint had all but reached breaking point when, one day in May in the Year of Our Lord 596, Prior Augustinus addressed our community after our morning meal in the refectory.

"Brethren, yesterday I met with His Holiness. I will come straight to the heart of the matter. His wish is to send a score or so from our monastery to bring the Faith to the Cantwara people."

Cries of surprise, delight, and concern swept through the refectory. I thought of the enormity of this, and also that a letter written two hundred years earlier by Bishop Augustinus of Hippo, would now be fulfilled by his namesake.

The prior waited for everyone to settle down. "Some of you may know that their kingdom lies in the southern part of territories formerly known as Britannia and ancient Albion. It is also Alric's homeland. His Holiness has instructed me, on his behalf, to lead this expedition to the Kingdom of Cantia." More cries rose in the refectory.

Again, Augustinus called for silence. "His Holiness and I have discussed together who might be best suited to undertake such a noble task, and I shall be speaking to members of our community, both monks and lay brothers, with a view to joining this venture. We have much to do in preparing for our journey, brethren. The hour is late, and the task is urgent. We depart from Rome in two weeks!"

Augustinus rang the small bell on the table and pronounced a benediction. We all stood and bowed, and most of us hastened to the outdoor reception area above the monastery steps to share their excitement and their concerns.

I found myself in turmoil. Two weeks! I couldn't believe it! From the decision to departure, the pope was allowing only two weeks! The scale of expectation now placed on our prior's shoulders was staggering. Fourteen days in which to shortlist, interview, recruit, prepare and provision a disparate group who, for the most part, had never travelled more than ten miles from Rome!

On the other hand, I could see how Gregorius—whose organisational abilities had energised the role of Prefect of Rome, inspired a monastic community, transformed the administration of the poor in this city and completely reordered the Office of Bishop of Rome—might place such an expectation on Augustinus. Perhaps, from Gregorius's perspective, two weeks to prepare for a mission to the outer reaches of the known world was not unreasonable! But the strain on those of us in the monastery was considerable.

These thoughts raced through my head as I hurried instead to the prior's office.

"Prior, I beg you to take me and Cadmon with you!"

Augustinus motioned for me to close the door and sit down. He said, "I spoke with His Holiness about you yesterday evening, Alric. There is every advantage in having you accompany us—and I do not doubt that we have much to learn from you—unless you have forgotten your homeland?"

"No, no, never! And besides, you may yet need someone who knows how to fish!"

The prior smiled. "And Cadmon, has he returned? He has been gone for a considerable time now. Nearly a year."

"I've had no word recently, but I will make inquiries at the barracks."

Augustinus nodded. "Then off you go!"

I turned as I reached the door. "Why now? Why two weeks?"

"King Agilulf returns sometime before the end of this year for his second tranche of gold. Frankly, we don't have it! His Holiness wants our expedition party away from Rome before Agilulf returns, lest we find ourselves trapped in the city by yet another siege. Besides, I doubt that Agilulf keeps a calendar! He will come whenever he wants, perhaps even tomorrow. But even more important, we must leave now if we are to arrive in the Kingdom of Cantia before winter sets in. Otherwise, we'll be stranded for months on the shores of Francia. And lastly, we leave now because no one knows how long this journey will actually take us!"

I half-walked, half-ran to the barracks, but there was no news of Cadmon. No one knew his whereabouts, when he might return, or even whether he was alive! There had been no word from him since the day he left Rome with Bishop Marinianus. I retraced my steps to the monastery.

Throughout the day, monks and lay brothers were summoned to meet with Augustinus. Most also sought my advice, asking how they should best prepare for such an undertaking, or whether they should undertake it at all. The days flew by, and our activity became frantic. Then, at last, I found an opportunity to see Paulina again at San Quattro Coronati.

"Come!" I said urgently, leading her into the grove.

"What is it Alric? You look so flustered!"

With my arm around her out of sight of the kitchen, I came straight to the point. "His Holiness has commissioned us to go to my home country, with Prior Augustinus and several others from the monastery. We leave in a matter of days!"

Her dusky cheeks turned pale as she stammered, "But ... when will you return?"

I had no idea, nor had I even thought about returning. "The prior has not said," I replied lamely, realising as I spoke that my joy was her heartbreak, throwing me further into confusion.

Paulina stared at me, stunned for a few moments, then for the first time threw herself into my arms and, with her head on my shoulder, began to sob so that hot tears ran down her cheeks.

"It will be well," I said without much conviction; "It won't be forever; I will return to you." But she was inconsolable. After a short while, I left, promising to try and see her again before we departed.

"I won't say goodbye, then, until I see you again!" she sobbed.

Every day I hurried to the barracks looking for news of Cadmon, but still, there was none. One morning, as I returned from another fruitless visit, I met our herbalist, Brother Anselm, as he made his way to the monastery's herb garden.

Seizing this opportunity, I said, "May I speak with you, please?" I joined him in the herb garden behind the oratory. I told Anselm what concerned me, something that had been running around my head ever since I had scribed for that fateful meeting of the Pope Gregorius's advisers the previous year. Now, this seemed my last opportunity to raise my question. "Do you think it is possible that someone could be poisoning His Holiness?"

Brother Anselm looked utterly shocked. "Alric, where does this idea come from?"

I told him of the pope's health and his symptoms. "He eats very little, mostly raw vegetables and he sips a little wine for his stomach."

"Yes, that I know."

"Could someone be giving him poison?"

"Or is it simply his severe diet?" Anselm countered.

We continued making our way slowly along the rows, our herbalist stooping every so often to examine his plants.

"Well, from what you say, I would rule out two obvious poisons that have a very long history in Rome!" We stood in the shade of a nearby tree as Anselm sifted through the possibilities. "I rule out hemlock because it numbs the limbs from the feet upwards and eventually stops the heart. These symptoms appear quickly, even in small doses. But His Holiness has had his condition for some years now." He paused, considering his remaining options.

"Another is mandrake—it causes hallucinations. The pope, from what you've described, has no such symptoms. Also, I would not think it is belladonna—it has a poison that creates wild visions and causes blindness. I do not think His Holiness shows any sign of either of these!"

I realised that these were unlikely to account for the pope's state of health, but Brother Anselm remained deep in thought as we resumed walking, stooping to sample one or other of his herbs, gently rubbing between finger and thumb and inhaling its scent.

Anselm continued, "So, even if someone did poison his food, it wouldn't be any of these obvious methods." After a few moments, he thought of another track he might follow, and prompted, "Did His Holiness have anything during the meeting? Anything at all?" I shook my head.

"Nothing.'

"Not even a drink of water?"

"No, not water. But he sipped a glass of liquor several times during the meeting."

Brother Anselm looked at me, his eyes alert and questioning. "Wine?"

"No, he said it was a liquor called cognidium; it gave his drink some flavour, and was also good for his stomach."

"Was it now. And where does this cognidium come from, Alric? Is it local?"

"His Holiness said from Alexandria. And like our lunchtime wine for the poor, it is also diluted with water."

As I mentioned the water, I recalled Cadmon and my unsuccessful attempt to escape from the city several years earlier. I babbled out our encounter with the wine merchant who supplied Abba with the local cognidium. I finished by saying, "I also remember that his men were watering-down the liquor, using the nearby Sallustiana stream."

Brother Anselm paused as he took in what I had said. "I shall keep thinking about this, Alric, and see what I can find."

I felt grateful my idea wasn't dismissed out of hand, but with little time before our departure, I had to leave the matter in someone else's capable hands.

On the eve of our departure, I finally received word of Cadmon's return. The light was fading, and the night watchman asked if I needed an escort, but by now I knew the way like the back of my hand. I thanked him for his offer, relying on moonlight for my return, but I had made a near-fatal mistake.

I quickly slipped out of the monastery's side gate near the library and hurried up the Via Triumphalis towards the Colosseum. In my haste I did not notice that there were three figures lying in wait on the slope of the Palatine Hill, hidden behind one of the arches of the Claudian Aqueduct. I only vaguely registered their presence in a blur of movement to my left as I hurried past. One shouted, "That's him! Take him!" and came rushing down from the hillside.

My path back to the monastery now blocked, I pulled up my habit and ran as fast as I could towards the Colosseum, the image of a corpse floating past Felix's ship six years earlier suddenly uppermost in my mind. My pursuers gave chase, but they were heavier and less fit than I. All the same, I was panting hard as I ran through the Arch of Constantine and turned towards the Arch of Titus, my pursuers all the while yelling, "Stop, you bastard, wait till we catch you!" Then just beyond the arch, my foot struck a stone, invisible in the darkness, and I stumbled and fell to the ground, my three pursuers panting and swearing as they reached me.

One shouted, "Time you learned a lesson, you interfering little bastard!" One of my attackers landed a hard kick on my thigh. I let out a long wail as they closed in, a torch flickering in the gloom, their faces hidden, hoods pulled down, cudgels in hand, ready for their finishing blows. I thought, this isn't going to end well; and even if they don't kill me, I won't be in any condition to leave Rome tomorrow!

Then, in all this noise and confusion, some soldiers on duty on the steps leading to the Palatine came running down towards the arch, shouting a warning to leave off the attack. At the same time, the relief guard for the night watch marched up from the guardhouse at the foot of the Palatine. Now outnumbered, and their exit cut off except by the way they had come, my attackers left off and ran back down the path. Sore and out of breath, I groaned as one of the guards rolled me over and pulled back my hood.

"He's one of the boys from the pope's monastery!"

I managed to gasp, "I need to see Trooper Cadmon at the barracks!"

A guard brought his torch closer and confirmed, "I know who you are, lad! I'll see you to the barracks. Here, put your arm on my shoulder." He lifted me to my feet, bruised and sore, but Deo Gratia, nothing seemed broken. I walked surrounded by four hefty soldiers like a felon under arrest, my limp gradually easing into a walk as we drew closer to the barracks. In a short while, I found myself standing in the doorway of Cadmon's quarters.

Cadmon's room looked sparser, if more spacious, than his previous accommodation a year earlier. The walls were unplastered brick and stone, functional enough for the barracks, but even with the flame of a torch in its ring on the wall, the room seemed shrouded in gloom.

"Not so hard!" I yelped, as he flung his arms around me in a bear hug. "Three men tried to kill me on my way over here this evening!"

"What? Who? Why?" His brow furrowed in a mixture of concern and anger.

"I don't know, but I think they've something to do with spies around the city. And I haven't made myself popular amongst some of the younger clergy at the Lateran."

"I see Rome has lost none of her charm! I did warn you!" he said. "My bet would be on Akakios, as your thugs were hiding out on the Palatine.

But it's good to see you again, Alric! What brings you here in such haste—and at such an hour?"

"I still pinch myself to see if I'm dreaming, Cadmon! But you and I are finally going home!"

He stared at me in shock, and then said in an unexpectedly gloomy voice, "I'm in the cavalry, Alric. I can't just leave!"

"Cadmon, you haven't spoken to your Commander, then?"

"He is away until morning. I spoke to Julius, the number two in command here, when I arrived a few hours ago, but he said nothing of this."

"Perhaps Castorius wants to tell you himself. I'm sorry to spoil it for him! But let me be the first! The pope has spoken to Castorius."

Cadmon brightened visibly.

"The pope? And what did Castus have to say?"

"Well, of course, he said 'No, the Law of Justinian forbids a soldier becoming a monk'. And also, he only has ten cavalrymen in the camp, so he couldn't spare you."

"Well, I'm not going to become a monk anyway! So, how did the Gregorius get out of that?"

"He said he's not asking to release you from the army. He's giving you a new commission—to protect us on the journey home!"

Cadmon roared with laughter. "Well, well! And Castus swallowed that?"

"I heard this from Prior Augustinus himself. He is leading this expedition."

"*Prior* Augustinus? Things *have* changed since I've been gone!"

"The Pope reminded Castus that the one who pays the piper calls the tune! And without the Church's money, no one's wages would be paid. So, His Holiness is now in full command of Rome."

Cadmon stood up. "I must verify this with Julius and get my documents for the journey! Come!"

We descended the stairs to the Duty Office at the entrance to the building.

"Alric's told me about my new commission, Julius! I'm sorry if he has spoiled the surprise!"

Julius conjured up the image of a giant woodland oak wearing a dark green tunic, its thick branches splitting the sleeves. Julius leaned back in his creaky chair and groaned. "No matter! You weren't to know, Alric!"

Cadmon and Julius spoke together for a few minutes. Julius picked up a document from his desk. "I've written out your military record to take with you, but you'll have to wait until Commander Castorius returns to give you your new commission. He's on patrol tonight—with your squadron, as a matter of fact, but they won't be back much before dawn."

Cadmon took the document and placed it carefully in his pouch. He glanced towards me. "I need to get Alric back to the monastery tonight; he was beaten up on the way here, so I can't take any chances!" Julius nodded. Cadmon said, " I'll stay over tonight, and return early in the morning for my commission and say farewell to Castorius and my unit."

We returned to Cadmon's quarters, and his packing continued in earnest. But was this sudden turn of affairs agreeable to him? Cadmon had also thrived in his few years in the military. Perhaps our homeland was too remote for him now; he could make his fortune better by staying. We remained silent for a while, each with our own thoughts, perhaps counting the cost of leaving Rome.

I said, "Are you sad to be leaving? You have a career and prospects here—and Castorius certainly doesn't want you to leave."

"I *am* glad to be going back, Alric. There's no future for me here—Romanus will see to that. He hates Rome and despises the garrison along with it. I can't rise in the ranks here. Besides, I have no desire to. Back home is my share of my father's estate, and a real opportunity for honour and glory serving in the King's Guard."

He paused; wearing an expression I had seen before when he spoke of home. "And I also have some unfinished family business that cannot wait for ever." Cadmon was silent for a moment then asked, "So, how does it stand with you and the fair Paulina?"

I felt awkward, shuffling my feet and staring at my hands.

"She is well," I managed to say, as a stab of regret pierced my soul.

"And?" His gaze found mine. I groaned.

"It's complicated, Cadmon. We feel something that brings us together, but now I'm about to leave, and perhaps we'll never see each other again. Besides all this, I promised Tola I would find her and bring her home; and that I surely must honour."

Cadmon nodded and probed no further.

"Well," I said, changing the subject, "How did you find Ravenna? And what delayed you for such a long time?"

"The journey passed without trouble," Cadmon said. "But it turned out that Marinianus was not only appointed to Ravenna but also as Bishop of Barium!"

I was puzzled, and my quizzical expression must have spoken for me.

Cadmon explained, “It’s further down the east coast, quite a way from Ravenna. But also, guess who appointed Marinianus to this? None other than the Patriarch of Constantinople! Even the pope didn’t know that! But it took a month before the bishop set sail down the coast to his unexpected diocese. Then before he embarked on the return journey to Ravenna, the patriarch summoned him to Constantinople to receive his formal commissioning! Marinianus insisted that I accompany him and Romanus agreed, which is why I have been away so long. But that’s a long story I’ll leave for another time. Let’s just say that for now, I’m truly overjoyed to be going home!”

The torch on the wall had begun to burn low as Cadmon finished his packing. Dressed in his full uniform and armour, he hefted his kit onto his shoulders, and pausing at the door, glanced back at his room.

“I can say this for certain, Alric. Rome and what’s left of the western empire will be abandoned to their fate. I can understand why the pope has turned his gaze to the north.”

We walked over to Belisarius in the stables. He greeted me with a snort and a nudge while Cadmon threw on the blanket, saddle, and armour. Then taking up his weapons, Cadmon and I set off through the garrison gate for the last time.

Like old times ast San Andreas, Cadmon and I had risen in the early hours and shuffled half asleep to the church for Matins. Afterwards I returned to our cell, lying awake in the gloom, unable to sleep, while Cadmon went over to the stables. We rose again a few hours later as dawn broke, and prayed for our journey in the church at the heart of the monastery. Afterwards, we made our way to the refectory for breakfast. Everyone was glad to see Cadmon back in his first home again.

A familiar mixture of excitement and regret wrestled in my heart as I thought of Paulina, the flower she gave me still in my habit pocket. I would miss, too, the comforting routine of monastic life, my studies and scribing and the friends like Alexius I now left behind at the Lateran.

With a belt I tied together my few possessions and collected parchment, ink and quills from the Library scriptorium, then made a short detour before I hurried down the monastery stairs. Perhaps I might not see Pope Gregorius again, but a good likeness of him had recently been painted on a circle of stucco in the apse of the church. I spent a few moments looking at his portrait, and then hurried down to the piazza.

Cadmon led Belisarius out of the monastery stables and along the Clivus Scauri into the piazza. With his few possessions tied behind him, Cadmon swung into the saddle as he trotted into the square, now filling with wellwishers. He was about to return briefly to the barracks when the sound of hooves came down the street. In a few moments Castorius, leading a squadron of cavalry at a fast trot down the ancient Via Triumphalis, drew up just short of Belisarius.

Cadmon saluted his commander, raising his sword in front of his face.

"You left this behind," Castorius said gruffly, handing over Cadmon's commission for the journey, and his second horse from the barracks stables. The Commander looked Cadmon up and down, noting that he wore his full cavalry uniform.

"Well," he said testily, "I see you are not in your monk's habit," a hint of relief in his voice that this whole episode was not merely a ruse to take his best cavalry officer out of the military, and back into the cloister.

"I know you have an appalling sense of direction, Cadmon! Your squadron will see you to Ostia!" Cadmon smiled and bowed his thanks to Castorius, while his troop, who had not seen him in nearly a year, beamed with approval.

My excitement grew as we gathered around the eight donkey-drawn carts carrying our possessions and tools for the journey. I carefully stowed my box of precious writing materials in the first cart, and waited alongside.

Taking five monks from a monastery of twenty-five brothers would leave a significant hole to fill, but the pope was adamant that a small expedition of only a few people would end in failure. Nor would a small number inspire confidence amongst the royal household in Cantia; and with that I fully agreed.

Prior Augustinus had also to consider the age and fitness of his travelling companions for this lengthy and arduous journey, as well as the skills they must bring for establishing a new monastery. Not everyone the prior approached felt willing or able to join the mission. It was important that those who joined had no ties of marriage or children to support. The lay brothers on the estate who did volunteer for the journey were essential to the venture's success, but they would also leave behind mothers and fathers, sisters and brothers—and friendships.

In the end, there were five monks, twelve lay brothers and Cadmon and me setting out, making a mixed party of nearly a score, standing in the narrow street below the monastery with eight mule carts, waiting to say farewell.

The whole community supporting our monastery estate had now turned out in the piazza. Families and friends of the lay brothers said last goodbyes with hugs and kisses. The monks murmured farewells with *pax vobiscum*, foreheads touching and hands clasping.

My heart felt as heavy as lead whenever I thought of Paulina. I had not been able to see her again before our departure. She should be here, or I should be staying behind. But I had made a promise to find Tola, and I must see it through.

Glancing up, I saw Paulina amongst the crowd, waving and smiling and crying; and then she was gone. Or perhaps it was someone else; or a figment of my vivid imagination? To clear my head, I glanced up and down the valley at the wild vines and groves between the Palatine and the Caelian Hills. Our urban wilderness spread all the way down from the Colosseum to Porta Ostiensis, the gateway to the Basilica San Pauli, and beyond to Ostia. Now our turn had come to walk this ancient way, and all the while excitement and hope and anxiety continued to churn in the pit of my stomach.

The arrival of Pope Gregorius coming from the Lateran on his white charger was a complete surprise to all of us, his retinue struggling to keep up as he rode. Loud cheers overwhelmed our initial shock as Augustinus came forward to greet His Holiness, exchanging greetings before the applauding crowd.

Gregorius now addressed us from the saddle of his white steed. He held aloft a magnificent crosier with an ivory carving of a ram, its head looking back, surmounted by a small cross. With a sweep of his right hand, he pointed up and down the narrow ribbon of pathway leading from the Colosseum down to Porta Ostiensis.

"My brothers and sisters," he began, addressing everyone at San Andreas; monks, laymen, mothers, wives and children. "You well know that in former times, down this same once proud Via Triumphalis, conquering emperors and renowned generals rode at the head of their armies, their carts laden as yours are today, but with the spoils of war, their captives coming behind, dragging their terrible chains. But it is not so with you." He paused, his orator's arm extended, the gathered assembly hanging on every word.

"Because the Gates of Hades could not prevail against our crucified and risen Lord when He came, bearing his Gospel of redemption—rescuing from bondage the souls of men and women, long departed and chained by sin, ignorance, and despair—and broke down the gates of their eternal prison. These wretched and forsaken souls he brought forth with Him on His great Day of Resurrection – not as unwilling slaves dragging their chains, but as freed men and women, following willingly behind their Saviour in joyous procession!"

Gregorius's gaze fell upon us, looking for a moment at each face as we stood beside our carts. In a quieter tone he said, "Know this, my brothers in Christ, that as you set forth this day, Our Lord goes before you to set prisoners free from their chains of ignorance and death in the Kingdom of Cantia, through this work that He has called you to perform."

In the hush that followed, Pope Gregorius turned to Alexius who now stepped forward, carrying an inlaid walnut casket. Inside, a wrapping of goatskin protected the thick leather cover of the Four Gospels, comprising three hundred pages of parchment. Each Gospel opened with an icon of an Evangelist, a decorated cover page and double-columned pages for the remainder. Miniature illustrations in gold richly adorned each Gospel. The whole endeavour had taken very nearly a year, starting on the day after Gregorius committed himself to send a mission to the Cantwara. I looked on with a touch of pride as, under Alexius's watchful eye, I had scribed two of the pages bound into the Gospels.

The pope made the sign of the cross over the casket then laid his hand on the polished lid, invoking the Almighty's blessing on the good news they contained. Alexius turned and held out the casket to a stunned Augustinus, who had not expected such a magnificent gift as this. After a moment he bowed down, kissed the casket's inlaid silver crucifix, and carried it carefully to our waiting cart at the front of the line. He took his place alongside the first of our eight carts, together with Petrus our teacher-librarian bringing books and teaching materials, and me as scribe, keeper of records and accounts, with my few personal possessions all tightly packed in the cart.

This was an intense moment for us all, and we put on a brave face. Only Cadmon genuinely smiled, content in the knowledge he was returning home to accomplish what he needed to do.

My own emotions were in turmoil again. I rejoiced that I might see my home once more, my mother Erlina and Galen my father, my siblings Godric and Greta. But would I recognise them, or would they recognise me? My conscience stirred as I thought of Tola. Would I ever find her? How could I find her, and was she still alive?

The monastery had given me so much that I would never have known otherwise—reading and writing, skills unknown to a fisherman. And also a community that cared for me as no other could or would have done. And not least, a freedom from the fickle gods of the Kingdom of Cantia—Thor, Wodin and all the gods and creatures that claimed sovereignty over our miserable lives and humble fortunes.

Looming largest were my feelings for Paulina, remembering her beautiful eyes, wet with tears and red with grief, as we said our farewells. How could I leave her after all that had passed between us? My head drooped in despair. Why did I get myself into such a mess? I did not know either my heart or my mind, and now it seemed that others were once again shaping the course of my life.

Bystanders from the Palatine Hill and neighbouring streets had also gathered to watch our departure, some of whom I recognised as locals, others I had not seen before. Had they come out of curiosity, or for a darker purpose, I wondered?

Still seated on his white horse, Pope Gregorius blessed our party with a sign of the cross. With a final "Amen", we turned our backs on the monastery that had been my home for the last seven years, and set our faces to the west—through the city gate, past the Basilica San Pauli to Ostia—unless the Langobards, whose spies seemed to watch our every move in Rome, lay in wait for us on the road.

Towering above us on Belisarius, Cadmon trotted down to the front of the line with his squadron as we set off. He greeted Augustinus and Petrus with a salute, the first time they had seen each other in a year. Petrus said, "So, Cadmon, your vision of four horsemen riding into a trap in Rome was indeed prescient! Doors have certainly opened in your absence!"

Cadmon shook his head and gestured towards me.

"No, Brother Petrus! Alric must receive the credit for opening the door that takes us home!" The memory of our earlier futile attempt to escape from Rome flooded back, and I said, "Are we going to make it this time, Cadmon?"

He smiled, leaned down and patted my shoulder. "Time will tell, Alric! Time will tell!"

CHARACTERS

Below are the names and brief descriptions of characters in the novel.
The names of **historical** characters are shown in ***italics.***

Agilulf, Frankish deacon, on pilgrimage to Rome from Turones (Tours), AD 590

Agilulf, Langobard King, d. AD 616

Akakios, Greek, an office holder under Romanus, Exarch of Ravenna, and his official in Rome notionally in charge of the military and other affairs of state in the city

Alexius, Roman, skilled scribe at the Lateran, becomes Alric's tutor

Alric, Saxon, narrator of this story; a fisherman, from Sandwic Haven, in the Kingdom of Cantia (later knows as Kent);oldest child of Galen and Erlina; elder brother to Tola, Godric and Greta; lifelong friend of Cadmon, with whom Alric shares this adventure

Anaxos, Greek, Felix's navigator

Angles, Angli. A Saxon tribe that settled in southeast England in the 5th century AD

Anselm, Roman, monk and herbalist, S.Andreas monastery

Appius Vulso, goatherd

Ariulf, Duke of Spoleto (near to Rome)

Augustinus, Roman, a Prior of San Andreas monastery, leader of the Mission to Cantia in AD 596

Cadmon, Saxon, second son of Earl Sighart, Ratteburg Fort, near Sandwic Haven

Caius Tiro, carpenter

Cantwara, Saxon people of the Kingdom of Cantia

Castus, Castorius, Commander of the Theodosian Regiment and the military barracks guarding Rome

Clementus, Roman, monk

Coifin, Saxon, a pagan High Priest to Eormenric, King of the Cantwara people

Constantinus, Emperor AD 312–337; founder of the city of Constantinople

Copiosus, Roman, a Prior of San Andreas Monastery from mid-580s to mid-590's AD

Decimus Valens, an ostler

Derian, Saxon, Cadmon's older brother and fierce rival

Dofras, Saxon-Jute word for present-day Dover.

Edoma, North African, slave on Felix's ship; later slave to a Roman noblewoman

Eormenric, Saxon, King of the Cantwara, father of Prince Ethelbert

Equitius, an itinerant preacher invited to Rome to show the priests how to preach

Erlina, Saxon, wife of Galen, mother of Alric, Tola, Godric and Greta; older sister of Helga

Falk, Saxon, son of Earl Hrothgar, exiled with his father to Francia

Felix, unknown, captain of a merchant-slaver trading from the Kingdom of Cantia to the eastern Mediterranean

Fortunatus, Roman, cardinal, oversees the San Quattro Coronati religious community in Rome

Frigga, Norse and Saxon goddess, wife of Wodin

Galen, British-Saxon, father of Alric

Gilling, a mythical figure of the Saxons

Godric, Saxon, Alric's brother, son of Galen and Erlina, also brother to siblings Tola and Greta

Gordianus, Roman, patrician, Gregorius's father

Graciosus, supervisor of the monastery's estates

Gregorius, Roman, Prefect of Rome, Legate for Pelagius II to Constantinople, Abbot, Pope

Greta, Saxon, Alric's youngest sibling; 4th and youngest child of Galen and Erlina

Helga, Saxon, younger sister of Erlina, midwife

Hippodamus, Roman, member of Cadmon's cavalry unit in Rome

Hrothgar, Saxon, Earl of Tanet, of the House of Horsa; exiled to Francia

John, a monk from the post-Benedictine period of Monte Cassino, resident at the Lateran Palace

Julius, adjutant to Commander Castorius at Rome's military garrison

Justus, Roman, monk at San Andreas

Kaeso Pollio, monastery vintner

Langobards (also known as **Lombards**), tribe of warlike Germanic stock occupying most of Italy; Arian Christians at odds with Catholicism

Marinianus, Roman, an Abbot of San Andreas and later Bishop of Ravenna, c. AD 595

Martinus, Roman, monk and sacristan at San Andreas

Mauricius, Emperor in Constantinople until AD 602

***Narses*, **Greek**,** general under Justinian (AD 478–573)

Neorth, Norse and Saxon, god of the sea

Numerius Etruscus, blacksmith

Numerius Albinus, potter and brick maker

Oslaf, Saxon, brother of Hrothgar, killed in battle

Paulina, Rome, lay sister at San Quattro Coronati**,** Alric's emotional interest

Pelagius II, Roman, Pope, Bishop of Rome and immediate predecessor of Gregorius I

Petrus, Roman, monk at San Andreas monastery; Alric and Cadmon's tutor

***Pontifex*,** 'bridge-builder', a papal title inherited from pagan Rome

Pretiosus, Roman, a Prior of San Andreas monastery

Quintus Lucanus, a monastery cook

Remus, Roman, captain of the Vigiles, a police-cum-fire service in Rome

Rollo, Hrothgar's youngest son

Rufinian, Roman, monk; a member of Augustinus's mission

Saba, Saxon, Earl Sighart's household slave at Ratteburg

***Saxons*,** people of Germanic stock who settled in East Kent from the mid-fifth century

Servius Tullus, potter and brick maker

***Seven Deacons of Rome*,** the seven appointed by the whole company of the original Christian community at Jerusalem and ordained by the Apostles. Their ministry was chiefly to attend to the poor, and the common *agape*. Both Gordianus and his son Gregorius served in this role

Souk, unknown, first mate to Felix on his merchant-slaver ship

Suttung, legendary figure in Norse mythology

***Sylvia*,** Roman, wife of Gordianus, mother of Gregorius

Theodore, Roman, friend of Alric and Cadmon; a lay brother at San Andreas monastery

***Theodosian Regiment*,** a regiment of the Eastern Empire billeted in Rome for the security of the city; under the command of Castorius (Castus)

***Tiberinus*,** Roman, king, elevated to the status of a god who ruled over the Tiber

Tiberius Centumalus, builder

Tola, Saxon, Alric's younger sister, captured at Sandwic Haven by Felix and his crew

***Totila*,** Ostrogoth King (died 1 July 552)

Vivius Servilianus, garment weaver and leather worker

Weal, Saxon, Sighart's slave, with charge over the Earl's ship

Wéofodthane, Saxon, priestly title (a person consulted for omens before getting married or planting new crops)

Wodin, Norse and Saxon chief god; sacrifice is made to him at his shrine, near the King's Hall at Eastringe

Wyrd, and her sisters, *(the Wyrdae);*Norse**;** also a concept in Anglo-Saxon pagan culture roughly corresponding to fate, or personal destiny, meaning "to come to pass, to become"; often personified as a goddess

MAPS

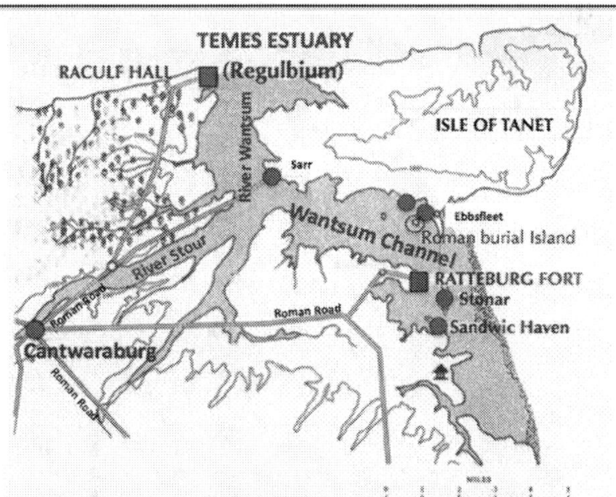

MAP 1 Kingdom of East Cantia, Late C6th

MAP 2 Key Ports from Sandwic Haven to Rome

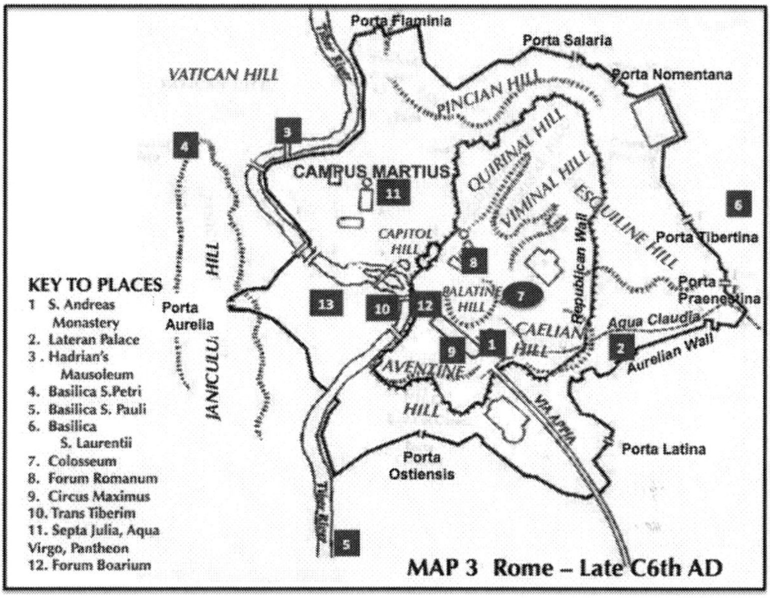

MAP 3 Rome – Late C6th AD

ABOUT THE AUTHOR

ROB MACKINTOSH, AFTER recently publishing a history of St. Augustine's sixth century mission to Kent, has now embarked on a Historical Novel Series. The Series begins in 579 AD against a backdrop of seventy tumultuous years—for Rome, for Merovingian Francia, and for Saxon England. The key fictional characters are not drawn from the good, the great or the terrible, but the ordinary, whose lives are made remarkable by their response to these extraordinary times in which they find themselves.

Since 2001, Rob has lived in Canterbury, and more recently in Sandwich, close to many of the events set in his historical novel writing. Rob has journeyed to Rome on several occasions for research, and as a pilgrim in recent years; and has also travelled extensively across France to explore Augustine's route from Rome to Canterbury.

Rob initially lectured undergraduates at Rhodes University in South Africa, and later served as a parish priest in England for fifteen years, before becoming Executive Director of the **Leadership Institute** (2000-2008: a national organisation for developing clergy leadership across the Church of England). He later served as **Director of Ministry** for Canterbury Diocese, and is a Canon Emeritus of **Canterbury Cathedral**.

In 2016, he was awarded the **Canterbury Cross** by the Archbishop of Canterbury, for his work in Leadership Development for the Church of England.

Other Books by Rob Mackintosh

(1) Robin Mackintosh, (2013); "**Augustine of Canterbury: Leadership, Mission, and Legacy;**"published by Canterbury Press, and available in both Kindle e-book and paperback format.

(2) Rob Mackintosh & Peter Ingrams, (2016); "**In the Steps of Augustine of Canterbury:** *A Pilgrim Guide in France,*"in pdf format.)

Sign up for Rob Mackintosh's email newsletter for readers at:

www.tckpublishing.com/robmackintosh

Visit Rob's websites for more information at:

www.robmackintosh.net

www.augustineofcanterbury.org

Get Book Discounts and Deals

28527227R10107

Printed in Great Britain
by Amazon